To Mam

This book is a work of fiction and, except in the case of historical fact, any reference to actual persons, living or dead, actual events or locations, and the use of any names or characters, is purely coincidental.

"Still Life" ©Copyright Geraldine Comiskey 2003

Geraldine Comiskey has asserted her right under the Copyright, Designs and Patents Act 1988 to be identified as the author of this work.

The moral right of the author has been asserted

Front cover illustration ©Copyright Geraldine Comiskey

A catalogue record for this book is available from the British Library

Also by Geraldine Comiskey:

Non-fiction:
Wacky Eire
Wacky Eire II – Wackier Eire

Fiction:
Shampoo & Sympathy
Floozies
Chasing Casanova
Skin Deep
Deadly

Acknowledgements:

Thanks to everyone who read the first – awful – draft of this book, including literary agent Jonathan Williams. Thanks for your advice, encouragement and proof-reading. And thanks especially to those who have indirectly inspired the characters of Chloe and her mum: the Lost Cinderellas. I hope you find Fairy Godmothers who steer you away from unreliable Prince Charmings.

Author's note

I wrote *Still Life* in 2003, when the Celtic Tiger was in full roar and greed had become the new religion. The widening gap between rich and poor had spawned a particularly poisonous kind of snobbery. The generosity, goodwill and self-deprecation which had been charming characteristics of Irish people for generations had largely been replaced by blatant vanity, aggressive rivalry and ruthlessness. I suspected then – and now know – that the 'boom' was little more than the proverbial house of cards. And I wondered what a sudden loss of fortune would do to a spoilt young woman – and what would happen if she fell in love with a man who seemed to represent everything that had gone wrong in her life.

About the author

Dublin-based award-winning journalist Geraldine Comiskey has spent more than thirty years covering everything from the district courts to wacky rural festival in her native Ireland, and, in the interest of research, has had many adventures. Some of her most memorable assignments have included "dunker training" in a submerged helicopter with the Royal Marines, boarding a trawler with the Irish Navy in a Force Nine gale, wingwalking over Galway Bay, scuba-diving with sharks and getting set on fire by stuntmen in the Wicklow Mountains. She has interviewed a wide range of interesting people – but finds that the best stories are those she can never tell.

Reviews of Geraldine Comiskey's work:

"...a riveting, rollicking romp of a read." – **author Niamh O'Connor (Sunday World)**

"[Wacky Eire is]...an eye-popping procession of dodgy faith healers, rural swingers, ghost hunters, GAA players, all of Irish life really. Gifted with a never say die spirit and an uncanny ability to find herself at the center of the wackiest stories, she's an ideal guide to the book's theme and this is one of the most singular books of its kind you're ever likely to read" – **Cahir O'Doherty (Irish Central)**

"Nothing escapes her eagle eye and her prolific pen" (ib.)

"Geraldine, in her own inimitable way covers the vast sprectrum of Irish life," (ib)

"...not a corner of Ireland goes untouched...the unusual stories criss-cross the country." (ib)

"[Wacky Eire] is unreal, everything you never associated Ireland with. It's specially fun coming from a field reporter who doesn't mind stripping down to a bikini to enter a pothole and take its measurements, or risking a ride with the country's worst driver...Geraldine is one hell of a storyteller." - **Anwesha Mittra (The Times of India)**

"Geraldine Comiskey...sketches a kaleidoscopic Ireland that is brimming with eccentric folks, eccentric rituals, eccentric gatherings, and some very eccentric animals whom she came across in the course of her career as a roving reporter." - **Anwesha Mittra (The Times of India)**

"[Wacky Eire] promises to be 'stranger than fiction' and on that count it delivers, for you keep flipping pages to find out just how weirder it can get." (ib)

"Geraldine's style of narration is casual with loads of cheek thrown in, but never once dull or impassive...she is so consumed being a reporter all the time that you almost envy her for getting to go on such interesting assignments, meet oddball folks and be one with them. Wacky Eire stands for the diversity, and a crazy amalgamation of cultures and philosophies Ireland is yet to be known for." (ib)

"...such an honest, witty, even downright cheesy, account of her country can only come from a person who is completely taken in by it, and can't stop exploring it for everything it is worth" (Anwesha Mittra, The Times of India)

"Ireland does seem an odd place indeed from the array of eccentrics and oddballs Comiskey has encountered in the course of her work. Not all are as charming or delightful as they would like to think but you can't help laughing at the naughty farmers, crazy football fans and eccentric racehorse trainers." - **Books Ireland**

Still Life

By Geraldine Comiskey

Life painting

So how had my life gone so dramatically wrong? I asked myself the same question every time I took the bus to the wrong side of the city and hurried through the shabby street, avoiding eye contact with passers-by who had been passed by once too often in life. I wiped my fingers after I had pushed the grimy bell on the red door with the peeling paint and waited for the receptionist, Brenda, to answer. 'Yeah?' 'It's me, Chloe.' Then I trudged up the narrow stairs and into the dingy, poky offices of Wrightman, Wrightman & Wrightman, solicitors.

I had been doing this for a week, and it hadn't got any more appealing. Maybe if I had come from a background like Brenda's – or any of the other five secretaries – I would have been quite proud of having a job as an office assistant with a venerable firm that supplied free legal aid to Dublin's dynamic sub-culture. On my first day, Brenda had recognised one of the clients, a shoplifter, as an old schoolmate.

There were fee-paying clients, too, but these were mostly fussy pensioners and squabbling young couples, as the firm specialised in probate, conveyancing and, more recently, divorce. Or 'wills, bit of land and broken vows' as my Gran would have called it.

Well, I had certainly learned a lot about that in the last few months; enough to know that I had no wealthy relatives (dead or otherwise) to help out, that Mummy might have to sell the house – and that my Daddy had broken his promises to all of us. I should have felt at home in a solicitor's office; after all, Mummy was always talking about what her solicitor had said and how much he was costing.

But I knew straight away that I hadn't found my calling – and I didn't want to. The dress code at Wrightman, Wrightman & Wrightman was a grown-up version of my school uniform – and I hadn't been out of school long enough to forget that particular frocky horror.

'Mummy, I'm not going back there', I sobbed at the end of my first day.

'You can't just walk out of a job, Chloe. You're not a little girl any more', she said, and then, as if I needed reminding, she added: 'Remember when you burst into tears on the stage during the Nativity play?'

'Mummy, I was five years old!'

'Doesn't matter. You've always been too quick to give up. You just take an irrational dislike to a situation or a group of people –'

'But this is different. I know why I don't like this job and those awful secretaries. They've all got common accents and plastic handbags.'

I paused, waiting for sympathy; Mummy's collection of designer handbags had multiplied at such an alarming rate lately, my brother Daryus had joked that those crocodiles were still alive and breeding. Surely Mummy would understand how awful it was for me to work with girls who didn't know a Chanel from a Cheapo. But she was just glaring at me as if I was guilty of a crime worse than fashion forgery. So I continued to vent:

'...they keep telling me I'm too thin and rolling their eyes at each other every time I talk. And the clients are those people you see on Crimecatchers – they've even got photofit faces from being in too many fights and wearing the arses of nylon tights over their heads.

And the things I have to look at – colour photos of their victims, who all look as if they modelled for Picasso.'

'Well, you'll have to put up with it', she said with a steely edge to her voice I'd never heard before. 'You're very lucky my solicitor recommended you to his friend.'

'Some solicitor! He can't even find where Daddy's hiding my trust fund. And Mr Wrightman is a grumpy old man. I hate working for him.'

Yet I was back the next day, trying to ignore Mr Wrightman's loud throat-clearing noises as he waited for me to finish typing his boring letters, which was nearly impossible as I had to keep rewinding the Dictaphone tape to make out what he was growling.

'Chloe, are ya usin de phorocopier?'

I removed my headset. 'Does it look as if I am?'

'There's no need to be so bleedin rude', Brenda said and Mr Wrightman walked back into his office with his hands behind his back, as if he was above all that bickering – the pompous old fart, I thought and pulled a face at his back.

My immediate boss was Sandra, the senior secretary, who told me her correct title was 'Office Manager'. She was a thirty-something mother of four who was only working 'to get out of the house'. 'Why don't you take up a hobby then?' I had asked and she had narrowed her eyes as if I had somehow offended her. She marched around the office, her shoulders thrust squarely back, arms and legs keeping time, the way I'd seen army sergeants do (not that I'd actually met any real soldiers; I'd only seen them in the war movies I used to watch on TV with my Daddy). Anyway, she had the kind of carefully cut, subtly tinted brown hair that aspiring career women think makes them look 'smart' and the kind of put-on accent you hear in private housing estates which are back-to-back with Council flats – which was bad enough, but she also had an annoying habit of using that peculiar brand of DIY grammar you hear among people who are trying to sound hip when really they're just uneducated. Her favourite word was 'do-able'. She sounded like my stupid maths teacher who used to speak like Ross out of *Friends* until he slipped up and his country accent came out. Vom!

Brenda, the receptionist, just missed being a beauty – by a few hundred years. She had what Sister Agnes in Art class would have called 'Pre-Raphaelite features', 'Titian hair' and an 'Ingres body'. She had turned twenty on my first day at work, so we had celebrated her birthday with a cake in the office ('Go on, it'll do ya good to purra birra weight on' she had sniggered as she cut me an extra-large slice). She wasn't married and lived with her parents and three-year-old son, whose father was going to marry her…some day. I would have pitied her if she hadn't been so catty to me.

The other three, Natalie, Beverley and Tina, spent half their salaries 'gettin rat-arsed', and the rest on the wardrobe to go with it. They had the most extensive range of ill-fitting acrylic clothes I'd ever seen.

Natalie was ancient – at least twenty-two. Her dream was to be settled down with her 'fella'; she was hoping her parents would let them move into their council house. Beverley and Tina claimed to be nineteen, like me, but already had the air of people who'd been on the world a long time and didn't like what they'd seen.

'Here, you can make yourself useful and make me a coffee', Tina said on my first day. She held out a mug but, as I ignored it, she goggled her eyes and elbowed Beverley, who smirked and turned to me: 'Chloe, I don't know what kind of place you worked in before, but in dis office we all have to take orders.'

'I don't take orders', I said, 'and anyway you're not my employers.'

'Oooh!' They all looked at each other and smirked.

Just then Sandra walked in. 'Listen, Chloe, I don't know what kind of job you were in before this, but in here we're a team.'

What kind of team? I wanted to ask. Shot-putting? But I just said: 'I might offer to make you a coffee if I'm getting some for myself. And, for your information, I have never worked before.'

There was silence for about two minutes, then Tina loudly asked Beverley to make her a coffee and Beverley said: 'Certainly, Tina.'

'By de time I was your age, I was on me turd job', Natalie (or, as she and the other girls pronounced it, 'Natalie', told me as she trained me (I tried not to look impatient as she showed me how the filing system worked and explained what exactly a desktop computer did; she was very proud of having a secretarial certificate). 'When I left school, I worked wit me Ma, cleanin offices out in de business park near our place, but it just wasn't *me*, ya know? Isn't it strange de way sum jobs just don't suit ya? Ma and Da tawt I was bleedin *mental* when I walked out in de middle of me shift. Den I got a job in a video shop, but my nerves got bad because we were always being held up, so I went to work in a clothes shop. I would've been happy to stay wurkin dere, but de bleedin supervisor accewsed me of nickin tings, so she fired me and I went on de dole and den I was able to do a secretarial course free.' She grinned. 'So here I am.'

I suppose, if you looked at it from her perspective, she had done amazingly well to get a job in a solicitor's firm, even if it was two bus rides from her Council estate and the pay wasn't much more than what she had been getting on the dole – which was why she was still living with her parents.

I hoped I wouldn't still be living with Mummy at twenty-two. I had always been sure I'd have a spacious apartment in the South of France at that age. I had visualised myself, fresh out of art college, living off my trust fund and building up a reputation as the most exciting neo-classical painter of modern times. And of course I'd have a hot millionaire fiancé, the kind you see in the Ralph Lauren *Polo* ad or *Hello* magazine. We'd fly to all the best parties in New York, Tokyo, Abu Dhabi, Hong Kong and London, I'd be photographed in the latest designers – and, every so often, we'd go on a McDate in Dublin, just so I'd get a chance to be snapped in my jeans for the tabloids. And my publicist would tell the paparazzi that I was really a simple girl at heart. Which would be true; after all, what could be simpler than expecting the best in life? It had been my destiny.

But now nothing in my life was certain. Daddy had left Mummy, my trust fund had totally vanished and I had had to drop out of Dublin's most prestigious art academy – which had been just a stepping stone to the Sorbonne but, all the same, dearly missed. I had just finding the remaining three months of my term and cried in the Principal's office as I told him my parents wouldn't be paying the fees for my second year. He hadn't offered to let me stay on free (which had been the whole point of my telling him myself). He hadn't even suggested I try for a scholarship – *that* had hurt most of all, because it meant he didn't think I was such a promising painter.

My friends didn't seem to think I was worth hanging onto, either. Once they realised I could no longer pay my way into Dublin's coolest bars, go on shopping sprees or travel all over Europe to music festivals, they had all faded out of my life like oil colours exposed to harsh daylight. My new reality was a boring, full-time job, a monthly clothes budget (like, I could afford *one* top or *one* pair of jeans – half an outfit) and a totally selfish mother who just sat in front of the TV drinking wine and not even asking me how I was feeling.

I used to think my life had been sketched out for me, and that all I had to do was colour it in. But real life isn't painted by numbers; like all true works of art, it is mysterious, unplanned, inspired by forces beyond the control of the artist. Or so Sister Agnes used to say in Art History class. Isn't it strange that her words have only come back to me now, years after the bloody exams?

I stopped painting when my father left my mother; it's hard to spread paint across a canvas with tears rolling down your cheeks. All through my childhood and teens, it had always seemed as if there had been a bottomless well inside me, ready to overflow, to drown me, if I didn't bail out all those ideas, whims, ghosts, mysterious images. But suddenly the paint had run out, and all that was left in the well was murky, stale-smelling sepia, the colour of old photos – photos of dead people.

Daddy had made a total shambles of the goodbye – he'd always been awkward with us 'children' as he still called my brother Daryus and me. He had pecked us each on the cheek as we stood in the doorway, trying to ignore the sound of my mother sobbing on the stairs behind us. I think Daddy wanted to get away quickly in case Mummy ran after him and damaged the car – the silver 'Fworrsh' as she had laughingly called it when he had bought it just a year before. He had called the car his 'mistress' – maybe he was dropping a hint.

You're probably thinking we should have been warned – well, everyone knows a flashy new car is just screaming 'midlife crisis; divorce alert!' But my Daddy had never seemed the type. Otherwise he would have left Mummy many years before. There were always women hanging around who wanted to work for him, learn from and…well, take him away from us. You don't get to be one of Ireland's richest self-made businessmen without attracting some gold-diggers.

But he had stayed loyal to Mummy all those years. 'My beautiful wife is every woman to me', he used to tell those tarts who used to interview him for Sunday supplement features on 'Ireland's most bankable men'. Mummy was sure they couldn't spell and really meant 'bonkable'.

So you can imagine how shocked everyone was when he moved in with a woman who not only lacked something upstairs but didn't even have a killer body to compensate. Mummy had thought it was a joke when we saw that photo of them in the business section of Ireland's sleaziest broadsheet, *Sins On Sunday*. The forty-ish woman linking his arm as they came out of a Paris hotel was just one of his secretaries. Daddy had always employed homely women because he firmly believed they were harder working – and less likely to run off to the Caribbean with one of his less morally scrupulous partners.

But I've often suspected the plain ones are more dangerous – like those innocuous looking camouflaged fish that lurk under the sand and then poison you with their concealed spikes. It's as if they have to make up for being overlooked all their lives. I went to school with a few girls like that – and they were experts at stealing boyfriends. One of them, Emmabelle McCowan (Emmabelle the Cow I called her), took my date from right under my nose at the graduation ball (or the 'debs', as it's called here in Ireland, where we still like to copy the English). I left him alone to go to the loo, and, when I got back, she had her lips locked onto his like one of those lampreys in the National Aquarium.

I had been wearing a custom-made creation that perfectly showed my tiny waist and long legs, and Mummy's blue coral necklace that matched my eyes so perfectly. Yet I, Chloe O'Doolahan, a girl who had turned away at least five model scouts on our hols in Sardinia that summer, had lost my boyfriend to a girl who looked like she belonged on a daytime TV chat show.

Anyway, I wouldn't be bumping into Emmabelle the Cow again; I didn't go to the school reunion. I couldn't bear to see her smirking at me. I'd rather be Emmabelle-less.

I tried to imagine how much worse it must have been for Mummy when Daddy left her after twenty years for a woman whose most interesting features were her bottle-blonde hair and the kind of beetling eyebrows you can only get away with if you've got big boobs and unshakeable self-confidence. But Carmel Delahanty had neither.

Worse, I discovered I had a half-brother – called Lexus. Imagine calling a child after a car. I couldn't resist pointing out to her that he seemed more like a souped-up dodgem.

I hadn't known little Lexus was related to me when Carmel brought him to our house the previous Christmas. I was sure he was the son of some maniac, even though Carmel had reassured me he was 'just going through the Terrible Twos' when he rammed his tricycle into my shins. Daryus and I only found out Lexus the Terrible was our brother five months later, when Mummy's solicitor told her Daddy had a baby son to support – oh, and lots of debts.

I didn't mind about the bankruptcy so much; it was cool, having a Daddy on the run from the Revenue and hundreds of creditor, most of them filthy rich themselves – quite a few of them part of our social circle. It was the *loss* of my Daddy that hurt the most.

Until then, I'd thought of divorce in an abstract way; it was something that happened to other people's parents – and you could always tell which ones, because they'd be fighting all the time or the man would be a total lech.

But the first Daryus and I heard of it was exactly a week after the *Sins On Sunday* photo appeared. Mummy and Daddy called us into the drawing room to talk about 'something important that concerns all of us, as a family.'

'They're probably going to tell us how much we've got in our trust funds', Daryus said with a grin.

I gave him my best disapproving look. 'All you ever think about is money'

'Not true – I'm thinking about what to *buy* with it. A nice gaff, somewhere sunny – yeah, I'll go and live in Greece! And I'll have a garage-load of motorbikes and a recording studio.'

'Well, I hope it's a soundproof one.'

He laughed. 'You'll be begging me to recognise you when I'm collecting my Grammy. I'll have to tell the tabloids my big sister tried to discourage me from becoming a rock star, and people will be afraid to buy your poxy paintings in case they're attacked by my angry fans.'

'What fans?' I laughed. 'Felim and Robert? Oh, sorry, they're going to be in the band, aren't they? You should call yourselves the Karaoke Kings.'

He pulled a face. 'Practising for your stage make-up, are you?' I laughed and dodged his pretend-kick.

We ran down the stairs, laughing and jostling, and into the drawing room. I've always felt embarrassed about Mummy's old-fashioned names for the rooms in our house: drawing room, scullery, pantry, Daddy's study, and her own little dressing room which is really just a walk-in wardrobe…though it is over two hundred years old so I suppose she's just respecting its history.

But this time it really felt like a drawing room; all formal and un-homely. Any minute now, I fantasised they're going to offer me a stark choice between marrying a rich old landowner or becoming a governess, just like in a period novel. Or maybe someone had died and left us a fortune, a little voice whispered in my head (probably the same voice that spoke to Daryus).

They made us sit down on the couch facing them. They sat in the armchairs, Daddy with his arms folded, Mummy with her hands on her lap, twisting one of Daddy's handkerchiefs. Her eyes looked red and puffy. That was nothing new these days; Mummy was going through the menopause and often cried for no apparent reason. Before that, she had always suffered from PMT. I was always grateful that I didn't have Mummy's 'artistic temperament', as my Daddy called it. 'Your mother has got the temperament and you've got the talent', he used to say as he brought me to meet yet another friend of his who owned a gallery (not that any of them had ever managed to sell a pointing for me; neo-classical just isn't in fashion, they told me).

Daddy heaved a sigh, and launched into his speech the way I'd seen him do at board meetings he'd let me attend. 'Your mother and I have decided to separate.' He raised his hand in a 'Stop' gesture – as if we were even thinking of interrupting. 'We've already decided so it's pointless trying to change our minds.'

It's not negotiable, I was thinking. That's what he was saying, wasn't it? I wasn't sure what he meant; nothing made sense any more.

Daddy's voice seemed far off even though he was right in front of us. 'Your mother and I haven't been getting on well for a long time. We stayed together for your sakes, until you grew up, but you must have felt the tension – and I'm sorry for that, believe me. We're both sorry.'

What tension? I asked myself. I glanced first at Mummy, then Daryus. The only one in the room who didn't appear to be in shock was Daddy. He looked very composed, the way he looked when he was speaking to a room full of investors.

He gave a little cough, the way he usually did with business acquaintances when he wanted to end a conversation that was 'going nowhere' as he would put it. 'Well, there's really nothing more to say.' He stood up quickly, reaching for his overcoat and scarf, which he had draped across the armchair as if he was a stranger who hadn't intended to stay long. His eyes rested first on Daryus, then me. 'I'm sorry, kiddos. It's not your fault.'

We know it's not, I wanted to say, but I just stared at him, willing myself not to burst into tears. Daddy had taught me to be tough back in the old days when he was making the transition from small-time car salesman to mega-rich wheeler-dealer. I had been bullied at national school and thought I'd find a more hospitable environment in the fee-paying academy, but my new classmates had made fun of my accent.

Now he was throwing me headfirst into another situation where I didn't fit in – and I was determined not to cry like Mummy, who was sniffling and dabbing her eyes with the handkerchief.

Daddy leaned down to kiss my cheek and I flinched. He looked hurt and tried to hug Daryus, but my brother's jaw tightened.

'Daryus, Chloe, you'll always be my children.' He looked at us, his eyes fleeting from one to the other. 'I really didn't mean this to happen. Someday I hope you'll understand. See you around, kiddos!'

And he put on his overcoat and off he went.

For a few weeks, I tried to pretend nothing had changed. After all, Daddy had never spent a lot of time at home; he was always abroad on business. He had promised to let Mummy keep our five-bedroomed house in the seaside village of Belgowan – which was Dublin's most upmarket district according to all the property experts. But he wasn't paying maintenance – and Mummy was rapidly realising that all those tearful sessions in her solicitor's office were only eating into what was left of her personal bank account (for one thing, she had to splash out on a new handbag for every meeting). 'You can always sell the house – or go out to work', Aunty Helen told her over a glass of champagne one morning. 'I mean, you're not as bad off as I am.'

Aunty Helen was Mummy's older sister, who had left school early to help out in the family business, a grocery-cum-newsagents, in their country village. She had married an accountant and they'd produced five kids by the time Mummy met Daddy at a cousin's wedding. I've often thought Helen begrudged Mummy her easy life. Helen had turned down a scholarship to study physics at uni – she'd sacrificed everything for love. On top of running the shop and raising my cousins, she had cared for Gran and Grandad until they died in their nineties. They'd been disabled for years but wouldn't let he get a carer for them, so Helen was on duty twenty-four-seven. Uncle Con was no help, working late and spending all his free time in the pub, watching soccer with his cronies – before running away with their savings. And their kids (a boy and four girls) had gone their separate ways as soon as they finished uni.

But Mummy just wailed: 'Helen, it's easy for you. You're used to working. You're good with money and budgets. You're so organised, you put everyone else to shame – especially the way you carried on with the shop after Con left you. But I'm not able for it. I'm just no good at coping on my own.'

'Sure you have the children. Chloe and Daryus will look after you – won't you, Chloe?' I tried to smile back at her, but my face was sinking under the sudden weight of the responsibility she had so casually thrown at me.

Mummy looked up at me from the table, with big, red-rimmed basset hound eyes. 'Chloe, pet, you won't go off and leave me, will you?'

Daryus walked in and Mummy turned her self-pity towards him. 'Ah, what would I do without my big handsome son?' She sighed and looked at Helen. 'He's the man of the house now.'

Helen nodded with tearful eyes. 'So was mine. Bee, would you mind pouring me another glass of that Moët?'

'Oh, I'm sorry, Helen. That was the last of it.'

Mixed palette

'So what do yewse drink on a night out?' Beverley asked me as she helped me put together a brief for Mr Wrightman (I was sure he was trying to embarrass us, the way he smirked and fumbled in his trouser pocket while he said: 'I want you to go through my briefs').

'Well, it depends on which crowd I'm going around with. When I'm with my boyfriend and his friends, and their girlfriends, I drink two breezers max because I don't want to fall over on the dancefloor. If it's a girls-only night, we start off with white wine spritzers and then by the end of the evening we're into slammers and martinis – a different drink in every club. If I'm at a party with my folks, I stay on the champagne.'

Even as I said it, I realised I was talking about my old life again. I tried not to look as if I was lying, but Beverley was giggling.

'Gerrup de yard! Little Miss La-di-dah! Next you'll be tellin me about your polo ponies and your yacht and de mansion in Marbella wirra swimmin pool, and the golf club.'

So I didn't tell her. Well, I was hardly going to tell her that the yacht and our Marbella villa had been repossessed or that I'd never had polo ponies but some of Daddy's friends had, and his golf club membership hadn't expired; that was why he could still play rounds and have lunch in the clubhouse despite being bankrupt. Meanwhile I couldn't even afford to continue my riding lessons and would have to forget about ever having my own horse.

'So, do yewse have any pets at home?'

'No.'

'A home wirour an animal – I tink dat's sad.'

'Well, I did have a dog – but she died.' Now why was I telling her that? It wasn't as if I wanted her sympathy – and anyway nothing could bring back Scarlet O'Hara; she was in the past, along with my memories of a happy family.

'Oh. Dat's terrible. What did ih die of?'

'I'd rather not say', I said, hiding behind my hair in case she saw my eyes were brimming with tears. I blinked furiously. Scarlet O'Hara had been knocked down by Daddy's mistress as they drove away. They hadn't stopped. I still have nightmares about crying over her broken body on the road. Someone had called the vet but he couldn't do a thing to save her.

'What sort of dog?' Beverley persisted.

'She was an Irish setter.' A tear escaped as I thought of my true friend, who had always known when to be quiet and just be there for me, her silky red head on my tummy as I cried myself to sleep after a bullying incident at school or a break-up with some silly boy.

'What was her name?'

'Scarlet O'Hara.'

'Jayz. After yer woman in de fillum. Hey, Natalie, you'll never guess what Chloe's dog's called: Scarleh! Scharleh Bleedin O'Hara!'

'Scarlet – I mean, Chloe – can I have a word with you?'

I quickly wiped my eye with the back of my hand and looked around to find Janet McStamp, frowning at me over her nasty brown-rimmed glasses (which made her look like a female version of Austin Powers). She was the junior partner in the firm, had only been practising law for a year and was supposed to be some sort of genius who'd won a scholarship to uni. But she was the most demanding – and the hardest to please. I just couldn't do anything right for her.

Now I followed her into her untidy office and tripped over a pile of files. I bent down to pick them up and she yelled: 'Leave them! Just sit down – before you do any more damage. And stop looking as if you're about to burst into tears. Only the likes of my uncle would fall for that.'

Gingerly, I removed a Post-It from the plastic seat where her clients usually sat (they were mostly what Mr Wrightman called 'deadwood' – people who paid late and whom he was anxious to lose).

Janet ran her raggedy fingernails through her greasy, shoulder-length brown hair and chewed on a pen. She always did this when she was gathering her thoughts. I dearly hoped some judge would find it offensive and tell her.

She handed me a piece of paper. 'Chloe, I don't give a fiddler's what you and the other girls call me among yourselves, but if you think you can make a mockery of me and...' She was going on and on in that monotone voice that she probably used to send her opponents to sleep. I was just nodding and trying to look contrite, wondering what she was talking about.

Then I glanced down at the page; I'd headed her letter 'MoreFee's Law'. I felt my cheeks redden as I wondered what else I had sub-consciously typed. This was exactly the kind of thing I had always been in trouble for doing when I was at school – except, with a pencil in my hand, I had drawn caricatures of the teachers.

'...Well, I've made my point and I'm not going to hammer it home again. I'm going to have to ask Sandra to check all your work before it goes in the post – these court documents are just too important to get wrong. Can you imagine if this had actually gone to the defendant's solicitors?'

The other partner, Mr Wrightman's nephew Barry, was easier to work for – because he hardly ever showed up. He simply appeared every day around lunchtime, smiled at everyone and waited for his uncle to come to lunch. Mr Wrightman always returned alone about three hours later, chuckling to himself, so I suppose Barry was there in a therapeutic capacity.

'Did you hear anything about Mr Wrightman's other nephew coming to work here?' Sandra was asking Brenda as I went out for my lunch, alone (Brenda and Sandra preferred to sit in the office, gossiping and swapping childcare tips over home-made sandwiches and instant soup; I had stopped going to the pub with the other three because they always chatted as though I didn't exist). Now I lingered a while, pretending to flick through my diary, as I tried to find out more about this nephew.

'Yes, but I'm not supposed to know yet. People give me faxes to send and dey tink I don't read them.'

'Is he a partner or associate? I don't see his name on the letterhead.'

'Not yet. You haven't met him because he went abroad just before you started – I tink it had sometin to do wit his wife leavin him. He got depressed or sometin.'

'She probably cleaned him out.'

'I'd say she did. She was a solicirror too – or so I heard.'

'So he's divorced?'

'Well, separayred anyhow.'

'Jayz. Is he anytin to look ah?' Sandra always slipped back into her real accent at some point in a conversation.

Brenda gave a dirty belly-chuckle. 'He's a looker all right! If I wasn't engaged to Clint, I'd go for him meself.'

They looked around at me. 'Are you goin out for lunch, Chloe?' Brenda asked.

'Yes. Do you want anything from the shops?'

'Yeah. You wouldn't mind gerrin us a packet of smokes, would you? I'll pay you later. Here.' She handed me an empty packet. 'Just in case you forget and get me de wrong ones. You're not really wirrit today, are you?'

'Wirrit? – I mean what?' That accent must be catching, I thought in horror.

'You're not concentrayrin. If Sandra hadn't opened dat envelope you put in the "Out" tray, all our liabilirry stuff would've gone to de bleedin defence.'

'You'll have to be more careful, Chloe', Sandra wagged her finger.

'Sorry.'

'Sorry won't be good enough the next time. Cop on to yourself, or you'll be ourrof a job.'

I nodded and tried to look concerned, but then I worried that I'd get a wrinkly forehead like Janet; she had obviously trained herself to look sympathetic to clients, but she'd be able to afford a facelift in a few years, whereas I'd be stuck with an anxious face and not even a career to make up for it.

'He'll go for Chloe; all dem posh blokes fancy skinny ones like dat. Not bleedin fair, is it?' I heard Brenda say as soon as I had shut the door behind me.

It was warm for May – and it had stopped raining. I could smell the black grime that clung to the grey buildings and farted out of cars and buses. It mingled with the putrid, salty stench of the River Liffey and, as I crossed the bridge, the halitosis of the brewery on the other side. It was a smell both seductive and repulsive, like an unsuitable lover, I imagined – not that I'd know, having never had an actual lover, unsuitable or otherwise. Snogging spotty boys didn't count. I stopped in the middle of the bridge, turning my back on the Four Courts building with all its negative connotations – my parents' divorce, my depressing job – and looked downriver. Out there was a sea, and beyond it Britain, which I remembered as a land of beautiful shops and country hotels and strange remarks about my 'Irish accent'.

I walked across the bridge to *my* Dublin. All my favourite shops were there, the pubs where I used to hang out on Saturday evenings, the clubs where I used to lean against the bar, too cool to dance.

And Daddy's office. As I came into the leafy square, I slowed down, wondering what I was doing there. After all, the bailiffs would have taken away the last of the office equipment and someone else would be in the office now. I wondered, idly, if it was populated by secretaries who said 'compewrer' and carried those ubiquitous plastic handbags everyone seemed to be carrying since I had entered the sub-culture of the secretarial lifestyle. 'There must be a jungle somewhere where poachers are risking their lives to trap plastic crocodiles', I had said to Mummy the previous night, but she had just sighed.

I stopped in front of the four-storey Georgian townhouse I remembered so well and gazed up at the big windows on the first floor, but all I could see was the reflection of the sun. I had been so proud of my Daddy the first time he had brought me and Daryus into his new office. I had been ten years old, Daryus nine, and we had got off school especially for our Daddy's big day. That was when we had realised we were 'rich people' and I'd be going to a new school where there wouldn't be rough girls who pulled hair (I soon discovered 'young ladies' were a lot more vicious, but with comments rather than fingernails).

Had Carmel Delahanty been Daddy's secretary then? I thought so. She'd certainly been working for him for a long time. She'd been the one who had organised all those trips to cities with exotic names that, after a while, became familiar ones: Budapest, Prague, Tallinn, and Dubai... I wondered where Lexus the Terrible had been conceived – probably Transylvania.

Feeling the way I imagined a burglar would feel casing a house, I walked up the steps and looked at the bell-panel. There were the names of an architects' firm, a food manufacturer's head office, a political pressure group and, where Daddy's firm used to be, an airline. Very appropriate I thought; Daddy had flown away from us.

It began to rain, so I walked fast down the street and found myself at the railway station where I used to get the suburban train home after a shopping spree – I had just walked there on autopilot, forgetting about work. It would take me a good twenty minutes to walk back to the office; I was going to be late back even if I ran. Oh well, I thought; I might as well be hung for the proverbial sheep as for a lamb. I toyed with the idea of going into a pub and getting drunk, the way people did in movies when they were down on their luck. But then I told myself it wouldn't be much fun.

So I went into the National Gallery. I hadn't been there since leaving art college, but I used to attend every exhibition at least twice. I'd always resented the hordes of raucous brats and their teachers who herded them through all the salons. What right did they have to be there, when they didn't appreciate the paintings? I used to wish the gallery would charge an entrance fee to deter them. But now I was glad it was free. Maybe it was true, what Gran used to say: 'Dublin is a grand city to be poor in.'

This time, I walked briskly past Sir John Lavery's works, even his charming portrait of Lady Lavery with her little daughter in the snow, which had always been my favourite because I fancied they looked like Mummy and me; now it only reminded me my Daddy was no longer in the picture. And Sir John's painting of Michael Collins brought me close to tears; I associated everything Irish with my father, who had always been a fervent patriot – I wondered if he still was.

I averted my eyes from the National Portrait Collection too; I was afraid I'd find one of Daddy's creditors smirking down at me from among the well-known Irish people whose likenesses were captured only too well. I wouldn't have minded so much if they'd been traditional, flattering portraits, but I couldn't handle an accusing stare from a Robert Ballagh soul-picture or a ghostly Louis Le Brocquy abstract.

Even the Flemish exhibition, on loan from various international galleries, reminded me of my former life and the contrast with my present situation. Normally, I'd find Vermeer's and Van Eyck's domestic scenes soothing, but now their underlying mysteries made me nervous; home life never really was as tranquil as it was supposed to be, once you looked at it closely enough. The mirrors within the paintings reflected more than the images in them. If Vermeer had been around now, he would probably have painted *Lady Reading a Decree Nisi*, and if you looked closely at the mirror on the wall you'd see a reflection of the husband's overcoat hanging up and the hairs of another woman on the shoulder.

The sculptures dotted around the gallery should have been a distraction. But I envied them their stony hearts, their plaster complexions that never blushed or paled, their smug invulnerability, their immortality.

What I needed was art that matched my mood and took it out of the shadows – something uplifting. El Greco? No; too pious. Rubens? Too carnal, robustly intimate – too sociable. I hungered for something about violence, injustice, betrayal... But what? Where? In a daze, I walked around, not really looking at anything now.

I drifted up the curved staircase and into the Italian Masters room…then stopped short as I always did when I entered; it was, as always, overwhelming.

The room simmered with ancient passion. Five-hundred-year-old eyes stared at me as if they understood my deepest thoughts and disapproved, some showing their scorn by continuing to converse among themselves. I had no right to have ever called myself an artist, they seemed to be saying – these characters that were so much more than colours on canvas. They were echoes of the artists' eternal souls, preserved in egg tempura and the blood of crushed insects.

I walked slowly over to Caravaggio's *The Taking of Christ*. The painting seemed to be speaking to me intimately, as if Caravaggio himself was sulking along with me over the unfairness of everything.

I remembered what I'd heard a guide say to a group of tourists the last time I'd stood in front of that painting: those Roman soldiers capturing Jesus were really portraits of the policemen who had arrested Caravaggio, who was by all accounts a yob. The painting had been his revenge against the authorities – a centuries-old hissy fit!

Of course, it had been unspeakably arrogant –and sacrilegious – of Caravaggio to compare his brush with the law with Christ's crucifixion. But maybe he could be forgiven. As I stared at the painting, I could feel the anger and humiliation that had inspired the fiery lad to paint those scowling, self-righteous looking, oafish faces in such detail. These were men he knew and despised. Art and the law just didn't go together – maybe that was why I hated my job in a solicitor's office.

I glanced at my Swatch (a present from Daryus when he still had pocket money) and panicked. It was four-thirty. I felt my stomach turn over. Tedious and depressing as my job was, I needed it to pay my gym fees and hairdresser – I couldn't face life as a mousy brunette. I was also putting a small amount by every week to visit friends in France in the hope that they'd find me a job there, working in a gallery or something...

Well, there was no point in going back to the office now; even if I sprinted back to the office, I'd just get there as Brenda was locking up. I'd just take the remaining half hour off and hope no one remembered the next day that I'd been gone since lunchtime. I suddenly felt pleased with my solution to a stressful situation.

The sky had clouded over again by the time I came out of the gallery. It was cold, for the brink of summer, and I was glad of my 'bus jacket' as I called the grey waterproof thing I wore to work to protect my clothes from the grime and sweat and general ickyness of public transport. My whole dress style had changed with my life, and these days I rarely wore skirts; I just didn't feel safe baring my legs in front of the criminal clients – even the female ones, who tended to wear leisure suits and yelled at me as I passed them on the street ("Hey, you over dere! Tink you're berrer dan us, do ya?'). Even the passing motorists behaved more laddishly in the rough part of Dublin. So I went to work in my purdah of loose trousers and shapeless tops (most of them presents from Aunty Helen, who had always been the opposite of what a godmother was supposed to be).

Here, in the nicer part of town, I could have got away with a mini-skirt; the occasional driver might hoot, but I could just turn up my nose and pretend not to hear him, and he wouldn't persist because I'd be just one of many attractively dressed women coming out of the offices, sashaying out of designer shops with bags full of goodies, relaxing at pavement tables outside the stylish bars and cafés where the cappuccino cost that little bit more but was totally worth it.

The great thing about Dublin, though, was that you never felt scruffy even in the upmarket parts. I looked like a casually dressed student, I supposed – which I would have been if I hadn't had my education rudely interrupted by my parents' divorce. It was all the fault of that floozy, Carmel Delahanty. I felt angry every time I thought of her.

I walked slowly along the street, not really wanting to leave the area around the National Gallery; it felt more like home than the house did these days. At least I could get the train all the way home today, instead of climbing onto that awful, stinking bus with its shabby passengers who were all, no doubt, heading for bleak housing estates full of working mums who left the kids with their grans because they couldn't afford childcare, and wore acrylic trousers to work. People like Sandra and Brenda – mothers like my Mummy most definitely was not.

Mummy had left some cash and a note on the table for me: 'Order a pizza for yourself and Daryus. Gone to Helen's. Might stay over.'

'Daryus!' I yelled up the stairs. I heard a thud from his room. I walked halfway up the stairs and yelled again: 'Daryus, I'm ordering a pizza. What sort of topping do you want?'

He popped a wet head around the door. 'Get what you like. I'm going out.' I caught a whiff of deodorant off him.

'Daryus, you never wash or wear deodorant.'

'He looked shifty. 'I'm going to a rehearsal.'

I took in the black shirt with the vertical grey pin-stripes, the clean jeans and what looked like a new pair of trainers. 'What sort of rehearsal? *Catch a Star?*'

'No-o-oh! Can you see the Saturday night telly viewers voting for an underground band?'

'Well, no – but your image is hardly underground – not with what's-his-face on the bass and his little brother on the drums. He doesn't even shave!'

'We're ironic', he said and fluffed up his hair with his fingers. 'Remember the New Romantics from the eighties? Like on *MTV Vintage?*'

I cocked an eyebrow.

'Well, it's not their look but their attitude.'

'A long way from underground, then.'

'No. We're a cross-over band. Sort of *Neo*-New Romantic, with underground overtones – without the grunge influences but, you know, sort of punk revival with a bit of metal…' His voice trailed off and he reddened.

'Oh, right. Well, for what it's worth, you look like an office boy or an aspiring off-duty supermarket manager or – or a blind date!' I laughed. 'Who is she?'

He flushed a deeper shade of red and slammed his bedroom door. Why was my little brother being so secretive? And what had happened to his grungy attitude? If Mummy had bought him a shirt like that just a few months ago, he would have scowled and refused to wear it. She used to use him as a fashion advisor for conservative occasions; if Daryus said 'It makes me want to puke', she knew she was appropriately dressed for a wedding, funeral or Neighbourhood Watch meeting.

Now I felt like I should be mourning the loss of my brother. It seemed as I his body had been possessed by the spirit of an original, pre-Celtic Tiger yuppie – he looked like Daddy did in photos from the eighties. I banged on his door. 'You're eighteen, Daryus. You look ridiculous in that shirt.'

I went downstairs and dialled the pizza people. Now that Daryus wasn't staying in, I could order a small vegetarian pizza instead of a large one with meat on one half and the taste of meat on my half. While I was waiting for it to be delivered, I heard Daryus run down the stairs and slam the front door. I ran into the drawing room and looked out the window; he was getting into a taxi. Mummy must have given him his allowance, which was very unfair; she had stopped mine since I'd started work.

I felt betrayed by Daryus, and not just because of the allowance injustice; it was mean of him not to tell me who he was going to meet. After all, it wasn't as if I'd tell Mummy.

The pizza guy arrived just as I was finishing off a packet of crisps. 'Thanks so bloody much', I snarled. 'When I ordered a genuine Italian pizza I didn't realise you'd be bringing it from Italy.'

'Well, you migh as well be over dere yerself, it took so long to find de house – would youse ever tink of purrin a bleedin number on yer gate?'

I looked at him. 'Are you by any chance from Ballyskanger?'

His cigarette fell from his mouth. 'How d'ya know?'

'You've got an accent exactly like some girls I work with who live there', I said and slammed the door.

Bloody cheek of him, I thought, delivering pizzas and not being Italian. I was sure he didn't even know who Caravaggio was – he probably thought he was a Mafia don.

'Chloe, dere's norra pick on you',Tina said as I stuffed a chocolate croissant into my mouth, hoping Mr Wrightman wouldn't come out of his office and catch me; he was always giving out to the others for eating *al desko*. I had missed breakfast because I'd overslept; I had forgotten to set the alarm. I had lain awake until three-thirty, when I'd heard Daryus sneaking up the stairs. Then I had fallen into a fitful sleep. Mummy hadn't come home and the house had seemed strange. I was still wondering if I should call to see if she was home from Aunty Helen's yet – and, if not, whether I should ring my aunt.

'You know, dat's de first time we've seen you eatin sometin fattenin', Beverley was saying. 'You're havin a blow-out, right?'

'Actually, Beverley, I eat what I like, when I like. I'm not anorexic or bulimic and, by the way I'm happy with my figure.'

Beverley and Tina looked offended, but before I could apologise for snapping or they could think of a retort, Natalie and Brenda walked in.

'Jayz, Chloe', Natalie said, 'you're eatin a croissant!' She pronounced it 'cross-ant'. She pinched the spare tyre that was just visible between the end of her tight top and the waistband of her elastic hipsters. 'I wish I had your figure.' I was sure she meant the reverse; she was scowling as she said it. 'Do you ever eat chips?'

'Of course I do.'

'From de chipper?'

'Yes. And last night I ate pizza.'

Natalie looked at the others and the four of them rolled their eyes at each other. 'Jayz', they chorused.

'Oh, by the way', Natalie said, 'Sandra's in a right snot wit you.'

'A snot?'

'Too right she is. Where were you yesterday afternoon?'

I thought for a moment. 'I didn't feel well. I had to go home.'

'Well, you shoulda called de office. You coulda left a message wit Brenda here. We had to work late to put togedder all dose books of pleadins Mr Wrightman gave you to do.'

I froze. I hoped they hadn't told old Wrightman.

'We didn't tell him, because he would've been in a major snot.'

'A major snot', I repeated. 'Thanks.' Maybe my colleagues were all right after all.

'Burrif it happens again', Natalie wagged a finger at me, 'we're not coverin up for you. It's not fair, expectin udder people to do your work for you –'

'– whedder you're sick or just skivin off', Tina cut in.

Sandra walked in then and we tried to look busy. She marched over to my desk and dumped a heap of files in front of me. 'Chloe, I need these letters put in date order.'

'Chronological order', I said. 'Right.'

'Oh, by the way, I'm deducting half a sick day for yesterday.'

Before I had the chance to ask her what 'half a sick day' was (did you spend the whole day feeling fifty-per-cent unwell, or plan a morning of vomiting?), Mr Wrightman came out of his office.

'Well, Miss O'Doolahan, how are you today?' His voice had a cheerful, Hooray-Henryish booming tone instead of the usual growl.

I looked up at him warily. 'I'm very well, thank you, Mr Wrightman.'

'Splendid. Very good indeed. Glad to hear it.' He seemed to want to say something very badly. He cleared his throat. 'I wonder if you would mind coming into my office for a moment?'

I ignored the smirking of my colleagues and tried not to shake as I followed him in. He was going to fire me, I was sure.

'Please sit down, Miss O'Doolahan. Now, I've been going through your curriculum vitae, and I see that you're fluent in French.' He removed his glasses and squinted at me (I wondered if he thought sight and sound ran off the same motor because he often did that when he was listening to clients). 'I take it you're not lying.'

If I was I wouldn't tell you, I wanted to answer, but I replied: 'Of course not, Mr Wrightman.'

'Excellent. Well, then you can help me with a rather tedious little job. It's for my nephew, you see. May I confide in you, Miss O'Doolahan?'

I nodded, hoping he wasn't going to talk about some fetish or his wife not understanding him. I was suddenly glad that he was elderly and overweight; if he leapt across his desk, he'd rupture something.

He frowned, as if he had been reading my thoughts, and I was annoyed to find myself blushing. 'I hope you didn't get the wrong idea', he said. 'I'm happily married.'

'Oh, Mr Wrightman, I'm glad to hear it – I never doubted it', I said, feeling even more embarrassed.

'I don't know why everyone thinks I should be a lecher. Must be my age or something. Bloody feminists started all that, you know.' He paused and wipes his glasses with a flannel, then put them on and frowned at me. I suppressed a sudden urge to laugh.

'Where was I? Ah, yes; my nephew John, my late sister's son. He's getting divorced, you see – from a French girl. Terrible state of affairs. Lovely girl, wonderful family.' He sniffed and shook his head. 'Anyway, for whatever reason, they've had their differences and now, after three years of marriage, they're packing it in.' He sighed. 'The documentation is all in French, of course, and I was wondering if you could translate it into English for John.'

'Yes, certainly', I said, wondering if a marriage guidance counsellor had ever told John and his wife: 'You just don't speak the same language'.

'Lack of communication, that's the problem between all young couples these days.' He wagged a finger at me. 'Don't make the same mistake when you get married –that's if you're not one of these independent women or lesbians or whatever all the young girls are supposed to be turning into.'

He opened a drawer and pulled out a manila envelope. 'Here you are, then. I'll need it done by this evening. Make it a priority.'

I took it; there seemed to be a lot of paper inside.

'Oh, by the way, John is coming to work for us. He's starting on Monday.'

I dumped the envelope on my desk and sidled towards the door; it was nearly lunchtime (well, quarter of an hour before) and I wasn't going to miss that bus. Brenda looked up so I told her: 'I'm just going to the loo.'

'In your coat?'

'Well, I will be if I have to hold it any longer. I need to get some things out of my coat pockets.'

'Ah', she nodded in mock-sympathy. '*Dah* time of the munt again, is it? Jaysus, dah's de second time dis munt !'

'I hadn't realised you were keeping count', I said haughtily and rushed out before anyone could stop me.

I ran to the bus stop and stood there, looking at my watch. The bus was due in one minute; it would drop me less than five minutes' walk away from the National Gallery, and I'd get to spend at least half an hour there even allowing for the fact that I might have to walk back if there wasn't a bus.

Twenty minutes later, I was still debating whether to start walking, or continue to wait, to hope... After another five minutes, I cut my losses and set off at a brisk walk – only to be passed out by the bus. Blast! My life had become so much harder since I'd had to give up taxis.

The gallery was busy that day. Crowds of tourists in waterproof windcheaters were being herded in by fussy-looking women, some with foreign accents. I wondered what it would feel like to spend the day yelling at people 'Follow me!' in five languages and patiently answering questions ranging from an urgent 'Where are the toilets?' (coach tours always seemed to attract people with bladder problems) to a cheerful 'Is it OK if I bring my camera in?' (philistine-speak for: 'May I vandalise the paintings?').

This time, I headed straight for *The Wedding of Strongbow and Aoife*, which depicted the Irish Medieval equivalent of a business merger (the bride was a Chieftain's daughter the groom a Norman warlord). I have always privately thought of the painting as 'gothic art', with its grandiose composition and violent sub-theme. The bride and groom looked as if they were enjoying the ceremony in an ironic way and there was an orgy in full swing right in front of them. I wondered what kind of party they'd throw if they were getting divorced. I'd read the ancient Celts had had divorce (the Brehon laws were quite liberal).

I kept an eye on the time. When it was time to head back to the office, I groaned and strode out of the gallery, dodging browsers who had all day to admire the art. Lucky people.

My stomach was rumbling so I bought a banana from a street vendor along the way. 'Just the one, lovie? You can have a bunch of ten for a fiver.'

'Can't afford them', I said handing her fifty cents and breaking off a large banana.

'Stingy fecker!' she yelled after me.' How do you tink I'm goin to sell dem wit one missin?'

I was actually one minute early – which was a pity, I thought, since I'd rather have had an extra minute in the gallery.

And – just my luck – no one else was in the office to witness my punctuality. Mr Wrightman's office was in darkness; he'd left the door open, which was uncharacteristic. Janet's was open too but the light was on and I could see her desk, piled with files.

Mr Wrightman's door was closed as usual. I was suddenly overcome by the urge to see what was in there surely I'd hear the others coming up the stairs. I turned the handle and, to my surprise, it wasn't locked.

Then I noticed the light was on.

And there was a beautiful woman sitting on his desk.

Portrait of a lady

She was just as surprised to see me as I was to see her. '*Ooof!*' she said and tumbled off the desk. She was wearing a knee-length beige dress, sleeveless with a boat-shaped neckline. She was about my size, I noticed, and her legs were as good as mine.

She blinked at me through big hazel eyes fringed with long black lashes, under arched black eyebrows. She had a strange beauty that couldn't be categorised. She looked as if she'd been painted by a team of artists, all blending their styles in harmony – first Gustav Klimt, then subtly softened by Renoir, and her stronger features enhanced by Graham Knuttel. And the play of sunlight through the green blinds was casting a yellowy-green dappled light over her left cheek, as if Matisse had leapt in and *fauve*-d her.

'Are you all right?' I asked as she got up fluidly, dusting down her dress with her manicured fingernails.

'Oooh, I sink so', she said and I realised her accent was French. 'I ave urt myself so many times, skiing and orseriding and dancing in ze *discothèque*.' She giggled. 'I am Veronique', she said. 'Ze wife of *Jean*.' She pronounced her husband's name the French way.

'*Jean*?'

She sighed and shrugged. '*Bof*! It does not matter. Soon ee is to be my ex-usband.'

Now I understood. 'Oh, John. John Wrightman. The boss's other nephew.'

'*Oui*. Mr Eely is such a good honkle-in-law, I will be most sad to lose im.' She sighed again. '*Alors*. Life goes on, *vrai*?'

'I suppose so', I said, wondering if she'd have to find a job after her divorce, the way Mummy was going to.

'Ah, well, it is bettair zis way. I know zis because I am a lawyair too. I spend my days arranging divorces for ozair people and now', she shrugged again, 'I am one of zem!' She opened a small red handbag – the latest Vuitton, I noticed, feeling sure it was the real thing – and pulled out a packet of cigarettes and a slim lighter. 'Smoke?'

'No thanks', I said.

'I ope zis is not an anti-smoking office. I ate zese anti-smokairs!' she purred, sounding like a mildly indignant tiger.

'Oh, it's not', I said, thinking of Sandra and Brenda.

'So', she said with a sudden, sweet smile. 'What is your name?'

'*Chloé*.' I pronounced it in French.

'Ah, you ave ze French name! Like ze designer.' She looked at my clothes and I wished I was wearing one of my *prêt-à-porter* designer outfits – or at least something chic instead of the over-washed shirt and trousers I had been planning to give to Oxfam as soon as I'd found a better job. Now I was painfully aware of the irony of having been named after a fashion house and not being able to afford the clothes. My parents had been upwardly mobile right from the start; I was sure I could remember them saying 'Gucci-goo' to me in my cot.

But Veronique's gaze seemed admiring; she was looking at me rather than my clothes. 'Ah, ow wonderful it is to see someone who can wear cheap clothes like zat and look so chic! So, is zair anyone French in your family?'

'Not as far as I know. Mummy just liked the name.' I found myself shrugging the way I always did when I was talking to French people (Aunty Helen had always said that was because I was so shallow and easily influenced; I think she was envious because I had learned the language on a six-week holiday while she had spent years going to classes and still couldn't book a hotel without reverting back to English).

'But you ave ze language, *non*?'

'*Oui*', I said and we had a boring, text-book conversation in French (we spoke about such things as our nationalities and how many parents we had).

I realised we were playing a game Continental women of all ages seem to play, making small-talk while trying to work out which one of us was the more beautiful (I based this observation on my experience as an exchange student in various European countries during my school years). After the initial dazzling effect of meeting her, I noticed she was not so perfect; she had fine lines around her eyes and her lips had been carefully outlined and coloured to look fuller. She was running her eyes up and down me, stopping around the waist every so often (my small waist is a feature that is much overlooked in Ireland but on the Continent it's something to be proud of). All the time, we smiled and shrugged at each other, bluffing and double-bluffing. It was a kind of joust – and we were worthy opponents.

Then I asked her how old she was, thinking I could always plead cultural differences as an excuse for being just plain rude – but she was flattered. 'Oh, you must think I'm so young you can ask my age! Well, I'm thirty-seven.'

'You're joking!' I was serious; I would never have guessed she was almost as old as my Mummy.

'But yes; it's true. And you?'

'Nineteen.'

'Well, I would have thought maybe a year younger. But nineteen is so young anyway', she laughed.

'Ahem!'

'Ah!' she squealed. 'Patreek!' I was amazed to see her fling her arms around Mr Wrightman.

He looked flustered. 'Well, well', he was saying. 'How lovely to see you – pity about the circumstances. I suppose Maeve and I can't talk you and John out of this?'

'Non!' she pouted, then laughed. 'But you're still my favourite honkle-in-law.'

He ushered her into his office and, looking back at me, indicated with his head towards a pile of files held together with rubber bands, with a microcassette on top. I picked it up, bending my knees the way my fitness instructor had shown me; I seemed to be getting so much exercise lately, between carrying files and running for the bus, that I could probably let my gym membership expire at the end of the month – though the thought of still being in this job another month depressed me.

'Where are you staying?' Mr Wrightman was asking Veronique as I closed the door behind them.

'Oh, you know zat charming hotel…"

When I came out into the main office, my colleagues were back at their desks.

'Who's in dere?' Natalie asked.

'Mr Wrightman's niece-in-law', I said.

'De French one? Ooh, she's gorgeous, isn't she? I wouldn't mind lookin like her.'

'In yer dreams!' Beverley laughed. 'But I still tink she's awful skinny. There's not – '

'– a pick on her', I finished, rolling my eyes the way I'd seen them do whenever they said the same about me.

This should have earned me some brownie points. But they all glared at me. I was still an outsider. Then Beverley turned to Natalie. 'You have to admit she *is* a bir anorexic-lookin.'

'But she's *French*. Dey've got de confidence to carry iroff.'

I've always noticed that working class people tend to develop either xenophobia or inverted xenophobia when they come across foreigners (the way they turn into snobs or inverted snobs when they meet people from a better part of town).

'Mind you', Natalie was going on, 'she has really hairy arms and a birrof a muss.' They all sniggered.

I felt a pang of compassions for Veronique. 'You lot have really studied her, haven't you?'

'Wait until she's our boss', Brenda was saying now. 'She's a top lawyer, you know. I bet she takes no shite from anyone. Even *you'd* have to toe the line, Chloe. No more long lunch breaks – where do you go for your lunch anyway?'

'Oh, I meet a friend', I said. 'In a café. You wouldn't know it.'

Just then, Veronique and Mr Wrightman came out of his office. She smiled at us. 'You've met my secretaries, haven't you, Veronique?'

'Oh, yes. I know all ze girls – ze beautiful Chloe I ave just met.'

Mr Wrightman smiled and walked to the door with her, kissing her on the cheek. 'I wish you'd come and work for us. You could deal with our international clients.'

She cocked an eyebrow and I found myself doing the same; Wrightman, Wrightman & Wrightman weren't exactly juggling multi-national lawsuits, unless you counted the fact that one of our cases concerned a fight between local lads and some Spanish exchange students outside an Indian take-away.

'Oh, you know I love Dublin – but only to visit for a weekend.'

'Well, come and stay with Maeve and me whenever you want. You know you're always welcome.'

'Oh, I will of course. You're too kind. And you must both come and stay in my chateau. It's so much nicer wizout your terrible nephew.'

Mr Wrightman chuckled and closed the door. Then he 'ahem'ed, shrugged his forehead back into the frown we all knew so well, and strode back into his office, closing the door.

I spent the rest of the day translating John and Veronique's divorce settlement papers. 'He must love her', I said to Natalie. ' He's letting her keep the chateau in Provence, the apartment in Paris, the Porshe, the Harley Davison, all the horses and dogs...and even the paintings – everything except his CD collection and clothes.'

'Jayz. Dey sound like de people off dem mini-series tings me Ma watches on de telly. Does it say what kind of mewzic he listens to?'

'Would you believe it does?' I looked down at the list of CDs. 'It's quite an eclectic collection.'

'Eclexia? Is dah a heavy metal band or sometin? I tink I heard of dem. Me brudder's into dah kind of crap.'

I tried not to laugh; the list of paintings helped. No wonder the glamorous Veronique and her husband couldn't get on together. How could anyone stay married to a man who didn't want a collection of little-known works by Chagall, Dali and Modigliani? 'He must be a complete philistine.'

'No. He's Irish. He's Mr Heel's nephew. I tawt you knew dah.' Natalie shook her head and went back to indexing the files.

'What are you doing at the weekend, girls?' Sandra asked.

'I'm goin to me brudder's twenhy-furst', Natalie said. 'We're havin it in de pub down de road and we're goin to gerrim a stripper. It'll be massive!' (I had a mental picture of a gigantic naked lady.)

'Oh, can I cum?' Beverley piped up.

Natalie looked embarrassed. 'Sorry, it's family ony. Me Da said we had too many spongers at me udder brudder's twenhy-furst and he didn't want to be buyin drinks all night for strangers.'

'Burr I'll pay me way.'

'Oh, all righ den.'

Sandra turned to me. 'And what are you doing tomorrow, Chloe?'

'I'm going to the gym.' I felt all five pairs of beady eyes trained on me. 'Not that I need to work out. I just go there to relax.'

Sandra contorted her face, so I added: 'Well I suppose it's like you coming to work just to get out of the house.'

It was true what I had told Sandra. I've never been one of those unfortunate people who need to work out to keep in shape; I've inherited all the good genes from both parents. But if I go a few weeks without any form of exercise, I feel tired and irritable. Running for the bus in the rain is just not as energising as jogging on a treadmill to music, looking hot in my designer gym wear and ignoring the muscle-flashers who try to chat me up in Belgowan's exclusive Ardnarock Fitness Centre, which has a stunning view over the Irish Sea and a fantastic range of pampering facilities. It was just what I needed after my stressful week, so I got up at eleven, waved away Mummy's offer of breakfast and walked the half-mile down the sea road.

There was the usual What's What of flash cars parked in front. I didn't see Daddy's Fworrsh but that was no surprise; he'd probably switched loyalty to a city centre gym since he'd moved in with Carmel and little Lexus.

I handed my swipe card to the receptionist and stopped smiling when I realised she was a girl who used to go to school with me and was pretending not to know me (maybe she was embarrassed to be seen in the yucky green T-shirt with 'Ardnarock Fitness Centre' stencilled across the front).

There were some young rugby types stuffed into the couches in the lounge, and middle-aged women in short white tennis skirts standing in front of them, trying to chat them up. 'We're thinking of setting up a ladies' rugby team', one of the women was staying. 'Are you interested in coaching us?' The guys were casting nervous eyes around at everyone who walked in. One of them yelled over to me: 'Hey, don't I know you from somewhere?' 'I doubt it', I said, thinking I didn't want to get into a catfight with those women; an angry floozy with a tennis racket could do a lot of damage.

I bought a small bottle of mineral water and strolled up the stairs to the aerobics studio. I smiled over at one of the fitness trainers, Vicky. She came over. 'Chloe! I thought you'd disappeared off the face of the earth.'

'No, just working.'

'Oh? But weren't you studying art?'

'Not any more. I've dropped out.'

She gave me that knowing look she usually reserves for people who've pigged out and piled on the kilos. 'I know what you're going through. I had to drop out of medicine – I failed my exams.'

'I didn't fail. My parents can't afford the fees.'

'Oh.' She tilted her head back. 'Well, enjoy your workout.'

It was as if I'd caught some contagious disease. Poveritis, I suppose you could call it. Everyone seemed to be avoiding me – even the girls I used to go to charity events with. I guessed they wouldn't be asking me to model a designer dress in aid of earthquake casualties or giant pandas now. The word had got round. It might be off the front pages of the tabloids, but Daddy's bankruptcy was still big news in the business sections of the broadsheets; they each claimed to have done an 'in-depth investigation into the mysterious disappearance of Donach O'Doolahan's off-shore accounts', his creditors were all giving interviews and *Sins On Sunday* was advertising a big exposé for the next day – with a photo of 'yummy Mummy' Carmel Delahanty with little Lexus in her arms, looking like a profane icon of the Madonna and Child.

'No wonder they call it an ABC1 paper', Mummy had snapped when I had shown her the ad. 'If that's what they call "yummy", they need a dictionary.'

'She looks old enough to be an Egyptian Mummy', Daryus said loyally, but Mummy was still glaring at the paper.

'And where did they get that picture of me?' There was an unflattering insert of Mummy looking red-faced and sweaty, with a forced smile.

'I think they took it when you were running the marathon, Mummy.'

Now I tried to forget about the papers and climbed onto one of the stationary bikes. I regretted not having brought my own music; the Number One hit thumping out of the speakers was a rap song about violent street gangs. It reminded me of Mr Wrightman's clients. It was amazing to think how much my life had changed.

'Hi Chloe.' Tarquin Pursewell was pedalling beside me. He would never have dared approach me a few months ago, when I was the belle of Belgowan (with the sash to prove it!). Guys like Tarquin, with his pimply face, prominent Adam's Apple and over-protective parents, only dated girls like Orla Upton, an elocuted gold-digger whose parents skimped on central heating to pay the mortgage.

'Isn't Orla with you?'

'Nope. We've broken up.' He smiled and nearly knocked me off the bike with the force of his halitosis.

I hoped she come into the gym to reclaim him, then remembered that poor Orla could only afford off-peak membership and had to work out alongside pensioners and lap dancers.

'I was just thinking, there's this dance I have to do to – black tie, tennis club thing, bit of a boozing session in the pub beforehand. Great *craic* and, well, I was wondering if you'd like to go?'

'I'd love to', I joked. Then, as I realised he was smiling, I added: 'But not with you.'

Just then Bryonella Banks walked in with some of her cronies. She gave a double-take as she saw me then rushed over to me on tippy-toes the way she used to in ballet-class when we were teenagers, and took one of my hands in both of hers. 'Oh, Chloe, you poor *thing*! I read *every*thing about it in those nasty papers. You must be *furious*...'

I just wished she'd go away, but she glanced down at my fingernails and squealed. 'Eeek! What happened to your nails?' I resisted the temptation to tell her I had broken most of them trying to stuff Mr Wrightman's briefs into his nasty metal (filing) drawers. I also had paper-cuts all over my hands and a plaster on my index finger, courtesy of a fight with a vicious stapler.

'I just think you're so courageous, coming here after all that scandal in the papers about your poor daddy. And all those nasty people gossiping about you – I'd leave Belgowan if it happened to my family.'

I kept pedalling and tried to ignore her, but she turned around and yelled: 'Caroline, come here and say hello to poor Chloe.'

I recognised Caroline from her Mummy's parties. I'd always pitied her, having a sausage figure and having to stuff it into designer gowns so her mother could look slimmer in the photos that appeared in the social columns. Her Mummy had even had the house painted in colours that set off her own eyes but clashed with Caroline's, and raised her hand in a 'Stop' sign every time the poor girl spoke. Now Caroline was jumping at the chance to feel superior.

'Oooh, Chloe, how are you bearing up?' she brayed. 'At least you haven't changed a *bit*. You're *sooo* skinny. I *envy* you, I really *dooo*. I mean, you're not comfort-eating or *any*thing.' She patted her mono-boob, which, flatted by her sports bra and spilling out under the armpits, was only slightly less ample than her tummy. 'I mean, look at me! This leotard does absolutely *nothing* for my curves. But you're like a *stick*!' She patted Bryonella's hockey-girl shoulders. 'Bryonella and I were just saying you can never be too rich or too thin – but you were *both*!'

Did I imply that only common girls slagged me about being too thin? Sorry. So did my ex-friends. The only difference was that these rich girls did it out of envy rather than amusement. They had been photographed in enough society mags to know that fat wasn't flattering; they had been exposed to high society from all over Europe and some had even done time in Swiss finishing schools alongside *Vogue*'s top ten debutantes.

Now I found myself wishing I hadn't brushed off all those model agency scouts who had offered me a glamorous lifestyle. I doubted they would look at the new-look Chloe O'Doolahan; I had dark circles under my eyes from getting up early every morning and was even breaking out in spots. The stress was getting to me because I couldn't see a way out of my new, grey lifestyle. I pedalled harder and harder on that stationary bike, but it was like my life: going nowhere. The gym equipment all seemed to be a metaphor for my life: the treadmill that was like my job, the stepper that felt like walking in quicksand...

I wished I could just paint a new life for myself. At last, I understood exactly how Stalin had felt – or whoever it was that got his enemies erased from photos. I wanted to paint a bright blue sky over all the unwelcome people in my life, and paint my Daddy back in.

'Mummy's having a party tonight', Caroline was going on. 'We'd invite you only it would be so insensitive, wouldn't it, with all your father's creditors there.'

When I got back to the house, I yelled 'Mummy? Daryus?' heard no response and went straight to the attic. I was suddenly desperate to daub colours on a canvas. I didn't have a clear idea of what I wanted to portray, which was a bit frustrating as I had always thought of myself as a neo-classical painter, but maybe I was just going through an abstract phase.

But there was someone else's painting on my ease. Someone had vandalised one of the large canvasses I had been saving up for a really important project! Now it was covered in blue and green splodges.

It had to have been Daryus. But why? I hadn't thought of my kid brother as malicious.

I heard the key turn in the front door, and Mummy yelled up: 'Chloe? Are you there?'

'Mummy, you'll never believe what Daryus has done', I sobbed, running down the stairs. 'He totally destroyed my big canvas!'

Mummy cast her eyes down.

'Mummy, you should have stopped him. You knew I was going to take up painting again.'

She sighed. 'I thought you had given it up – well, you haven't painted anything for at least six months, around the time your father left.' Her eyes filled up and I suddenly felt ashamed of making a fuss about my canvas. 'Anyway, pet, Daryus didn't do it; *I* did.'

'What?'

'I've decided to stop moping around and find myself some hobbies. Helen told me she'd read somewhere that painting was a good stress-reliever.'

I couldn't believe what I was hearing. Painting had been a compulsion for me, a need as basic as eating, sleeping or breathing. And now Mummy had casually decided to take it up, as a hobby – a 'stress-reliever', no less.

'Helen told me painting was supposed to be calming', she added.

'Well, it's not! Why do you think Caravaggio was wanted by the police? For murder! And Michelangelo Buonarotti got his nose cut off in a swordfight with another artist – oh, and I hardly imagine Van Gogh cut off his ear in a fit of serenity.'

Mummy looked momentarily puzzled, then rolled her eyes and fluttered her hands: 'Maybe he would have cut off his whole head if he hadn't had that lovely hobby to calm him down. If only he could have channelled all his negative energy into a painting, maybe he would never even have cut off his ear.'

I sighed and she seemed to think she'd won the argument. She was smiling now, her eyes shining with enthusiasm. 'We can share the attic, can't we, darling? It can be our studio. A mother-and-daughter artistic team – I might even get Barbara to do a feature on us in *U Know Who* magazine.'

'Oh no, Mummy.' Not that old cow, Barbara Burrows! 'She's doing a feature on Daddy and Carmel in *Sins On Sunday* tomorrow. I saw the ad for it in the newsagent's.' She was claiming they spent a fortune on clothes, jewellery and meals all over Europe. There was a picture of Carmel and Daddy on a beach with their bastard. I had meant to break it gently to Mummy.

Mummy's face suddenly fell and I realised she had new wrinkles; she looked wearier than she ever had, even when she and Daddy had been quarrelling back in the old days. 'Oh dear', she was saying. 'Well, I suppose I'll have to cross Barbara out of my address book – along with the rest of our acquaintances from our old life.'

I hugged her. 'Mummy, I'm sure we'll have our old life back some time – but without all the horrible people. I'll paint a picture, and it will just happen.'

'If only it were that simple, darling.'

'Didn't Daddy always say art was a form of prayer?'

Mummy nodded. We both remembered a time when my father had been a regular Mass-goer and really seemed to be that rare thing: a true Christian. That had been before he had become a millionaire. He had sworn wealth wouldn't change him, and to prove it he had donated tens of thousands to charity, but then he had undone all the goodness by running off on his creditors – even the small-time investors who had trusted him with their lives' savings. And then he had run off on us.

Chiaroscuro

We went to Mass on Sunday morning – even Daryus, who had stopped going when he was sixteen. 'At least we can find some comfort in the church', Mummy was saying as we got into the Merc. 'Thank God the liquidator let me keep the car', she added as it started raining.

My parents had been bringing us to this church since we were very young – even before we lived in the area. 'Daddy, why do we have to go to Mass in *Belgowan*?' I used to ask as he drove past our local church at the other end of the motorway. Daddy never had a good answer. 'We can go for an ice-cream later.' 'But we can get one from the ice-cream van.' (It used to stop outside our door but we were never let join the neighbours' kids in the queue.) 'And we can go for a walk along the seafront.' Our own seafront had a carnival with dodgems, a ghost train and a glass case full of teddy bears; you put a coin in and if you were lucky, you'd win one. The kids in Belgowan didn't have anything like that. It was a pretty boring place, full of restaurants, cafés and shops selling the kind of knick-knacks that always ended up going for a fiver at the parish sale-of-work.

I soon realised that the big attraction of going to Mass every Sunday in Belgowan was the congregation, who were all familiar faces from TV and the newspapers. 'There's that film director', my parents would murmur to each other. 'No, don't stare; he'll think you're looking at him.'

Now Mummy parked at the end of a row of stretch limos on the pavement, and we walked the quarter-kilometre to join the large crowd that was trying squeeze into the church. Belgowan certainly seemed to have a lot of devout Catholics, quite a few of whom regularly boasted of their faith in tabloid interviews. All the salt-of-the-earth types attended too: local conservative politicians, Chamber of Commerce stalwarts and the righteous brigade who sat on residents' association committees, held anti-litter campaigns and wrote apoplectic letters to the newspapers about such abominations as dog turds on the pavements or unemployed people dossing on the dole while there were plenty of jobs available in the fast food industry. These were the good citizens who had got the homeless people's drop-in centre closed on the grounds that it would attract 'unsavoury elements' to Belgowan.

But there was a quiet minority among the congregation too; the people who did lots of little acts of kindness which didn't make headlines. I recognised a lady who used to hold coffee mornings to raise cash for famine victims until the local ladies-who-lunch took over the charities and informed her that they only accepted direct debits.

But now even that lady and her friends were scrutinising our Merc and our clothes. 'There's Donach O'Doolahan's wife and daughter in the height of fashion', I heard someone stage-whisper. 'If I owed that much money, I'd be wearing something out of Oxfam. And look at that big waster of a son with his leather jacket. You'd think they'd be ashamed to show their faces.' 'They've got hard necks to turn up here where everyone knows them!'

I looked around and recognised one of the old biddies. 'Hello, Mrs Landbag. Have you evicted any more tenants from the bedsits lately? Are you still putting dog-food in the stew in those nursing homes you own?'

'Well, did you hear that?' her friend barked, while Mrs Landbag gaped. The rest of them smirked and I immediately regretted my comments – they didn't deserve free entertainment.

Mummy was going as red as the beetroot. 'Chloe, you're making a show of us.'

But Daryus sniggered and gave me a Rasta handshake – the ultimate compliment from him.

I shrugged the way I imagined Veronique would have done in this situation. 'Since we're obviously pariahs, we might as well get some fun out of it. It's a great stress-reliever – much better than painting.'

I hardly listened to the sermon, I was so conscious of the nudges, winks, pursed lips and furtive glances. As we came out, a smartly dressed woman who ran an estate agency came over to Mummy, handed her a business card and murmured: 'I can get you a very competitive price for the house. Just call me when you're ready to sell.' She flitted off into the street before Mummy could answer her.

Then Father Nick emerged from the side-door. He had a concerned look on his face. Mummy walked over to him. Daryus and I followed at a discreet distance; Father Nick looked as if he wanted to say something in private to Mummy. 'I'm always here if you need to talk', he was saying. 'Or you can join the group therapy sessions every Tuesday evening in the parish resource centre. They're run by Dr Finklestein – you know, the celebrity psychotherapist who's over from New York? He's studying Irish Catholic guilt for his new book.' Father Nick relished his role as parish priest in Ireland's snobbiest neighbourhood.

Mummy grimaced and shook her head.

Sunday afternoon had always been a family occasion when Daddy had lived with us. He could even persuade Daryus to come and watch a golf tournament – though Daryus always enraged him by dressing all in black ('When I'm a famous rock star, this club will be begging me to join', Daryus used to point out). Sometimes we'd go to the races and Daddy would give us modest amounts of cash to bet; he had always warned us about gambling, which now made his bankruptcy harder to believe.

But these days Mummy just wandered aimlessly around the house, Daryus went off to meet his friends for a rehearsal that seemed to require cans of lager from the off-licence, and I skulked in my room with the magazine out of *Sins On Sunday*, scowling at photos of people I knew in the social diary.

I was just thinking how preposterously pompous they all looked (especially Mummy's ex-friends who had all gone to the same orthodontist and had identical rabbit capped teeth), when the doorbell rang. I ran to the window and groaned; Uncle Jemsie's ugly big Rangeroller was parked on the kerb, and he was helping Aunty Shivawn out. As usual, she was barking at him not to rush her; her designer trousers were too long for her high heels and she was in danger of falling flat on her face (pity she wouldn't, I thought).

They had come to gloat, of course. Daddy's older sister had always resented Mummy for taking away her biddable brother who used to look up to Shivawn and her car dealer husband until, with Mummy's encouragement, Dad had told Shivawn and Jemsie he wouldn't be taking the job as a salesman but wanted to go into business for himself. Daryus and I were supposed to be the poor cousins, grateful for hand-me-down clothes. But their first-born, Shona, had got pregnant by a trainee doctor at her debs ball around the time Dad had turned into a millionaire, and Shivawn had never forgiven us. Now she could finally blame us for his downfall.

'Mummy, don't answer it!' I hissed. Uncle Jemsie was peering in the bay window of the drawing room. 'Coo! Bridget!' Mummy had been named after the Irish Saint Brigid but, ever since *Bridget Jones's Diary* had come out, Shivawn and Jemsie had spelt it the English way on Christmas cards. From then on, Mummy had insisted on being called 'Bee' even though Dad had reasonably pointed out that no one would confuse her with a fictional character who happened to be single. Now, of course, she was single again and her life had taken on the quality of fiction; she was always saying she was certain she'd wake up some morning and find Dad there and realise it had all been a dream.

'Breege!' That was Aunty Shivawn's new pet name for Mummy (she used to call her 'Bridie' until Dad left, when she pointed out that Mummy no longer seemed like a 'Bride type').

'Aunty Biddy!' Oh no, that was my cousin Shona, getting out of the back of the jeep with her five-year-old twin brats Whitney and Britney. 'Mummy, it's the Defrocked Debutante and the Doctor's Wild Oats!'

The whole extended family was casing the house, tapping on the windows and trampling the flowers we couldn't afford to replace.

Mummy sighed. 'I'll have to let them in.'

I grabbed my coat. 'I'm going out – I'll go for a walk, even if it is bloody raining.'

'No please, Chloe, don't leave me alone with them. You know I can't tell them to leave when they've got the children with them – they'll tell the whole family I'm the wicked witch!'

'You can always say you're going out.'

But then the timer on the cooker buzzed; no one would believe Mummy had cooked Sunday lunch if she was going out.

'We don't know what to call your mother these days', Aunty Shivawn was saying as Mummy went into the kitchen to put on some more food. I heard her angrily clattering pots and emptying stuff from packets into them. 'I mean, she's not busy enough to call herself a Bee.' She tittered.

'How about Brigitte – like Bardot', Uncle Jemsie chipped in, and they guffawed. 'Can you imagine your mother if she dyed her hair platinum blonde?'

'She doesn't need to', I snapped. 'She's glamorous enough already.'

They swapped sneering glances and I made a big show of staring them up and down, especially Shona, who was twenty-five but looked older than my Mummy (in my opinion, anyway, and that was what counted).

'Wasn't that woman your father ran off with a glamorous blonde?' Uncle Jemsie persisted. 'What was her name? Ah yes, Carmen, like the opera.'

'Carmel', I corrected him. 'There's an order of nuns named after her – made up of wives who were Carmelised by their husbands.'

'That's a blatant lie!' Aunty Shivawn said, looking as if she was about to have a fit.

'So?' I shrugged. 'It's no more false than Carmel Delahanty's hair.' Or my parents' wedding vows, I felt like adding, but didn't; I wasn't going to let them see how angry I was at Daddy.

'Her baby boy is the spitting image of her, isn't he?' Aunty Shivawn was gushing. 'Such a beautiful child. Like my little Britney – good enough to eat! Yummy!' I felt sorry for my niece as her granny pretended to devour her chubby cheeks, making awful gummy munching noises.

'Britney', I said, 'do you know the story *Hansel and Gretel*?' The stupid kid just stared at me blankly, so I added: 'Well, your granny is the witch. She eats children.' It didn't work on the child – she was as thick as her mother, and her granny was thick-skinned enough to smirk.

We got out our worst crockery – the stuff we had since we were poor – and slapped the lunch onto it. I could see them thinking: 'So, they've sold the Wedgwood dinner service.'

'Gran, why is Aunty Chloe eating smoked salmon?'

'Because she's on a diet, dear.'

'I am not on a diet. I eat what I like!'

Aunty Shivawn smirked. 'Well why don't you eat some of this casserole, like the rest of us?'

Because it's from a packet and tastes like Readymix, I wanted to say, but Mummy was glaring at me so I said: 'I don't eat anything with meat in it.'

'Chloe is a vegetarian', Mummy cut in. It really annoys me when people label me a vegetarian just because I don't eat beef, pork or chicken, but I decided to let it go.

Aunty Shivawn, though, was like a dog with a bone. 'Such nonsense. No wonder you're so skinny. You surely don't want people thinking your mother can't afford to feed you?'

Uncle Jemsie guffawed: 'You can't be a vegetarian and eat fish! Are you saying one kind of animal has less of a right to live than another?'

'If that's how you feel', I said, 'why don't you turn to cannibalism like your wife?' Aunty Shivawn stopped making gobbling noises on little Britney's cheek and sat up straight. 'And anyway, I'm not a bloody vegetarian.'

It was impossible to make them feel unwelcome; they just couldn't take a hint. 'You're obviously used to going where you're not wanted', I said, but they just laughed. Ha bloody ha, I thought.

The kids were whining about the scarcity of soft drinks, so I had the perfect answer when Aunty Shivawn asked me: 'Well, Chloe, when are you ever going to find a nice boy and have children like your little half-brother and Shona's two little angels?'

'Hell's angels, you mean. Thanks for totally putting me off the idea of having children – I've just realised there are pest genes in the family.'

Aunty Shivawn pretended to look offended (I knew she was faking because, with a face like that, she must have been well used to insults). Then she swelled up the way she always does when she's about to boast, and turned to Mummy. 'You know, Andrew's still crazy about our Shona. They're getting engaged as soon as he finishes his studies.'

Mummy shot me a please-don't-say-a-thing look so I didn't ask if he was studying biology.

Shona, who has a skin as thick as rasher-rind (and not just physically), sat with a smirk on her big round face, looking like a particularly smug sow, while Whitney and Britney dashed around the house, knocking over lamps (bang goes Daryus's college fund, I thought as they smashed the Tiffany lamp) and hurling ornaments at each other. 'Aren't they a bit old to be going through the Terrible Twos?' I asked Shona. I saw Mummy's worried face as they ran up the stairs, so I went up after them.

'But we were only playing hide-and-seek', they whined.

'Wait until you get back to your Granny and Grandad's', I suggested. 'You can do what you like in their house.'

'But we're not allowed – there are too many expensive things there.'

Eventually they left. As they were getting into the car, I heard Shona ask the brats: 'And what did you see in the big bedroom?'

Abstract male

'Well, girls, what do yewse tink of him?' Brenda was leaning back against Mr Wrightman's door. We could hear Mr Wrightman roaring with laughter as his nephew told him something about his gaffes with the French language. 'Well, how was I to know it meant "arse"? I was asking her to massage my stiff *neck*.'

'He's a birra all righ', Tina said.

'What do ya mean, a bit? He's a looker!' Natalie said.

That seemed to be the general consensus. Then Brenda turned to me. 'Cum on, Chloe, you're very quiet over dere. Tell us what you tink of yer man. Is he a fine ting or what?'

'He's abso-bleedin-lutely gorgeous', I said, doing my best to put on their accent.

They all stared at me and burst into laughter. Then Brenda went flying as the door opened suddenly. 'I'm terribly sorry', John said, trying not to laugh as he helped her up. 'You seem to be accident-prone.'

'I'd go for him if I wasn't engaged to Clint', Brenda sighed, holding out her ring finger for us to admire the sparkler. We'd all seen it before, but the others felt obliged to go 'Aaah, isn't it bee-ewiful?' I pretended to look impressed. I couldn't decide which was worse: the ring or Clint, a semi-employed nightclub bouncer who often came to pick Brenda up on his 'scoorer'. I found it hard to believe he was the father of her little Barney, whose photo smiled out at me every day from a gilt frame.

'Have you gorra bloke, Chloe?' Tina asked and they all looked at me.

'Sort of', I said, suddenly feeling as if I should.

'What does he wurk ah?'

'Well, he don't work.'

Tina nudged Brenda. 'So he's on the dole, den?' Tina was grinning; clearly she thought I was having her on. But Sandra was swelling up with indignation. Middle-class sponger, I could hear her thinking.

'He's still at university – in France.'

'Oh.' They rolled their eyes at each other and went back to typing.

Well, Philippe was 'sort of' my boyfriend; we had spent all the previous summer kissing and cuddling. I had been on a language exchange and had instantly hit it off with the boy next door – much to the envy of Claudine, the girl whose family I was staying with. Philippe and I still kept in touch but I knew he'd met someone in university, where he was studying architecture – someone who'd let him do more than just cuddle.

I walked at a brisk pace to the National Gallery this time; I wasn't taking my chances with the bus timetable again. It was quiet, and I could have lingered in front of Roderic O'Conor's painting of a stag, as I had planned to do, but I suddenly felt an urge to go up to the Italian

Masters room – not to look at the Caravaggio again, but another painting that seemed to be haunting me these days.

There it was, on the far wall. It depicted an old crone whispering something to a girl about my age - something naughty, judging by the older woman's lascivious expression. She was trying to encourage the beautiful girl to do something that she, herself, would do if she wasn't too old and ugly to get away with it. They reminded me of the mothers and daughters I used to see at high-society balls; the mothers beckoning their daughters over to whisper something, tug a neckline down to expose just a little more cleavage, nod coyly at eligible men – and cast sly glances at all-too-eligible Salomes…

The girl in the painting was plump, but it was a luscious plumpness. I supposed she'd look awful in a modern designer frock; she'd probably be miserable in the twenty-first century unless she was lucky enough to be born into the Dublin working-class suburbs where being 'too skinny' was worse than having a big cellulitey bum. If the artist time-travelled to modern Dublin, he'd probably ask a girl like Brenda to model – and get his nose flattened by her fiancé.

I glanced over at *The Taking of Christ* as I left the room; it was still my favourite. This time, one of the soldiers arresting Jesus reminded me of Brenda's fiancé, Clint; I could imagine him ejecting someone from a disco because they weren't wearing acrylic or had the wrong accent.

It was raining as usual as I came out of the gallery. My trench coat didn't cover the end of my trousers and there was no sign of the bus. So I was feeling quite miserable by the time I had walked back to the office. I was late yet again, and had run out of excuses. I groaned when I met Janet going in. She was wearing a new pin-striped trouser suit and, for the first time I'd known her, make-up. Even her Austin Powers glasses had been replaced by chic red-rimmed ones. And her hair had highlights.

She looked around. 'Oh, hello Chloe', she said with a smile.

'Janet, I'm really sorry I'm late – '

She flapped a freshly manicured hand at me. 'Don't worry about it, Chloe.' She glided into the office in front of me, beaming around the room and saying 'Hello, girls!' before disappearing into her office. I noticed he left the door open a crack.

I sat down at my desk and reached for my copy of *U Know Who* intending to stuff it into my backpack as I should have done earlier; it wouldn't do for any of the bosses to see a magazine on my desk. But I couldn't find it. Then I realised Tina and Beverley were flicking through it, keeping a wary eye on Mr Wrightman's door.

'Jayz, look at de state of dah. Yer woman must be the same age as my granny', Tina was saying.

I looked over her shoulder. She was scrutinising the social diary column and I recognised the woman in the skimpy outfit as Poo Anchorbottom. My parents used to be regulars at her charity balls, which raised almost as much money as she was reputed to have spent on designer clothes. But the invitations had stopped arriving in our letterbox since Daddy left. 'Poo only invites couples', a neighbour confided in Mummy. 'Otherwise her dinner-table seating plan would be in *chaos*. She doesn't want any separated women prowling around.'

Now I was glad to see someone taking Poo down a peg – even if Poo herself would never get to hear my colleagues' comments, and wouldn't pay any attention to them if she did. In Poo's world, people who were outside her social circle simply didn't exist – apart from the token deprived people who were occasionally invited to her charity dos to declare publicly that Poo's fundraising efforts saved them from a hell of homelessness and drug-addiction.

'Showin off her body at her age', Tina was sniggering.

'Well', I said, trying to sound casual, 'mid-riffs are supposed to be the latest thing.'

They looked at me. 'Maybe for J Lo, but not bleedin coffin-dodgers', Tina laughed. 'Me granny wouldn't go out like dah – and she suffers from bleedin Alzheimer's!'

'I wonder how an aul wan like dah keeps herself so skinny', Beverley was saying.

'Oh, she got her stomach stapled', I said. 'It's true. I know because my mother met her cosmetic surgeon at one of her parties; he was boasting about performing the operation.'

Well, I made that up – but this was a woman who had single-handedly wiped my mother off the invitation lists of every society matron in Dublin, so I was only getting my own back. Anyway, she should have known that the mid-riff is never a middle-aged lady's bet asset, no matter how many sit-ups she does with her personal trainer.

I felt my indignation rise as I realised that Poo Anchorbottom could afford to wear the kind of outfits that were designed for bodies like mine (maybe that was shy she had warned the photographer from *You Know Who* magazine not to take my photo at the last charity ball I'd attended).

We pored over the "Social Whirl" column and the girls continued to criticise the photos. I had fun telling them exactly how much the clothes had cost and why the identical-looking high-street knock-offs were not regarded as a bargain if your self-esteem depended on impressing the likes of Poo Anchorbottom. 'You see, the important thing for these people is the label. You can buy something that *looks* cheap – you can even look cheap in it – but it has to cost more than the price of the ticket for the ball.'

'Well, I tink dese people are bleedin stupid to waste all dat money just to make demselves look like hookers', Tina said.

I agreed. 'I actually think the designers are inverted snobs – they're always playing cruel jokes on their snobby clients.'

'Out of the mouths of babes', a baritone voice joined in. We looked up to see John Wrightman. He was standing with his hands in his pockets. He could have been listening to us for ages. I found myself blushing – more so when John actually tweaked my cheek! Then he sauntered out, singing the theme from *The Emperor's New Clothes,* which I had remembered having seen as a panto when I was about five: 'Oh, the King is in the altogether, the altogether, the all-together…'

We were giggling again when Janet bolted out of her office and galloped down the stairs after him. 'She's not used to wearin high heels', Brenda said. We rushed to the window to see her chasing John across the street. She caught his arm and he turned around, looking surprised at first, then smiling. He gestured with a clutch of keys towards a dark green BMW convertible on the opposite path, then ushered her towards it. Janet was beaming as he opened the door for her.

'Miss O'Doolahan.' The others went back to their desks and left me standing in front of Mr Wrightman, who was back to his old, frowny self. 'Have you finished translating that divorce document for John?'

'I finished it this morning.'

'Well, why didn't you leave it on my desk?' he snapped, then added: 'No, please ignore that question. I haven't got time to listen to excuses. Give it to me.' I went meekly to my desk and handed it to him. I could hardly tell him I had been holding onto it in the hope that John would ask me for it.

'Tell me about de divorce stuff', Tina asked, then clammed up as Sandra entered.

She was carrying two paper bags. 'Here's the new letter headed paper', she said, leaving them on the receptions desk in front of Brenda. We each took a batch for our desks.

I noticed that John Wrightman's name had been added to the letterhead and, with it, another 'Associate': Veronique Chatelaine.

'Who left who?' Tina murmured to me while Sandra was on the phone.

'Oh, she initiated the divorce.'

Tina shrugged her eyebrows. 'Must've had a reason. Was he playin around?'

'What?'

'Did he geroff wirra nudder woman?'

'The divorce documents don't say.' I couldn't imagine John – or any man – cheating on the beautiful Veronique. Certainly not for an 'udder woman'.

But then I remembered my father had left my mother for an old cow.

Janet was in a terrible mood the next morning. She arrive late, slammed her office door and barked orders over the intercom. She even told reliable Sandra to 'get the bloody finger out and get off your fanny and bloody-well *do* something with this fucking filing system.'

'Must have gor our of bed de wrong side', Sandra sniffed and went into Janet's office as if she was going to prison.

We heard Janet yelling at her. 'You can start at "A" for arseholes and finish at "Z" for all the dozy old farts who insist on changing their bloody wills.'

Mr Wrightman came out of his office. 'Is something wrong?'

We tried not to laugh. He rapped on Janet's door. A sulky-looking Sandra opened it. 'I hate to interrupt, but one of your clients has been on the phone to me while you were out – a Mrs Coughlan. She's in a hurry to change her will before she, you know, pops off to the next world –'

'Tell her to leave it all to the Cats' Home!' Janet snarled and Mr Wrightman shuffled back into his office fiddling with his glasses.

When Janet told a juvenile offender he'd 'definitely go to prison this time' and the boy's tough-looking mother dragged him down the stairs, both of them uncharacteristically quiet, we realised she had to be having more than a dose of PMT or a bad hair day.

'It's sometin to do wit John Wrightman – I'm cerhain ir is', Brenda said after Janet and Mr Wrightman had left for court. 'Didn't we see dem gerrin into his car togedder yesterday afternoon?'

Tina giggled. 'I bet she made a pass ar him and he told her where to gerroff!'

'Yeah', Beverley chimed in. 'I mean, after dah Veronique one, he'd hardly look ar an old wagon like Janet.'

'I hope he cums in today', Natalie said. 'I'm wearin me best mascara.'

'Fat chance you'll have wir him', Beverley said, and we all giggled – Natalie too, fluttering her lashes and saying: 'Yewse never know. Maybe he fancies a change. After bein married to a stick insect, he migh want sometin a bit cuddly.'

'Nah', Tina said. 'I know his type. He'll go for yer woman over dere. Hey, Chloe! We're talkin to you. Do ya fancy John or not?'

I shrugged.

'Go on, tell the trewt and shame de devil – dah's what me granny would say to you.'

I laughed. 'The granny who wouldn't even have the nerve to dress like this?' I help up a copy of *U Know Who*, still open at the social column, and pointed to the photo of Poo Anchorbottom.

They screamed with laughter and then John Wrightman walked in. He grabbed the magazine off me, grinning. 'That poor lady doesn't even know she's being slandered.' He walked into Mr Wrightman's empty office, flicking through the magazine and chuckling to himself. Then he popped his head around the door. 'I'm working through lunch. Which of you ladies is going to get me a black coffee?'

'I will!' Natalie shouted and John handed her a tenner. 'I'd say "Keep the change" only I'm soon going to be a poor divorcee.' 'Ah you're all righ luv. Dere won't be any change where I'm goin to get your coffee.' She winked at us and went out.

I looked at my Swatch. There was still ten minutes to go to lunchtime. I tried to look busy; then, at a minute to, I grabbed my backpack and coat and dashed off before anyone could hold me up. I met Natalie as she came up the stairs. She was clutching a bag of doughnuts and two cardboard cups of coffee. 'He needs a birra nourishment', he said. She winked at me, then winced. 'Ow! Me flippin false eyelash has cum off. Will you gerra out of me eye, Chloe?'

We giggled as I tried to fish it out with a tissue. John Wrightman appeared at the top of the stairs looking puzzled, just as she spilt the coffee. 'Did you say you wan-hed ih in a *cup*?'

I was especially keen to get to the National Gallery that day; there was a once-off exhibition of a little-known metaphysical work by Giorgio de Chirico, on loan from a private collector. I'd never been a fan of surrealism – and rummaging through our clients' files, which included photofits based on victims' descriptions had done nothing to change my preferences. But I felt I had a moral duty to welcome what I called 'paintings on parole' –I wished I could rescue all the masterpieces languishing in private collectors' homes. People such as Poo Anchorbottom bought them as 'investments', the way they bought antique furniture and Ormolu clocks and cameo brooches and other beautiful things. Even their houses were bought only to be hoarded for a few years until the price rose enough.

The de Chirico was there for one day only, so there was a queue to see it. I eavesdropped on a group of elderly Italian women (the language was a souvenir from holidays and art-college trips). The ladies were saying that the de Chirico had been bought by someone who didn't even speak Italian and had never been to Italy. They were complaining that a lot of their country's artistic heritage seemed to be in the hands of foreigners. I sympathised with them until I realised that they were also referring to the Caravaggio. 'At least it's not buried in a private gallery', I interrupted. They looked round in surprise. 'Anyway, Caravaggio had to flee Italy and live in Malta.'

'That's true', one of the women said.

'He's welcome in Ireland too', I added. 'Even people who can't speak Italian appreciate it because art is a language everyone understands.'

'Not everyone. He would be better understood at home – in Italy!' one old lady insisted.

They were squabbling among themselves now, and I regretted having spoken to them at all. I wanted to disappear into the canvas like the grey pigments in de Chirico's painting, which depicted a sculpture of a horse rearing on sturdy haunches, partially submerged in a nightmarish red sea. I found the horse was strangely comforting; maybe it was because it appeared to be made of granite – literally solid as a rock. Or maybe it was because there was always something dependable and yet free-spirited about a horse; it would carry you where you wanted to go.

I tried to block out the squabbling of the Italian women and just enjoy the painting, but they drew me into the conversation. 'You seem to know something about art. What do you think of his compatriot, Sassù?'

'Ah yes, the sculptor', I said. 'You know, I was just thinking how this horse reminds me of a bronze statue I once saw by Sassù in Busto Arsizio near Milan –'

'Yes, yes! I know the one. So you've been to Italy.'

'Of course she's been to Italy', her friend scolded her, and turned back to me. 'Your Italian is very good, *signorina*.'

'Thank you.' I smiled politely and tried not to remember those lazy days sipping real cappuccino in Florence.

'*Allora*, you're an art student? A *pittrice* yourself, perhaps…?'

'Well, I used to be – both. But this year I dropped out of art college and gave up painting.' I couldn't stop the tears escaping. 'I'm sorry, I always get emotional when I speak Italian.'

'*Poverina*!' the women chorused, and suddenly I was the centre of attention, not de Chirico. They were all mothering me – one dabbing my eyes with a handkerchief, another wiping my nose, her friend handing me a bar of chocolate, all of them wanting to know why I was no longer an artist and why my parents could no longer afford to send me on art appreciation trips to Italy.

Suddenly I realised the time. 'I have to get back to work!'

'You had to leave college to work?' they gasped. I wanted to tell them I swept ashes from the grate in my new, wicked stepmother's dungeon, but guilt got in the way, so I told them the truth. They all wrote their addresses on the back of an exhibition leaflet, urging me to contact them if I ever needed decided to move to Italy, and wished me 'courage'.

When I got back to the office, there was a tense-looking couple sitting on the leather couch in front of the reception desk. They were waiting for Janet, who was in her office with the door locked and a 'Do Not Disturb' sign on the handle. I called her on the intercom but she just hung up. Just as the couple were about to walk out, Janet opened her door, looking flustered, and herded them into her office.

John and Barry came up the stairs, laughing. 'So, you'll come out for a pint tonight, Barry?'

'Looking forward to it, cuz. And then I'll show you the city. It's changed a lot since you used to live here. We can go to a club, pick up a few young wans…' He disappeared into his office, chortling.

I started to type some letters, but stopped when I realised John was standing in front of me. I noticed for the first time that his eyes were racing green – the colour of his car. I wondered if he had chosen the car to match his eyes – and if they had the same effect on girls in France. Was that why Veronique had left him?

'I was just wondering if you'd like to come out with me after work.'

I felt my heart thump and my stomach plummet, the way they did on the big wheel at the carnival. I had broken out in a sweat, too – and my cheeks were blazing! And my tongue was paralysed!

'I take it that's a no?' But he smiled.

I took a deep breath. 'I'm not a young wan.'

Now it was his turn to look sheepish – but he managed to do it with dignity. 'I am so sorry you heard that. I have no intention of picking up "wans", young or otherwise. I'm asking you on a date.'

Had he really said 'date'? Until then, I'd thought only Americans on TV talked about 'dating'. It was nice, though…. I realised I was confused about John Wrightman. I wasn't sure I could trust him and didn't even know whether I liked him or not. All I knew was that I found him achingly attractive – so much so that I wasn't going to let him get too close. After all, my parents had been in love twenty years and it had all ended when an old slapper caught his eye.

I didn't tell the other girls I had a date with John; I knew they'd tease me, and then I'd go all awkward with him. I had done enough blushing for one day.

So I kept my head rigged up to the Dictaphone machine and, by the end of the day, even Janet was impressed. 'You and I are the only ones who do any work around here', she said. Not that she eased up on my load. So, as soon as she'd left the office, I hid her pile of 'urgent' letters under my desk and went to the ladies' to make myself look dateworthy.

I had no make-up with me (I never bothered these days, with no parties to go to and no money to justify hanging out at the shopping mall with my old friends) so I licked my finger and used it to tease my eyelashes into shape, then subtly coloured in my eyebrows with gentle, upward strokes of a black biro, so they looked fuller. I hoped it made me look sultry, like Veronique.

'You look different, Chloe', Sandra said as we were finishing up for the day. 'I don't know what it is, but you look sort of – *foreign*.'

'It must be contagious', I laughed and went out to grab my coat. 'See you tomorrow – have to run for the bus!'

'I'll walk wit you', Brenda said. 'I'm meerin Clint for a drink in dat pub beside the bus stop.'

Blast, I thought; that was where I had arranged to meet John. Well, I'd just have to tell the girls now, wouldn't I?

Just as I was scrabbling around for a way to break it to them, John dashed in. 'Chloe! Thank God you're still here. Listen, I can't meet you this evening; something urgent has come up. But, look, we'll do it another time. Byeee!' He tweaked my cheek and ran back out.

'Wooo!' Tina's grin was splitting her face in two. Brenda Beverley were gaping. Natalie had gone pale – almost green.

Sandra broke the awkwardness. 'Chloe, I hope you won't take this the wrong way, but…' She hesitated and put on the 'concerned' expression she used for clients who were definitely going to jail. 'It's never a good idea to get too, well, involved with your employers. It's just not *righ* – d'you know wharr I mean?'

'My social life is my own business!' I bolted down the stairs, tears welling. It was still raining, and I'd left my umbrella in the office, but I didn't want to go back to get it – not while the gossip was fresh. So I stood at the bus stop, letting the sky pour down on my head letting it drench my hair – which, anyway, needed a trim and some highlights. Even if I could afford to go to my favourite salon, it was hard to fit in an appointment on the weekend, which was the only time I was free nowadays. Life as a student with a rich daddy had been so much simpler.

I was under my own personal black cloud so I didn't realise someone was calling me until I felt a warm hand on my shoulder. 'Chloe, you'll catch cold.' It was John. 'Come on, I'll give you a lift.'

He opened the door of the BMW and I got in, shivering. The rain drummed on the soft roof, sounding like Janet's recently acquired false nails on her desk. John Wrightman certainly had a knack for lifting women's spirits and then letting them plummet; he was a human rollercoaster.

'Put your seatbelt on, Chloe. I'm not giving the cops the satisfaction of catching a solicitor breaking the law.' I obeyed, feeling like a child. 'I really am sorry about this evening. It's just that Uncle Patrick has finally realised that I'm just a name on the letterhead, so he's dumped some of his worst clients on me.'

'The legal aid ones?'

'Lord, no. I wish he would; I like the idea of convincing myself someone's innocent even when they've got a face like the picture of Dorian Grey. No, he's given me all the conveyancing and probate ones. Can you imagine anything more boring than talking to old people about their wills?'

'Well, if they're millionaires leaving priceless collections of art –'

'Unfortunately not. This man I'm meeting tonight wants me to divide his stamp collection between his three sons and leave the house to his drinking buddies who want to set up a "smoke-easy" – a private pub where they don't have to obey the smoking ban. His sons will be furious.'

'At least he's not leaving it to a floozy.'

He laughed. 'What would you know about floozies?'

'My dad ran off with one.' I didn't feel like crying this time; I didn't know what I felt like any more.

'I'm sorry to hear that', John said. He drove in silence for what seemed an eternity, then stopped outside the railway station. 'This is where you get the train home isn't it?'

'Yes, thanks – saved me a bus journey.' I opened my seatbelt. John put his hand over mine.

'Marriage is not always simple. I'm not trying to patronise you, but some day you'll understand. Before you judge your father, wait until you're at least thirty and paying a mortgage and worrying about crime in the neighbourhood.'

'Never! I'll never get a mortgage – or a husband.' I felt my eyes well up again. He cocked an eyebrow. 'And I'll probably turn to crime!' I bent down to reach for my bag, and was all set to storm out of the car, slamming the door, when he pulled my hair back from my face. 'You look as if you coloured your eyebrows in with biro.'

I felt my cheeks burn. 'Actually, it's waterproof eyebrow pencil – for waiting at bus stops in the rain.'

'Oh.' He smiled. 'Well, it's very artistic.' He tweaked my cheek, then reached his hand behind my neck, under my hair, and kissed me gently on the lips. It was very exciting but it was over in a split-second – and I didn't know what to make of that mirthful smile. And I was furious with myself for blushing.

'OK, well, bye then', I said.

'See you tomorrow, Chloe.'

As I got out, my legs felt like spaghetti.

I blushed all the way home on the train. I was vaguely aware of a man sitting opposite me, who probably thought I was shy of him – maybe he even thought I was crazy. But I didn't care.

I nearly missed my stop, and caused a scene when the doors of the train briefly closed on me; only the sensors prevented me getting squashed to death. I really was living dangerously these days: nearly getting killed, greeting criminals at work, kissing a soon-to-be divorced man... If only I could take the best parts of both my new and old lives, and blend them together, like mixing colours on a palette.

When I got home, the house was empty as usual. Cool, I thought; nobody here to interrupt me. I threw my coat and backpack on the floor and hurried to the attic. I rummaged through the canvasses until I found a big one that Mummy hadn't destroyed with her awful abstract efforts. I put it on the easel and got out my old paints. There would be no sketch, no planning; I'd paint life as I wanted it to be – freehand. Hadn't Caravaggio worked without outlines?

I was still painting when Mummy came home. I only stopped when she yelled my name. 'I'm up here, in my studio', I yelled back, looking at my handiwork and finding something pleasing in the way my figures had arranged themselves on the canvas. It was as if they had just walked on and taken up positions – actors on my stage. They were shadowy, muslin-clothed creatures, male and female but still without facial features; those would appear later if they wanted to.

'Do you realise it's midnight and you haven't eaten?' How did she know? I went downstairs, suddenly hungry. Mummy was in an elegant cream-coloured trouser suit with grey pinstripes, and her face looked flushed under the make-up, as if she had been drinking wine. 'I was out with Helen. I left you a note on the table – and some money for pizza.'

Pizza was all I seemed to be eating these days, while Mummy was dining out with Aunty Helen. The pair of them seemed to be going through the mid-life crisis in a spirit of sisterly camaraderie. Normally, I'd be pissed off about all this; being neglected and expected to live on junk was not what a loyal daughter deserved. But now I couldn't be angry if I tried.

'Mummy, you look wonderful', I said and gave her a hug. 'Where did you and Aunty Helen go for your meal?'

She walked away from me, flapping her hand limply. 'Oh, you know, a little restaurant. I can't remember the name. Where's Daryus?'

'I don't know. I've been painting since I came home.'

She spun round and suddenly she looked angry and worried. 'You mean you don't know where your little brother is? But Chloe, he's only eighteen!'

'That's old enough to be tried in an adult court and go to a men's prison. It's old enough to be married. And I'm just a year older and six inches shorter and four stone lighter – hardly the big sister!'

She looked me up and down, her eyes unfocussed; I realised she was too drunk to have driven home safely. 'I know what you're shaying to yourself: "I'm nosh my brother's keeper." Well, you *are*, Chloe.' She was yelling now. 'You're the eldest; you're responsible for your lishle brosher!'

'Mummy, stop it', I said, feeling all tight inside, the way I used to when I was a little girl and my parents were fighting. I used to sit beside my little brother on the carpet, forcing myself to smile at him so he wouldn't cry, and he'd look at me with those big blue eyes, putting all his trust in me. And now I'd let him down – and I was still afraid to cry, because that would upset Mummy even more. 'I'll call his mobile, Mummy.'

She was sitting on the couch, sobbing, saying over and over again: 'Helen and I, we were good wives, too good for the men we married – too good for our children. We should've shtayed shingle.'

Daryus didn't answer his phone, so I texted him, then boiled the kettle and made Mummy a mug of tea. 'Here, drink this, Mummy. You'll feel better.' She pushed it away, scalding both of us. She got up, livid-faced, went up to her room and slammed the door.

Just as I was about to call the *Garda* and report him as a missing person, Daryus texted me back: 'Gone 2 a gig. CU tomoro.'

I worried myself to sleep. I wondered what Daryus would do when he finally left school the following year. He'd either become a rock star or end up on the dole. And I could see Mummy turning into an old floozy like Aunty Helen – like Carmel Delahanty, who had stolen my Daddy. I worried most of all about Daddy. The only contact we'd had with him since he'd left had been through Mummy's solicitor, who'd passed on a message from Daddy's solicitor to say that he was living in Carmel's city centre apartment with her and the bastard, and that he had signed on the dole.

Bizarrely, when I finally slept John swam into my dreams, but Veronique was with him. Our kiss became their kiss. I woke up wondering if the kiss had been a dream.

'It must've been de age-gap dat broke dem up', Natalie was as I pretended to ignore them. 'I mean, six years is a massive bleedin age-gap between a couple – especially when it's de woman dat's older.'

'They wouldn't be listening to de same mewzic or fancyin de same fillum stars', Tina pointed out.

'A man and a woman wouldn't fancy de same fillum stars anyway – unless one of dem was gay.'

'Ah, would yewse two ever shut de fuck up about age-gaps', Beverley snorted. 'My Christie is eight bleedin years older dan me an we don't give a fuck. We're gerrin engaged as soon as he gets on the housing list. And look at Sandra an Keet: he's nearly as old as her aul fella. And wharrabout Brenda an Clint? He must be a good bit older.'

'Twelve years older', Brenda confirmed, with a smile, shoving her engagement ring in front of us all. We dutifully admired the sparkler. She winked at me. 'Like Chloe and Jonno.' I was furious to feel my cheeks redden, and I turned away, shuffling the papers on my desk to hide my embarrassment.

'By de way', Brenda was saying now, 'yewse are all invired to me hen night. It's next week in de Flyin Brick – yewse know dah big posh pub?'

I hoped none of our criminal clients would be at Brenda's hen party. After all, a lot of them knew she was engaged – and most of them lived in her neighbourhood. Probably drank with Clint in the Flying Brick.

'I wonder if these kids are born with charge sheets clutched in their little fists?' I asked John as we pored over some of the files in Barry's office. I couldn't believe John had actually volunteered to represent these thugs. 'Look, some of them have juvenile prison records going back to when they were in primary school.'

He chuckled but he was shaking his head. 'It's not their fault they came from a disadvantaged background.'

'No, but that doesn't give them the right to mug innocent people.'

'Shh – here comes the mammy of them all. Tell my uncle his favourite client is here.'

Old Wrightman had clearly been looking out his office window and had seen Mrs Gouger. He popped his florid face around the door. 'John, I need you in my office for back-up in case this woman gets violent.'

John signed. 'So I'm on bouncer duty. We probably should employ Brenda's fiancé in this place.'

48

'And Miss O'Doolahan, I want you in here as a female witness in case she accuses John of sexually assaulting her.'

But Mrs Gouger wasn't in a fighting mood today. She sat there with the injured dignity of a proud mother. One of her sons had been beaten up by a curmudgeonly shopkeeper over the matter of some borrowed goods, and she was hoping Mr Wrightman would take civil and criminal proceedings on her boy's behalf.

'It doesn't work that way, Mrs Gouger. The State will have to prosecute the perpetrators – including your son for shoplifting. Have you filed a complaint to the Garda?'

'The pigs? Sure, dey'd only laugh in me face. Dey're on de side of dat animal dat attacked him.' She began to sob. As she opened her handbag, Mr Wrightman recoiled and went white, but Mrs Gouger was just taking out a photo. 'Dat's him as a baby, in his cot.' She kissed it. 'He was behind bars right from de beginnin.'

'He must have had a bad start in life', I cut in, trying to sound sympathetic (only because John was there).

My attempt to get bleeding-heart-brigade brownie points backfired, as Mrs Gouger glared at me. 'Sure, what would you know?' She looked me up and down. 'I bet you went to university.'

'Art college, actually – but I dropped out.'

'Isn't it well for some, droppin out when de fancy takes ya? Me own sons an daughters never had de opportewnity to finish deir education. I sent dem to elocewtion lessons when dey were little, and dat was as far as dey got.'

I was getting hot in the face and even John's hand on my shoulder failed to calm me down. 'I couldn't finish college because my parents couldn't afford to pay my fees. They're getting divorced, you see, and my father has gone bankrupt.' Tears stung my eyelids.

Mrs Gouger cackled. 'So he's one of dem white-collar criminals dat has de country de way it is. Youse lot tinks youse is berrer dan de rest of us!'

She walked out giving us the two-fingered salute. 'Tanks for feckin nottin. I'm goin to find meself a berrer firm of solicirors – even if I has to rob banks for de money to pay dem.'

John turned to his uncle. 'I think we should invite Chloe to lunch for getting rid of the Gouger clan.'

Mr Wrightman chuckled, then shook his head. 'I'm afraid we can't this time. We've got to talk about your role in this firm – and Veronique's.' He frowned at me. 'Miss O'Doolahan, can you leave us alone? And shut the door after you.'

I glanced at John, who shrugged and smiled at me from behind his uncle.

'Off to meet your friends again, Chloe?' Sandra said as I gathered up my backpack and coat. When I didn't answer her, she persisted: 'Where are you going for lunch?'

'We're meeting in an art gallery. There's a café there.' I regretted having told her and dashed off before she could invite herself along; it wouldn't do for my colleagues to discover that my friends in the gallery were centuries-old ghosts who spoke to me silently, through the medium of paint and canvas. They were the only friends I had these days.

I did go to the café in the gallery this time; I needed comfort food and they did lovely hot apple tart with cream. I was also in the mood for people-watching; cafés were always ideal places to indulge in this guilty pleasure.

And I no longer felt the urge to dash around the gallery, staring at paintings; they were all so familiar to me now, I was no longer over-awed and hardly even noticed them. I wondered if it would be the same a few weeks into my affair with John – if it ever happened.

The café had been empty when I'd arrived, but suddenly a large group of old people came in. I cringed as they debated loudly whether to go for double-cream cakes or banoffi; they could hardly walk all that off. And I winced as they scraped chairs noisily; they had destroyed my tranquillity. Then I felt guilty for having such uncharitable thoughts – after all, stuffing their faces in the midst of all that art was probably the height of sensory pleasure for people their age; they'd never have an affair with John Wrightman to look forward to.

'Excuse me, would you mind awfully if we shared your table?' I looked up and saw two old ladies. The one who had spoken had brilliant blue eyes and dramatically pencilled eyebrows under a vibrant red fringe. Her hair was cut in a blunt bob that ended just below her strong cheekbones and drew attention to a sharp nose and long, elegant neck (I admired the artily knotted scarf which was obviously there to hide wrinkles). She was a Toulouse Lautrec model come to life!

'Of course you may', I said, taking my backpack off the other seat and putting it on the floor. The two ladies sat down in a cloud of strong but refined perfume and I noticed the short, plump one had a less angular version of the same face, and grey hair scraped back in a tight bun. Whereas the Toulouse Lautrec lady was draped in wispy, vibrantly patterned scarves, her sister (they were clearly sisters) wore a smart lilac trouser suit. She offered to get tea and disappeared into the crowd, fiddling with an expensive looking beige leather handbag.

'We see you here every day', Madam Toulouse Lautrec said. Her accent was Irish but clipped, as if she'd spent years abroad.

'Oh?'

She patted my arm and smiled. 'Don't worry, dear; we weren't spying on you and we're not going to tell your headmistress.'

'I'm not a schoolgirl.' I was offended; did she really think I looked like a kid?

Her eyebrows flew up and she fluttered her hands, which had long red fingernails. 'Oh I'm so sorry. Everyone looks so young to me – I must be getting old.'

I felt awful for having made her feel old (and worried that someone might do the same to me if I ever reached that age; I half-believed in karma). 'You don't look old at all.'

She threw her head back and cackled. 'Oh, that's so kind of you.' She leaned forward, fists under her chin. 'I'm seventy-seven. Both of us are – my sister and I. We've just had our birthday. Isn't that right, Francesca?'

Francesca put the two cups and saucers down, and eased herself into the chair. 'Oooh, my poor hip. Are you telling everyone our age again, Eleanor?' She snorted, a rude laugh that didn't really go with her elegant clothes. 'This young lady must thing we're as old as the paintings.'

'And nowhere near as beautiful', Eleanor chortled.

What was I doing here with two giggly old dears? I wondered. But I nibbled at my apple tart; I needed the energy before my long walk back to the office.

'We didn't want to disturb you when we saw you looking at the paintings', Francesca was saying. 'You looked lost in them.'

I wished she and her sister would get lost.

'So', Eleanor persisted, 'you're not at school. Are you a university student, then?'

'I was an art student. Then I dropped out.' My mantra, my tragedy, the story of my life so far; I had really messed up, hadn't I? If it wasn't for John, I'd have nothing to look forward to. I know that sounds irrational but that was how I felt at that moment, when I was nineteen with no social life, no education prospects, a grey job going nowhere, a mother and brother who had no time for me, and a runaway father.

I looked at my Swatch and suddenly felt sick. 'Please excuse me; I have to get back to work.'

Eleanor scraped back her chair to let me out. 'So you work?'

'Yes, in a solicitor's office; I'm a secretary.'

Francesca smiled. 'That's nice, dear.'

'No it's not. It's boring and my boss is cranky and my colleagues are always teasing me about being skinny and having a different accent', I said, realising even as I said it that the girls had been nicer to me lately – Brenda had even invited me to her hen party. And Mr Wrightman wasn't so bad to work for.

'Well, I'm sure you'll get back on your feet and go back to your studies. After all, you're still young', Francesca said with a warm smile.

'I think it's tragic', Eleanor cut in.

'I'm really sorry; I can't stay and talk. It was a pleasure – but I have to go. Byee!' I said and dashed out of the café, down the elegant marble staircase and out into the summer rain. Blast, I thought; I'd left my umbrella in the office again. If I were as old as Eleanor and Francesca, I'd be diagnosed with dementia and locked up in a nursing home.

I was seriously late this time. I didn't even have five minutes to gamble at the bus stop, on the off-chance that the twenty-past-three would arrive five minutes late instead of what-felt-like-never; I'd never been late enough to find out. Now I was going to be two hours late!

John's BMW was parked at the meter across the street from the office. My heart somersaulted and I slowed down, catching my breath, frantically slicking my hair behind my ears to make it look less ratty; I hoped to arrive in the office looking as if I'd just stepped out of the sea-foam like some modern Venus, rather than the way I appeared in the glare of the bus-stop shelter.

John eased his long legs out of the car, walked around to the passenger side and opened the door. I thought he was reaching in for his briefcase but then Veronique emerged, all elegant legs under a very short beige business suit. *She* certainly didn't care if our less savoury clients ogled her legs. Her hair had been cut and waved, and she was wearing a black-and-white scarf around her swanlike neck. Something glittered at each ear. John held his umbrella over her head as they walked to the door. I caught my breath as he pressed the buzzer. They must have gone off to meet a wealthy client or barrister, after that lunch with old Wrightman, I supposed; there was Wrightman Senior's car in its usual place beside the door.

I lingered on the pavement, getting soaked. I didn't want to walk up the stairs with them; I would feel uncomfortable around Veronique, knowing that I was soon to be her replacement in John's personal life. I felt a twinge of guilt as I wondered if Carmel Delahanty thought of my Mummy in the same way.

Then John put his hand on the small of Veronique's back. At first I just thought he was ushering her through the door, because he had pushed it slightly ajar. But now their heads were disappearing behind the umbrella, and he was pulling her close. I saw her hand hesitate, then reach up along his pin-striped arm until it rested on his shoulder.

I stood watching them until they had disappeared into the building. Then I wiped the tears away with a rain-soaked hand, and went over to press the buzzer, thinking to myself that I was touching exactly the same spot that John had touched just seconds ago.

I trudged up the stairs and pushed open the door, thinking how grimy it was – like the whole bloody office and my whole miserable existence. Brenda put her finger to her lips as I entered. The others glanced up nervously.

Then Mr Wrightman burst out of his office, his face like the proverbial thunderbolt. He motioned to me with his finger to come into his office, closed the door firmly after me and flapped his pudgy hand in the direction of the seat in front of his desk. He sat down opposite me, removed his glasses, wiped them with a flannel – he seemed to take forever –

then put them back on and fixed his frown on me (the glasses seemed to set the wrinkles in place, like a kind of gelling agent, I found myself thinking).

'Miss O'Doolahan', he growled, 'I am most disappointed in you.' He paused for effect, as I imagined he would if he ever had to cross-examine a witness in court (just as well he had to do everything through a barrister, I thought).

Tears welled up and I angrily blinked them back; I didn't want him to think the tears had anything to do with him and his rotten job. It was seeing John with Veronique that was making me miserable.

'You got this job on the recommendation of a good friend of mine, whose judgement I have, until recently, never questioned. I realise now that I made a grave mistake.'

Anyone would think he was sentencing me to life in prison – which would be a lot more pleasant than spending eight hours a day in this office, just a few feet away from John and Veronique.

'You seem to have no regard for the working hours, the people working with you or, for that matter, the work itself. Do you have any idea of the chaos you caused this morning?'

'No', I said, wondering if he was implying that I was an evil temptress destroying his nephew's already-broken marriage. Mr Wrightman seemed like the type who would disapprove of that kind of thing (he made no secret of his contempt for his divorce clients, as soon as they were out of the office).

'Cast your woolly little mind back to yesterday evening, when you were entrusted with the Book of Pleadings in a certain case we were defending – does the name "Simon Wong" ring a bell?'

'Simon Wong', I said, trying to think clearly. 'Mr Wrong – I mean Mr Wong.'

Mr Wrightman banged his fist down on the desk, breaking the pencil clenched in it (if he had been a judge, the top of his gavel would have flown off and hit me in the eye). 'He's our best client! And you have just made a liar out of him – and out of us, his solicitors.' He leaned across the desk and narrowed his eyes. He was growling like an old tiger I'd seen on a nature documentary once; it was too weak to run after a buffalo, so it was puckering up its nose and closing in on an injured chicken.

'You sent me the bloody Book of Pleadings – complete with our barrister's Opinion – to the solicitors representing Mr Wong's rival. He's going to lose the fucking restaurant because of you! He won't be able to pay off his debts.'

'Oh, I'm really sorry, Mr Wrightman', I said, my surprise at his use of the 'F' word mingling with visions of Mr Wong being attacked with one of those axes the Chines use to chop up vegetables. 'If I can do anything to help – '

'You can't!' He snorted a few times, glaring at me, then went silent. The storm had passed, I thought; he was once again just a harmless, grumpy old man who paid my salary into my bank-account and gave me mountains of boring work.

He stood up, walked over to the window and stood with his hands in his pockets, his solid silhouette nearly filling the frame. He was a de Chirico man, I thought to myself: bulky, basic-looking, almost a still life, yet *animate* – he seemed to be pulsing with a kind of rage under that thick, bland shell.

Suddenly, he turned round to face me. I couldn't see his expression with the light behind him. 'Miss O'Doolahan, I'm giving you one minute's notice.'

'What?' I felt as if the blood had drained from my face and trickled into my stomach.

'You're fired.'

I just stared at him, trying to see the humanity and failing. He was pure de Chirico Man now. He coughed and added, waving his finger in the air: 'You're not entitled by law to a lengthier period of notice because you haven't been here a wet day. I will of course pay your salary to the end of the month, but I want you out of the office before you do any more damage to my firm.'

He went over and opened the door, his hand gesturing towards it, looking like Oliver Hardy's doppelganger – the humourless version.

'I got rid of Mrs Gouger – '

'Out!'

As I passed him, I resisted the urge to give him 'the finger' the way I'd seen Tina give one of the clients earlier that day, an obnoxious juvenile delinquent who'd made a pass at her ('Cheeky little bugger – I went to school with his big sister', she had fumed).

I walked slowly across the office to my desk to get my backpack, feeling as if my legs had turned to lead. I kept my head down, my hair shrouding my face. I heard Mr Wrightman's door close and then I looked up. The other secretaries were staring at me.

Then Tina growled: 'I'd like to give him a kick up his big, pin-striped arse!' She made a kicking motion with her platform ankle-boots.

'You'll find anudder job, no probs', Brenda said, and they all hugged me – though I noticed Natalie was suppressing a smile, which vanished when Tina said: 'Jonno will give you a reference – he's mad abou ya. I'll give him your number.'

'And you're still comin to me hen party', Brenda reminded me.

'Yes, of course – I'd love to. Thanks so much.' I was smiling through my tears now.'

'And de weddin afters. I'll introdewce ya to me cousin who's broken up wir his girlfriend.' She winked at me and nodded towards Mr Wrightman's office, from where I could hear John and Veronique chuckling. 'I've invited Jonno too – but not yer woman Veronique.'

'You're meerin us for a jar after work –and we're not taking "No" for an answer', Sandra said.

'Thanks', I said, overwhelmed by their kindness. I just hoped they'd invite John too – without Veronique.

I crossed the bridge and spent the rest of the afternoon in the nice part of town, near the National Gallery. I walked into a few fine art galleries and asked them if they needed staff, but the well-groomed men and women invariably told me they always advertised vacancies. I doubted it; they looked like the kind of people who would hire on personal recommendation only. One lady smiled kindly at me and said: 'You're very young. Why don't you finish your studies and then drop us in your CV?' I even plucked up the courage to ask the receptionist at the National Gallery if they could give me work, even part-time. 'I'll do anything – I'll work in the café, sweep the floors, you name it.'

She shook her head. 'You really do love this place, don't you? I see you in here every day. I'm sorry I can't help you, but we advertise all job vacancies. Drop your CV in but I can't promise anything.'

As I was walking out the door, Eleanor and Francesca grabbed me, one on each side. 'Oh, you're back, dear. But we thought you were working.'

'I was, but I got fired.'

I could see them thinking: first she drops out of college, then she gets dropped from her job. But Francesca was reaching into her bag and pulling out one of the notebooks they sold in the gallery shop with images of the paintings on every other page. 'Write your phone number on this, dear. We'll help you find something.'

'Come back in for a cup of tea', Eleanor added. 'Tell us all about your terrible job.'

I was about to say no, then I thought: why not? After all, I had plenty of free time now. So I let them buy me tea and tart and told them everything – even the stuff about John.

Eleanor was wiping black streaks of mascara across her eyelids by the time I'd finished and her sister was dabbing away my tears. 'I know exactly how you feel, pet', Eleanor wailed. 'The same thing happened to me when I was younger – and Francesca.' Her sister nodded, though she seemed to be laughing at the memory. Eleanor was snorting: 'Men like that think they can lead young girls on and then go back to their wives. I bet he's broken many a heart.'

I thought of Janet's sour face after she'd had lunch with him, and Veronique's feigned nonchalance the first time I'd met her, when they were still considering divorce. Had I wasted my time translating all those documents into English for John? Was he going to move back into their chateau with the paintings and the horses and dogs?

I wasn't in the humour for meeting my ex-colleagues in the pub across from the office, but I wasn't going to break my promise; they had been so nice to me. So I trudged across the River Liffey again and went into the dark little lounge. There was a stink of beer and damp clothes. The last time I'd been in a proper pub, it had smelt of cigarettes; that had been before smoking in pubs was banned. Daryus and I had been little then, and our parents had brought us for lunch in our local out in the suburb where we used to live before we got all posh and moved to Belgowan. I'd guessed something wonderful was about to happen, and Daddy had waited until we'd finished our dessert. Then he'd told us: 'We're going to be rich.'

'What?' Mummy had asked, her eyes shining, a smile breaking across her tired face.

'I said, you can give up the job in the bookies' because I've got the contract.'

I had no idea what 'the contract' was (my mind always seemed to wander off in another direction every time my parents talked about 'business') but now I realised it was very important indeed, as Mummy was flinging her arms around Daddy and squealing. I had pulled Daryus out of their way, afraid they'd knock him over in their happiness.

Daddy had turned to me. 'What would you like, sugar? Just tell your rich Daddy.'

'A horse', I had replied. 'An Arabian stallion – dark chestnut like the one in my book.' I showed him my favourite book at the time, which was about a stable lad who had been charged with looking after a precious racehorse.

Daddy had laughed. 'Well, maybe I'm not that rich – yet. But you can certainly have riding lessons.'

'Chloe, stop pouting!' Mummy had snapped, her face suddenly wrinkled again. 'You really know how to ruin everything, don't you? Nothing is ever fabulous enough for you.'

And now here I was, back in the same kind of pub, with a slightly different fog in it, wondering if my life was going to veer off in another direction.

I ordered a glass of orange juice and sat down in a corner, where I could see the door. I looked at my Swatch: it said five-fifteen. The girls would be here any minute, I thought.

They came in giggling, then stopped as if they felt guilty for laughing in the face of my misery. Brenda came over and squeezed my shoulder. 'Wharr are ya drinkin?'

'It's OK, thanks Brenda; I've got an orange juice.'

She stared at me, then whispered: 'You're not – don't tell me you're up the bleedin duff!'

Now I was laughing . 'Jayz, ya gave me a frigh', Brenda said. Tina pointed at my tummy. 'Does she look as if she's gorra bun in de oven! Here, get dis down ya.' She plonked a pint of lager in front of me. 'Ya need dis to drown yer sorrows.'

I wasn't used to lager; I had avoided everything alcoholic since my debs when that slut, Emmabelle McCowan, let my drunken boyfriend smooch her on the dancefloor. My ex-friends at art college had nicknamed me 'Clean Chloe' and even the girls from my ballet class had stopped inviting me to go dancing with them because I actually liked to dance (they were usually legless at the end of the evening, fair game for all the rugby players who circled us like lions around a crowd of gazelles).

But being teetotal had got me nowhere, so I sipped the dark beer. It tasted lovely! 'Get dat down ya!' Brenda was still egging me on three pints (and a few tearful trips to the Ladies') later. 'You'll feel berrer. Lerrit all out.' 'Yeah', Tina said. 'Let de drink talk.'

So the drink spoke – and told them everything: about Daddy going bankrupt and running off with Carmel Delahanty, about my suddenly discovering I had a half-brother, about having to give up my studies, the neighbours snubbing my mother, my former friends sneering at me in the gym, and how much of a shock it was to have my life changed so dramatically, through no fault of my own.

Brenda, Tina, Beverley and Sandra were nodding sympathetically. Brenda even pointed out to the others: 'It would be like de way we'd feel if we were purrin a Turd Wurld cuntery – no, I'm norrexaggerarin, I'm bleedin not!'

Natalie, however, was pulling faces and saying: 'We all have to work in offices. We can't all be bleedin art stewdents', over and over again, like a mantra.

I turned to her at last. 'I forgive you, Natalie, because you're drunk. You've no idea – hic! – whatsh your shaying.'

'Tank ya, luv', Natalie said, and gave me a drunken hug, knocking my pint onto my lap. We giggled as we tried to mop it up with tissues.

John chose that moment to walk in with Barry – and Veronique. John and Veronique sat down while Barry went to the bar, passing us.

'Hey, Barrree!' Natalie yelled. He didn't seem to hear her, so she followed up with an ear-splitting roar. 'Mr Wrightman Junior, wharrever the fuck you want us to call ya! C'mere to us!'

He nodded and smiled weakly.

'Ah, Natalie, he's scarlet!' Beverley said. 'He don't want to be seen with us.'

'It's cos of Chloe', Tina cut in. 'He's afraid she'll cry about lewsin her job. Men are petrified of dah.'

'Would youse look at de luv-birds over dere', Natalie said, pointing to John and Veronique. 'Dey're jus pretendin not to see us.'

'Oh, don't say anything', I pleaded, clutching her arm. I suddenly felt very sober indeed. John and Veronique were *tête-à-tête* – and they were clearly not talking about work. They hardly noticed when Barry put a glass in front of each of them. A mini-skirted blonde lounge-girl carried over his drink and he said something to her that was obviously flirtatious. She looked flattered – I supposed she would be, with a bum as big as hers.

'Barry's gone wild since his wife divorced him', Brenda was saying. 'She took half his fortewn – and de house he inherited from his parents.'

I quietly sipped my pint, letting their small talk drift over my head, until Sandra said: 'I heard Jonno on the phone just before I locked up. He was bewkin a nigh in dis swanky cuntery house for himself and Veronique. Look, I took de brochure to show it to my Keet – fat chance he'll take me dere!'

I looked at the picture of a stately home with a tweed-trousered woman playing golf in the foreground. 'I know that place', I said. 'It's really a retirement home.' Well, Poo Anchorbottom and her army of ageing gold-diggers were always holding charity balls there, so what was the difference?

Sandra snorted and stabbed her fingernail into the brochure. 'In me arse! Look – it's got bleedin four-poster bed!' She was obviously indignant that I'd spoiled her romantic daydream.

'I'm going home', I said, feeling tired. 'Have you got the number of a taxi rank?'

'You can't afford a bleedin taxi', Sandra pointed out. 'You're unemployed.'

'You'll have to sign on the dole until you get another job', Brenda said. 'The money's not much but it'll keep you in bus fares and phone credit while you're going around to job interviews.'

It all sounded very bleak. And I realised that I'd have to dip into the small sum I'd saved from my last month's salary, because I wouldn't be signing on the dole; Mummy would hit the roof, and I couldn't imagine a social welfare inspector coming to our house in Belgowan to do a means test.

'I'll find a job – any job. I'll just have to be less choosy', I told the girls.

'Well, here's your chance to be less choosey about blokes', Tina sniggered. 'Barry Wrightman is eyeballin ya.'

As soon as I looked to check, he came over to our table, dragged up a stool and sat down beside me. 'Well, girls, how are you?' he said brightly. 'Fine.' 'All right.' 'Ho-hum.'

I ignored him, but he moved his stool closer until we were welded together at the hip, like John and Veronique – it sickened me to see them.

'Chloe, I was sorry to hear about your being, ah, em, well, fired.'

'It's for the best', I said.

'Oh, but it's not, you know. What am I going to do with nothing pretty to look at?'

'Ya have us!' Tina snarled, then giggled. 'Not dat we want ya gogglin at us.' The other girls laughed.

Barry looked mortally offended. He pulled his card and a silver pen out of his breast pocket and scribbled a number. 'My mobile. We must get together sometime.'

I didn't take it from him, but folded my arms. He obviously thought he could take up where John had left off – maybe they'd even place bets on whether he could bed me, the way I'd heard my brother betting with his school friends over a prudish girl their own age.

'What? You're not going to take my card? I could be a useful contact for you, you know. I could get you another job.'

I felt very drunk, and it took some effort to focus on him while I explained: 'I don't trusht men who've broken their marriage vows.'

His face coloured – more much from anger than alcohol, I realised. 'I was a faithful husband. My wife just decided she wanted half my money and another man. You're all the bloody same, women! Bloody tarts!'

There was only one answer to that; I emptied my lager over him. He stood up, spluttering and swearing, as the girls laughed hysterically. Veronique was gaping as John came over. Now I've ruined it for good, I thought.

But, to my surprise, John grabbed his cousin by the tie and punched him under the jaw, sending him flying into the path of the flirty lounge-girl, tipping her tray of brimming beer glasses over all of us. Everyone in the pub stared. The lounge-girl, now on her hands and knees, looked up through her blonde curls towards Barry – but he wasn't in the mood to be her hero.

Natalie was the first to speak. 'Jonno, me brudder an all me cousins are amateur boxers, an I've never seen anytin like dat. You're shaggin leetal, y'are.'

John grinned. 'That's a real compliment if ever I heard one. Chloe, you've been baptised in beer! Go and clean yourself up. One of you go with her.'

Brenda came to the Ladies' with me. As we dabbed away at the beer stains, we giggled. 'We're goin to miss ya. Ya really have a way of livenin tings up. I knew ya would be fun de day you started – do ya member when dah young lad who was up for shopliftin tried to grab yer backpack and ya belted him wirrit?'

I'd forgotten that incident until now. 'That was a good backpack. I bought it in Milan. His nasty nose-stud scuffed it and I had to throw it in the recycling bank.'

'Jayz, Chloe, I dunno what planet ya've been livin on but yer a scream!'

When we got back to our table, John, Veronique and Barry were nowhere to be seen. 'He got Barry barred from the pub', Tina said. 'De manager is gerrin us two taxis – one goin your way, d'udder to bring us home.'

I didn't tell Mummy I'd been fired (or Daryus because I knew he'd tell Mummy if he wanted to distract attention from some misdemeanour of his own). Mummy was in a world of her own, anyway. She'd given up painting (I was relieved to have my studio to myself again) and had found a range of new 'power hobbies', as she and Aunty Helen called them.

'Helen said the best way to cope with divorce is to throw myself into something absorbing', she said.

'Well, she'd know' I said, remember how Helen had joined an amateur dramatic society, taken up scuba diving and gone back to school after Uncle Con dumped her. She'd had a few affairs too, and was her neighbours' favourite topic of gossip, but I wasn't going to remind Mummy of that – it might give her ideas.

'I'm starting bellydancing lessons', she was saying.

'Mummy, how can you pay for bellydancing lessons if we're supposed to be broke?'

She suddenly looked shifty. 'I – I had a little bit put by.'

'Oh.'

'Well, Chloe, what do you expect me to do? Sit here in the house worrying about money? Maybe if I do well at the bellydancing, I can get work dancing in restaurants and – and at weddings. Soraya says most of her students go on to be professionals.'

'You'll get a big tummy!' I warned her. 'Why do you think it's called bellydancing?'

'Who cares? That's considered very attractive where Soraya comes from.'

Mummy's other new hobbies included writing a romantic novel and singing. 'I've been practising every day, singing alone with the radio', she said. 'I'm going to ask your brother to let me join his band.'

'Mummy, Daryus won't let you anywhere near the band. He won't even introduced them to you in case you embarrass him. They're a metal-punk cross-over at the moment. You wouldn't fit in.'

'My son will let his mother join the band –or I'm throwing those bloody drums out!'

I would have warned Daryus, but he was out; it was Wednesday night, so he was practising in his friend Felim's house.

'I'm going down to Felim's to surprise him', Mummy said about half an hour later, clumping down the stairs in what sounded like my old biker boots – an impulse buy after I'd read an article saying the look was back in. Of course, that was before Daddy had left and poverty had rained down on my life; I wouldn't be spending over three hundred euro on boots I'd never wear now. I ran out to see Mummy getting into Helen's car. And, yes, she was wearing my biker boots – with a leather jacket and trouser that looked new. I texted Daryus: 'Mummy coming 2 get U.'

Then I surfed the web, looking at my horoscope in three different language and daring myself to join an online dating service. I got as far as filling out the profile, then my head was flooded with visions of toothless old men tapping their keyboards in bedsits with posters of Pamela Anderson on the walls, and I decided that, no, blind dates were all very well if you happened to be blind, but I was an art lover.

I also looked up the jobs websites, but they were depressing; most of the 'top jobs' were for managers with experience, and the rest were McJobs like the one I'd lost – and even they required experience or qualifications. I doubted Mummy's solicitor would put in a good word for me again even if I swallowed my fear and told Mummy – and she wouldn't grovel to him again. He had sent a few letters demanding his fees, which Mummy had told him she couldn't pay until Daddy found some of his missing millions.

Now I wondered if Mummy would end up in prison for non-payment of her solicitor's divorce fees. Was there still a debtors' prison? Would they take away Mummy's designer handbags in case she used them to fight with other prisoners? No wonder I'd been useless as a legal secretary if I couldn't even be bothered to find out about legal matters that affected my own family. My father would probably end up behind bars at some stage, too; bigger businessmen than he were serving time.

I was so engrossed in the internet and my visiting-Mummy-and-Daddy-in-jail fantasies that I didn't hear Mummy coming back. I became aware of her yelling: 'Chloe! Daryus's run off!'

I ran out onto the landing. Mummy was sitting on the floor, in floods of tears, Helen fussing over her with handkerchiefs.

Helen's eyes narrowed and her lips pursed. 'You should have been keeping an eye on your brother', she said.

I ignored her. 'Mummy, what are you talking about?'

She sobbed. 'I went to Felim's house, and he said he hadn't seen Daryus for at least two months – told me he was in Flings.'

'The lap-dancing club? But Mummy, he's only eighteen. They have an over-twenty-three rule.'

Mummy glared at me. 'I know that.' She sobbed again. 'Felim said Daryus was in a – a relationship – with one of the girls – '

'A lap dancer', Helen clarified, as if I was thick. 'Daryus spends a few nights a week at her apartment, over the club. Here, Bee, drink this. It'll calm your nerves.'

'Mummy, you promised you'd stay off the drink – '

'Ah would you ever shut up!' Mummy screamed and I realised that she was already stotious. 'Little Miss Know-It-All. You think you're so perfect with your job and your boyfriend! You'll just run off and leave me and poor Daryus.'

Now I was confused. Boyfriend? The last guy I'd gone out with was Philippe while I was on that language exchange the previous summer. Before that, I'd gone to a few parties with boys I knew from the neighbourhood – they were part of our social circle at the time. One of them, of course, had been my errant escort at the debs ball. The only guy I wanted now was John.

'He left a message for you on the answering machine', Mummy was saying. 'He's a solicitor from your job, isn't he? Off you go with him to Paris or wherever he's taking you.' She gulped some of the champagne and sobbed again. 'My Daryus, my baby boy, he's going to leave me too. He's going to run away to Lithuania with that woman – that prostitute!'

Helen helped Mummy to her feet. 'Lie down on the couch and stop worrying. That woman won't take Daryus back to where she came from – she must have been glad to escape from it. Why do you think she came here to work in a seedy nightclub?'

The pair of them staggered into the sitting room, Mummy leaning on Helen.

I sighed. So Daryus had found himself a glamorous foreign girlfriend, most likely a bit older than himself; I was happy for him.

And I was even happier for myself. I went into the kitchen, closed the door and played John's message. 'Hi, John Wrightman here. I'm just calling to make sure Chloe got home safely. Can you get her to call me tonight? Doesn't matter if it's late. I'm leaving for Paris tomorrow – for a few days. And – .' He hesitated and I was worried he had been cut off. 'Eh, Chloe, if you get this message, I want you to know that I – I really want to see you again. Please call me. Tonight. Any time. Or call the office and I'll leave my mobile number with the girls for you.'

I played it at least ten times, half-fearing I had just imagined it. But no; it was more real every time I listened. There was no way I could have misinterpreted the words.

Eventually, I went up to bed, passing Mummy and Aunty Helen, who had both fallen asleep on the living room floor, new handbags clutched in their hands, looking like two drunken bag ladies – which I supposed they were. I felt a pang of pity for them; they had lost what I'd just found. I wished them well and hoped they'd find love again. I even hoped Daddy would find true love with Carmel, if Mummy really was wrong for him – after all, John and Veronique had cut their losses, hadn't they? And it was for the best, now that he'd found me. He was probably going to Paris to finalise the divorce.

I thought of Daryus and his Lithuanian lap-dancer. I was overwhelmed by affection for him and goodwill towards both of them; my sensitive kid brother who had never had a girlfriend because he'd always come across as 'too intense' (according to my ex-friend whose sister he had asked out) and the foreign woman who had come to Ireland in search of a decent standard of living and had found love – with a future rock star! Now *that* was a real Cinderella story.

I didn't call John back that night; I didn't want him to think I'd just fall into his arms after having seen him kissing Veronique and then looking so intimate with her in the pub. No; I'd let him sweat a bit – at least until the next day. I hoped Veronique and he wouldn't get too cosy together on the plane to Paris.

Brenda was gagging for some gossip when I rang in the morning to get John's mobile number. 'Maybe he just wants to give me a reference', I said. Ah gerrup the yard! You'll have to come for another jar with us and tell us everytin!'

I thanked her, and feeling my heart pound, bought a pre-paid call card; I planned to spend a lot of time on the phone to John in Paris.

But his voicemail answered. I hesitated, trying to think of something that wouldn't sound naff, then hung up and texted him: 'Miss U2. Chloe.' I hoped he wouldn't think I was referring to the rock band (I was a U2 fan but I fancied John far more!). Then I realised I was just being neurotic and tried to put him out of my mind for a few days. Now that he had my mobile number, it was up to him to call. Brenda had told me he had a full diary at work. Meanwhile I still had plenty to do; I had to find a job.

But today was Friday; it was never a good idea to look for a job close to the weekend, was it? I decided not, and went to the gym instead.

I brought my own music this time, just in case any of my annoying ex-friends tried to talk to me. I hadn't been there during the off-peak period since my lazy student days, and had forgotten how pleasant it was, having a whole room full of machines to myself and empty mirrors all around. I enjoyed having all this space.

I asked Daryus about his girlfriend on Saturday evening, when he briefly returned home to grab a sports bag full of clothes. 'She's cool. She'd love to meet you sometime', he said vaguely.

I looked at his smart, silk pin-striped shirt, tucked into his jeans instead of hanging outside. The grown-up clothes made him look more childish. I scruffed his hair, which was fluffy and, well, babyish. 'Daryus, be careful.'

'What?' He blushed. 'You don't need to worry about me, sis. We use protection – and she's had all the tests for STDs.'

'I didn't mean that – though that's important too. What I meant was, don't let her use you. She's not the only girl in the world.'

'She is, for me.' Then he laughed and looked like my kid brother again. 'Until she does something to annoy me – like turn out to be a tranny or something.'

He turned up at Mass on Sunday morning. Mummy was relieved to see he hadn't totally rebelled against his upbringing, until she saw the woman with him. After Mass, he introduced her to him. Mira was very polite to Mummy and me. She was smaller than I imagined she'd be, not so pretty close-up, and she was a brunette. She confided that he often wore a long blonde wig at work and lot of make-up. Like everyone else in my life she was a disappointment.

'Mira's all right, isn't she, Mummy?' I said as we walked home. I so wanted everyone to be all right.

'She's not having my son! That woman must be as old as myself!'

'She's twenty-seven – just nine years older than Daryus.'

'Well, even that's too big an age-gap. She was the age of consent while he was making his First Holy Communion.'

I thought of John and the fact that twelve years older than me. Mummy must have seen me smile, because she looked sharply at me. 'How old is this John fellow?'

'I haven't asked him. But he's the youngest solicitor in the firm. He's not even a partner – just an associate.'

'Oh.' She tossed her head. 'So my husband is shacked up with his former secretary, my son is living with a lap dancer and my daughter is going out with a struggling solicitor. Great. This family is really going down in the world. Next you'll be telling me he's married.'

Capolavoro

It ought to be easy to find another job, I told myself as I took the train into the city on Monday. I'd told Mummy I was off to work as usual. Instead, I walked into a city centre recruitment agency. I was quite proud of my typing speed, and even the woman in the agency was impressed. But she didn't look so friendly when I told her I wasn't willing to take two buses to an industrial estate on the wrong side of town.

'Most of the jobs are there', she said. 'The city centre office blocks are being turned into apartments.'

'But there must be some firms still working in town. I mean, you have your offices here.'

'We're not looking for staff – and, even if we were, we'd give priority to people who have relevant experience, a degree and, preferably, a Masters in human resources.' She gave me a nasty little smirk.

But I wasn't going to be crushed to easily. 'What about a translating or interpreting job? I can speak French, Spanish and Italian fluently.'

'Have you got a degree in them?'

'Well, no, but I speak them like a native – the slang, idioms, colloquialisms. I spent two months every summer as an exchange student in either France or Italy and my family used to have a villa in Marbella.'

Her pupils turned to pinpricks as she widened her eyes and nodded. 'How lovely. But I'm sorry. Unless you have a qualification, none of that counts.'

Now I understood what old Wrightman had been going on about in all those speeches I'd typed for him, when he'd pleaded 'leniency' for criminals on the grounds that they'd been 'disadvantaged'. I was like them now. I felt as if doors were slamming behind me. 'There but for the grace of God go all of us', Wrightman Senior used to say, shaking his head as he went off to court to defend a heroin addict on a burglary charge or a young girl who'd been caught stealing perfume from a fine department store. 'You young ladies are very privileged to have well-paid jobs.'

And now I had lost that job through my own fault – and that was why I was sitting across from a haughty "human resources" hag.

I tried a model agency but they said I'd need to be available to go for castings and regular work was not guaranteed, then left my CV in the fast food joints (minimum wage, stinking work environment, yucky uniform – and the hours were irregular).

At what would have been my morning tea-break, I took a break from job-hunting and found myself in the National Gallery again. I planned to grab a bite in the café, then lose myself in the art for the afternoon. I wanted to forget about salaries and three-month trial periods. The gallery was my oasis in the middle of a hostile world. I wished I could live there, among the paintings.

The gallery was quiet this time. There was no lunchtime crowd. I had the place almost entirely to myself. I walked over to Sir John Lavery's portrait of the handsome Irish patriot Michael Collins, lying in his coffin. No wonder the painter's wife had (allegedly) tried to steal him from his fiancée. And no wonder the painter had still loved her; Lady Lavery was the subject of several of his paintings, including one which had been watermarked onto the old Irish pound note.

'A fine thing, wasn't he?' I turned round and saw Eleanor. 'My mother was in love with him too', she said.

She opened her handbag, took out a card and handed it to me. 'Eleanor and Francesca Fitzwalton, 7 Fenian Square', it said in cursive script. 'My sister and I would like you to come and work for us. We've got a house full of old paintings which were left to us by our late father, and we need help cataloguing them, deciding which ones need restoring, and identifying the artists in some cases. It would be a full-time job – and of course we'd pay you properly. That's if you're interested.'

I stared at her. It was too good to be true, I thought.

'Well, do you want the job or not?'

'Yes – of course! Thank you!'

Francesca came over, her face glowing like a Renoir lady's. 'Chloe, dear, I'm delighted you said yes.'

I didn't tell Mummy about the new job; I felt she'd somehow ruin it. But I rang John. When I stopped to take a breath, he congratulated me. 'You won't be needing my reference so', he said.

To celebrate, he took me to a pizzeria in town. Afterwards, we went for a walk in Stephen's Green. His hand brushed against mine, but something was holding him back. As we sat on a bench, feeding the ducks, he squeezed my knee but didn't look at me. 'Chloe, there's something I need to tell you.'

I looked at him but he was gazing into the pond. 'I don't want to leave Veronique.'

Now it was my turn to turn my eyes away from him. I rubbed them with my sleeve, not caring that my mascara was smudged.

'She wants a divorce; I never did.' Then he blurted it all out; Veronique's jealousy, his innocence. 'Her definition of flirting is very broad. She can't bear it if I so much as glance at another woman or remark on how pretty some stranger is.'

'I thought French people were open about that sort of thing.'

'No – they only pretend to be.' He looked at me now, his pupils dilated. 'Chloe, I love her.'

I should have been devastated, but I felt strangely relieved. So Veronique was human, after all. The world wasn't a cruel place where couples could break their vows and move on to other relationships – they could still love each other. Like I hoped my parents did.

'I think that's so romantic', I said. 'I think you should try to win her back.'

He cocked an eyebrow. 'Really?'

'Yes. Go for it! What have you got to lose?'

His eyes glistened. 'Nothing, I suppose. She doesn't want me.' He sighed, then suddenly smiled. 'It's her loss. And it doesn't mean I can't fancy other women.'

Now why was he doing this to me? I wondered. Before I could walk away in fury, he put his hand on the nape of my neck, pulled me gently towards him and kissed my lips, softly first then harder as I melted against his broad chest. I felt dizzy. My ears were ringing. It was nothing like the way Philippe had kissed me the previous summer, or the awkward snogs I'd endured with boys my own age at the teen disco.

He finally released me, stroking my cheeks tenderly. 'How do you feel about dating a married man?'

'A soon-to-be-divorced man?' Not that I cared anymore; I wanted him at any cost.

He laughed, kissed me again, for longer this time.

He walked me to the train station, or, rather, we staggered along the street, wrapped up in each other, and only stopped kissing when the train was about to leave. He promised to book a table for the following Friday evening; he'd call me during the week.

I tried to slip into the house quietly; I felt charged up with images to splash on canvas, and wanted to get straight to work without any interruptions. The subjects in my painting had taken on the features of people I knew, and now I was curious to see what expressions would flicker across their faces with a flick of my brush. It was a sort of séance in which I was just the medium.

But Mummy had heard me come in. 'Chloe, come here for a moment.' I sighed.

'Poo Anchorbottom has been on the phone. She said she heard you were looking for work – some woman from a recruitment agency showed her your CV.'

I felt faint. Mummy was flapping her hand at me. 'I don't care why you left that solicitor's firm. I never could imagine you as a secretary, anyway; you're too scatty.'

So Mummy thought I'd left voluntarily. Oh, well, I wasn't going to spoil her illusion.

'Anyway, Poo was very nice and said she'd love to have you on board. You could help her with the PR work she's doing for some charity – handicapped children in Africa, I think, or did she say homeless people in Dublin? Do you know, I can't remember? Anyway, it's all in a good cause – and Poo is a good person to know. She'll get you mingling again.'

Get Mummy into the outer orbit of Poo's social circle, she meant. 'Mummy, that woman has been snubbing us ever since Dad went bankrupt. She's stopped inviting you to the ladies' lunches. She acts as if she doesn't know you – you saw the way she was in the shops.' Poo had done a double-take when Mummy had greeted her in the supermarket.

'Water under the bridge, dear. And you always got on well with Poo's daughter.'

'No, I didn't.' Fanny Anchorbottom believed she had an automatic right to be the belle of every ball, despite having a tummy as big as her ego (I called her the "belly of the ball" once and she threw a hissy fit) and a natural ungainliness that no amount of ballet lessons could correct. Whenever I stood near her, she'd reclaim the attention by whinnying: 'Oooh, Chloe, I'd love to be a stick insect like you.' I once pointed out to her: 'Fanny, if you stopped lunching with the ladies and went on that diet you're always talking about, your Mummy wouldn't need to raise money for famine relief – the two of you could donate your meals.' Poo always passed on her leftovers to Fanny; she used her daughter as a slimmer's sin-bin.

And now Mummy wanted me to become a minion in the court of the Anchorbottoms, where I'd be expected to pander to Poo's every whim and flatter Fanny. I'd always pitied those lower-middle-class girls who'd been taken under Poo's wing – aspiring journalists who wrote sickeningly sycophantic magazine features about how she was single-handedly solving the world's problems by eating five-course meals at €150-a-head charity balls, and how she and her 'stunning daughter Fanny' were doing Ireland proud by wearing expensive gowns at international celebrity events.

'No, Mummy. I'm not going to brown-nose Poo Anchorbottom. I've found a new job – a creative job. I start tomorrow.' I told her about the Fitzwalton sisters.

'But who *are* they, dear?'

I reassured her that I'd leave if they didn't pay me by the end of the month, as they had promised.

'Well, I suppose you can't come to any harm. They sound a bit, well, surreal, but then who isn't these days?'

'Don't worry, Mummy; someday I'll be a famous artist and we'll be able to afford our old life – even if Daddy doesn't come back.'

She wiped a tear. 'I thought it would get easier with time, Chloe, but I still miss him.'

I cried. 'So do I, Mummy.'

I went up to my attic and painted Dad more firmly into the painting; I added the slightly ruddy colour of his cheeks and the dimple in his chin, and changed his charcoal-coloured tailored suit to the old brown chain store one he used to wear when he was a car salesman on the make.

Then I painted John, sitting in the foreground on a park bench. I left room beside him for myself, but hadn't the courage to paint myself in just yet; I was afraid to tempt fate.

Eleanor and Francesca Fitzwalton lived on the top two floors of a four-storey townhouse on one of Dublin's elegant Georgian square. The first and ground floors were occupied by a firm of architects and the basement was an expensive crèche. As I arrived, a trousersuited woman was listening with barely concealed irritation as a girl about my age, dressed in a pink tracksuit, was explaining why little Marcus had to be taken home.

'He's got measles. We can't let him spread it to all the other kids.'

'Well, what am I supposed to do? Leave work? I pay you all my salary to look after him.'

'Can your husband take a day off?'

'Of course not! He's a doctor. Lives depend on him.'

Little Marcus was sucking his thumb and staring at the gravel. He didn't look well. I wanted to pick him up and cuddle him, measles and all. Then I felt cross with myself; I was only nineteen, too young to be thinking about children. And he was about the same age as my half-brother, Carmel Delahanty's brat: Lexus the Terrible. But this little boy didn't look like the sort who would run a tricycle into my shins or steal my Daddy.

I fantasised about the name John and I would choose for our children – in the distant future, if we had children.

'Eblana! Come to Mummy!' I looked round and there was Eleanor, crouching by the flower pots in front of the basement. 'Cooee! Eblana. Pss-pss-pss.'

A Siamese cat sauntered out from behind a rose bush and rubbed itself against Eleanor, languorously, from head to tail – getting the maximum pleasure anybody could get from an old lady's nylon-stockinged leg.

'Hello, Eleanor.'

'Oh, Chloe! I'd forgotten you were coming.'

Well, that was a good start to my new job, but Eleanor was smiling and leaning over to kiss my cheek. 'Welcome to our home, dear. Now, will you be a pet and carry Eblana up the stairs for me? Careful! She scratches.'

Eblana wriggled in my arms but settled down once I held her close.

'Oh, you have a way with her!'

I followed Eleanor up two steep flights of stairs to the second floor, marvelling at her agility for her age.

'You'll have to forgive Francesca if she's a bit unsociable today, dear. She's been quite ill – I imagine she's caught something from those little monsters in the basement. Children spread everything, you know – and germs travel up the air ducts in this building.'

She rapped on the door. 'Yoo-hoo! Francesca? Francesca! You've locked me out again.'

The door opened, a gust of musty fabric and lavender-scented talcum powder assaulted my nostrils, and Francesca's plump face appeared. 'Chloe, how lovely to see you here at last, in our humble little home.'

I put Eblana down and scanned their living room. A dusty yellow crystal chandelier dangled from a plaster wreath in the high ceiling, and cast-iron fireplace as adorned with gargoyles. Above the black marble fireplace was a convex mirror like the one in Jan Van Eyck's *Arnolfini Wedding Portrait*. 'Bought it in a car parts shop it's one of those mirrors people use on their pillars to get a good view of the road as they drive out. Francesca and I decorated it with some plaster.'

The room was stuffed with what at first looked like tasteful throws over antique furniture but what, on scrutiny, turned out to be wooden storage palettes masquerading as coffee tables, a miscellany of garden furniture tarted-up as a dining table with matching chairs (they'd painted them to look like mahogany) and two armchairs made out of recycled car seats covered in nylon (they looked as if they'd been cut from a particularly lurid collection of cheap nighties).

'This place is incredible', I said.

'We knew you'd love it. Francesca, dear, can you get Chloe a cup of tea? And some biscuits?'

'No thanks', I said, my imagination running wild (I wondered what they'd use for tea, and the biscuits didn't bear thinking about). But Francesca was bustling out of a door to 'rustle up something in the kitchen.'

I noticed another Siamese playing with Eblana. 'That's her sister, Annalivia. Do you like cats, Chloe?'

I've always thought that a strange question (like asking 'Do you like people?') but Eleanor was fixing me with a stare that demanded a reply, so I said: 'I'm more of a dog person. But these are lovely cats.' Now they were slinking in and out between my legs. 'Lovely names, too.'

'Patriotic names. We called Eblana after the old name for Dublin and Annalivia is the Latin name for the River Liffey. We used to have two tomcats called Big Fella and Long Fella after Michael Collin and Eamonn De Valera, but they kept fighting – just like their namesakes.' She chuckled. 'It was a mistake to call them after two leaders on the opposing sides in the Civil War, but you see our father supported DeV and our mother was besotted with Collins – so handsome! That's why we always visit that painting of him in the National Gallery.'

She motioned to what looked like a sofa but turned out to be a huge trunk, the kind used as a dressing-up box.

'That was Mamma's old stage wardrobe. Our parents were actors, you see, with the fit-ups. You know what they were, I presume?'

I shook my head, wondering if they had something to do with the Old IRA – maybe Mrs Fitzwalton RIP had been an agent carrying explosives in her frilly drawers.

Eleanor flapped her hand. 'Oh, you must have heard of the fit-up. They were travelling theatre companies that went to every town and village in the country, performing on makeshift stages. The actors were like circus and carnival performers; they came from everywhere. Our Mamma was Italian; she named Francesca after our Nonna.'

Francesca brought me a china cup and saucer and matching teapot filled with what I reckoned smelt like Earl Grey – the man, not the tea: there was a definite aroma of old snuff. 'Pour it out yourself', she said. 'I'm not your servant, you know!' She disappeared into the kitchen again, muttering something about 'the last of the bloody biscuits'.

Eleanor patted my arm. 'My sister's a bit out of sorts. Not feeling well at all. It won't be long now.' Her eyes took on an eerie gleam. 'Drink your tea, dear!'

I spluttered and put down the cup and saucer. 'Ah, Eleanor, I hope you won't think I'm rude but I've got to tell you something. You see, I've got another job. I'm supposed to start today – I just, ah, took the morning off to tell you both in person.'

I bolted down the stairs, ignoring their cries of 'Come back, Chloe! Come back at once!' and out into the sunshine. A procession of little people in designer kidswear was toddling across the road and into a gated park. I wished I could join them – if only I'd had a Pooh Bear flask and a pink frock with little lambs printed on it. If only I was a little girl again, and not having to worry about finding a job or being a magnet for eccentric old ladies drawn to my 'outsider status'.

Still, there was my date with John to look forward to. Work and responsibility could wait, I decided. 'I'll think about it tomorrow', I told myself, feeling like Scarlet O'Hara as I set off to find something amazing to wear.

There should be enough money in my bank account to buy something decent, I was sure. I could max out my credit card if necessary. I wasn't going to let debt bother me; Daddy had always worried about debt and see where that had got him.

Anyway, I hadn't had time to spend much, and there would be no more drinks with the girls now I'd been fired; they'd soon forget about me, I thought. I kinda missed them now.

I drifted towards my favourite shopping area, a network of narrow lanes honeycombed with exclusive little shopping malls. A lingerie shop caught my eye. Not that I had any intention of letting John get anywhere near my underwear on a first date, but there was no harm in being well prepared, was there? I mean, who knew what would happen? I found a set that flattered my small curves. Years of working out alongside girls whose parents gave them boob jobs for their eighteenth birthdays had given me a complex about my cup size. I'd never dared ask Mummy for such a gift because she'd have sent me for psychoanalysis, and Daddy would have refused to pay for his daughter's mutilation.

Next up was a dress shop. I wanted something that would show John that I was as sophisticated as Veronique, only younger, fresher and less cynical – and less likely to write him 'Dear John' letter that would break his heart. Was it possible for a dress to say all that?

Browsing in a boutique where Mummy and I had bought mother-and-daughter dresses for Ladies' Day at the races, I ignored the beige-clad owner's attempts to find me 'something young' – the last thing I wanted was to make John feel like a lech – and eavesdropped on some ladies who looked as if they belonged in a Rubens or Ingres painting. 'But I absolutely refuse to wear a size eighteen. I'm a twelve, darling.' 'It's these sizes, they've shrunk! I'm convinced those nasty fashion designers despise real women!' 'Well, that's hardly surprising – most of them are gay.' 'That's it! They only design for boys!'

The shop assistant, who I recognised from art college rolled her eyes at me and guided me towards the size eight rack. 'Us skinny bitches have to stick together', she said with a wink.

'Sorcha! May I have a word with you?' The beige woman beckoned her towards the back of the shop. 'Did you tell Mrs Anchorbottom she should wear a kaftan?'

'Well, I just suggested –'

'She was our best customer, but I doubt she'll return after the way you spoke to her this morning. And I've just had a complaint from two ladies who said you were sneering at them with another stick insect. You're fired.'

'Stuff your poxy job, then. You'll regret it when I'm a famous designer.'

'I doubt that we'll be buying any of your designs. I saw the photos of your student fashion show. Bin-liners and sticking tape? I mean, hel-*lo*? Can you see anyone going to the Hunt Ball in that?'

'Better than wearing a dead-fox necklace, like Mrs Anchorbottom.'

'Just leave, please.'

'I might come back and buy something – if I ever get fat.'

By the time I'd chosen a dress, Sorcha had left, and was probably roaming the streets looking for another job to see her through until the beginning of her next term at art college. Or maybe she'd been forced to drop out, like me. I'd never thought about other people's financial problems until now.

'I'm the stick insect who was talking to Sorcha in front of the fat ladies', I told her ex-boss.

She beiged paler under her powder and gaped, then pursed her lips (people who wear safe colours generally know how to hold their tempers). 'I'm sorry if you overheard that.'

'I'm sure Sorcha will be an amazing fashion designer. I'm devoting my entire column to her in next month's You Know Who.' I doubted she believed me but it felt good to stand up for another impoverished girl.

I chose a dress with a discreet cleavage and bare arms, and the hem was just high enough to show some leg without looking tarty. Best of all, it was red; it made me look confident. It was the sort of dress I imagined Veronique would wear to dinner.

All I needed now was a pair of killer heels. It was so strange to be wearing stilettos again that I wondered if my feet had changed along with my whole life, but after a few minutes tottering around the shop, I felt like the old Chloe who could dance all night on six-inch stilts; the belle of every ball.

I paid with my credit card, realising that I had now spent all of my last salary and some of my savings. I sighed. Maybe Daddy would be home by the time my credit card bill arrived.

If not, I'd soon be rummaging in Poo Anchorbottom's charity fundraising shop, like some of our social-climber neighbours who'd rather wear another person's Gucci than buy a new chain-store dress.

Still, I could hardly talk; after all, I was taking Veronique's cast-off husband. I wondered if John would have creases in all the wrong places after years with her – maybe she'd left her shape in him, frayed him and pulled him apart at the seams. Could I stitch him back together – or would I have to flatten him with the emotional equivalent of a steam iron?

It was lunchtime and, instinctively, I found myself hurrying in the direction of the National Gallery. Then I remembered I didn't need to run; I no longer had a job to rush back for.

Anyway this was the worst time of day to visit the gallery because the Fitzwalton sisters would most likely be there as they had been every lunchtime since I'd known them. I'd have to restrict my browsing to mornings – which was fine as long as I had no job, but I couldn't manage without one for much longer.

I couldn't do without my art fix, and there was nothing new in the windows of the commercial galleries in this part of town (anyway I always felt guilty about admiring paintings on sale and then not buying them), so I ambled towards the Gallery of Modern Art which, like the National Gallery, had no entry fee.

'What were they like?'

'Weird but fun', I said, before I realised Mummy was asking me about the Fitzwalton sisters, not the installations in the Gallery of Modern Art. 'They've got an interesting collection in their house.'

'Oh. Anything good?' She meant expensive.

I decided lying was the best policy; otherwise she'd put me to work with Poo Anchorbottom. 'Actually, they've got some obscure works by De Chirico, Modigliani, Rembrandt – '

'That must be worth a fortune!' She actually believed me!

'Well, the Rembrandt is in very bad condition.'

'What's it's of?'

'Oh, it's *very* Rembrandt – you know, a woman with lots of children, all rosy,chubby cheeks, sitting on the stoop of a canal house in Amsterdam.'

She nodded, her eyes awash with wonder. 'How did they get these paintings?'

'They inherited them. In their family for generations.' Now I'd gone too far, I thought; any mention of families was enough to bring tears to her eyes. But she was fascinated. I hadn't seen Mummy enthusiastic about anything for a long time; even the power hobbies had just been a manifestation of nervous energy.

'I wonder if they'd let me catalogue them.'

'Oh, Mummy, I don't think so – they've threatened to sue me if I tell anyone.'

That shut her up; Mummy was terrified of losing the house.

I took her silence as a cue to go up to the attic and work on my paintings. This time I did a wash over the figures of Eleanor and Francesca. First I covered their faces in pale grey mist so they looked like two Miss Havishams in dusty bridal veils. Then I blended black and green paint, and covered their bodies in cypress trees – 'graveyard trees', as I used to call them when I was a little girl, making my Daddy laugh.

Charcoal drawing

The sun woke me and I realised I had fallen asleep over the easel. There was paint on my face and in my hair.

My painting was no longer what I could call 'neo-classical.' My parents and Daryus were paler, their facial features reduced to hints, as if they were wearing nylon tights over their heads like old Wrightman's clients in the CCTV footage of a bank hold-up.

I shuddered. This was terrifying; I had lost control of my own painting and even my own artistic style. No matter how beautiful and serene I tried to paint everything, it just turned out weird.

Did this happen to other artists? True artists? Those works by the Great Masters had always seemed to have been meticulously plotted, sketched in fine detail before they ever allowed paint to touch canvas. But now I wondered if the nuances of expressions on their subjects' faces had appeared spontaneously, bringing the paintings to life and shocking the people who had presumed to be their creators – the artists who had dared to play God. Had *La Giaconda* (that's the *Mona Lisa* to those who didn't study art) suddenly woken up and smiled at Leonardo? Maybe the duty of an artist was simply to channel whatever happened to be floating by – and to be grateful to get an interesting picture out of it

But at that moment I just wanted a pretty picture. I stifled a sob and turned away from my very own Dorian Grey experience.

I looked down and saw my pink backpack, and a green paper shopping bag poking out from it. I took out the dress I had bought, and the shoes and underwear. I felt the colour flood back into my world like a watercolour wash.

Mummy was at her yoga so I had the house to myself. I walked around the house in my new clothes, then took them off and applied fake tan, and read *You Know Who* as I waited for it to dry – there was Poo Anchorbottom in the social diary again, smiling with just her mouth. They all did that, Poo and her cronies; they never let their smiles reach their eyes because they didn't want to look wrinkly. One of my art college classmates had interned as a photographer for *You Know Who* but had a nervous breakdown after a few months working the social diary beat; he'd gone off to work for a famine relief charity, driven by an artistic hunger to photograph people with 'authentic smiles'.

A text from Brenda, reminding me about her hen party that night gave me a new what-to-wear dilemma. The girls had booked a corner of the lounge in a pub two buses away – in a rough neighbourhood.

I hoped I wasn't turning into a snob – or, worse, an inverted snob, like Harriet Upperly who brought a council estate boy to her debs and went around saying 'bleedin'' and 'shaggin'' to shock everyone. I reckoned she was getting revenge on her parents, who used to send her to elocution lessons, and had even held her granny's funeral in a Protestant church because the Catholic priest we'd had at the time had a common accent. The last I heard of

Harriet, she'd been serial-dating immigrants and her own mother was considering reporting he to a human rights organisation for misleading asylum-seekers into thinking she'd marry them.

I texted Brenda back to say I'd meet her in the Flyin Brick at eight.

Then I went to the gym and ran on the treadmill while watching TV. Flicking around the channels, I came across a scene that sent me flying backwards. The pain of landing with all my weight on my wrist was nothing compared to the shock of seeing my Daddy sitting on a sun-lounger on the balcony of an apartment that certainly didn't look like Carmel Delahanty's flat in Dublin. A blonde bitch in a white towelling robe and shades was coming out and kissing my Daddy – on the lips!

'...Our reporter went to the island of Santa Moneta, where the disgraced Dublin tycoon now lives with his personal assistant, Carmel Delahanty, and their two-year old son.'

Just then little Lexus toddled onto the balcony and put his chubby little arms around Daddy's leg – the way I used to when I was his age. His face was pixelated, a legal requirement due to his age, but I thought it made him look like a baby criminal – well, he *had* stolen my Daddy.

It was just as well I had the aerobics studio to myself, because what followed next brought me to tears.

The reporter stood below the balcony, like an mock-Romeo, and, using his hands as a loudspeaker, yelled: 'Mr O'Doolahan, hundreds of investors lost their life savings and you've made no attempt to repay them. What do you have to say to them?'

What did he expect my Daddy to say? I found myself thinking, suddenly indignant on his behalf.

Dad was totally cool; he raised a champagne flute and went back to reading a pink-toned newspaper, little Lexus still hugging his leg. I wondered if Daddy was already tiring of him, and would abandon him the way he had me and Daryus. Would he leave Carmel too?

Carmel looked around, smiled and waved, Marilyn Monroe style (not that she looked anything like the movie legend; her ankles were thick and that belt on her bathrobe didn't flatter her waist).

The newsreader was interviewing the reporter now. 'Mr O'Doolahan's creditors will be upset to see him enjoying a life of luxury while their companies go to the wall', she suggested. 'Yes', the reporter chirped with a cocky wait-till-I-tell-you smile, 'but as yet there is no extradition agreement between the government of Santa Moneta and Ireland.'

And that was it. Nothing at all about the family my Daddy had left behind. I hope Mummy wouldn't look at the news.

She was crying when I got home. Helen was feeding her biscuits and whiskey – and glaring at me whenever I suggested that turning her into an alcoholic comfort-eater was a recipe for even more misery. 'What do you know about misery, about life?' Helen scolded me. 'You're only a teenager.'

Well, there was no way I could win that argument, so I went to my room and sat on the edge of my bed, blinking and breathing slowly until my head stopped spinning and the ringing in my ears ceased.

The first time I'd had a panic attack – about two weeks after Daddy left – I had thought I was dying. My heart was racing and I could actually hear it thumping. My breath had caught in my throat and I had forced myself to exhale very slowly until my lungs were empty, the way I'd learned in yoga. The family doctor had given me a check-up and reassured me that there was nothing physically wrong with me, but since then I had felt as if everything in my life, including my life itself, was as fragile as my parents' relationship.

Now I struggled to suppress my fear again. I tried to shut out the images of Daddy with Carmel and Lexus, to squeeze them into a tiny space deep inside my memory, like a painting-within-a-painting, like a Van Eyck's with a mirror showing what's happening behind the painter.

Aunty Helen was staying for dinner; she was going to cook some crap she had learned to make in an evening class and, no doubt, planned to chastise me yet again for being 'selfish', 'irresponsible', 'cold and uncaring'. I never was sure what she or Mummy expected of me these days, because if I let the tears flow they accused me of 'attention-seeking'. Brenda's hen night was suddenly looking very enticing.

Not that I'd ever been to a hen party; my former friends had all been my age, and marriage was a distant dream. So I wasn't sure what to wear. I reckoned Brenda's friends would go full-on tarty; she'd mentioned they liked to go 'on the prowl'. But I had found my prey – or he had found me. In the end, I settled for skinny jeans with ankle boots and an off-the-shoulder red top that showed a hint of midriff. I'd left it too late to wash my hair, so I scraped it into a messy ponytail.

Anyway, there was no shampoo in the house; Mummy had forgotten to do routine things such as shopping, and our weekly housekeeper had vanished once Mummy had asked her to buy groceries 'on the tab').

I ran out before Mummy or Helen could ask me where I was going. I took the train into the city centre, then, because it had started to rain and I couldn't face the misery of waiting at a bus stop, I got into the taxi.

'Where to, love?'

'Em, well, do you know a pub on the Clonbollard dual carriageway called the Flying – the Flyin Brick.' I wasn't sure if the name of the pub was meant to be pronounced in the local accent or not.

'Course I do. Sure that place is famous.'

'Great! How much will it cost to go there?'

'A bleedin arm and a leg. I wouldn't go near that dive for love nor money.'

'Excuse me?'

'Isn't that where that fella got stabbed to death at the weekend – a gangland killin, they're sayin. What's a nice young one like you doin goin to a place like that?'

'My friend is having her hen party there.'

'Tell you what, love, I'll drop you out as far as the Ramblin Roundabout; that's a nice big pub where all the people stuck in traffic jams go on the way home from work. You can get a bus from there – the Flyin Brick is only two or three stops away from it – or walk it cos the bleedin bus-lane is always blocked too.'

He reminded me of the coachman in one of those old vampire movies, who refused to drive any nearer the creepy castle on the hill. 'So you won't even drop me off outside it?'

'It's not just the pub; that stretch of the dual carriageway has a bridge over it, where young lads stand and drop bricks down on the cars. Why d'you think the pub is called the "Flyin Brick"?'

He gave me a lecture on self-defence all the way out to the Ramblin Roundabout, then left me with a shake of his head. His parting words were: 'I just hope I don't turn on the radio and hear a young girl has been brutally attacked.'

I didn't fancy going to the Flyin Brick straight away and waiting until Brenda arrived, so I went into the Ramblin Roundabout, ordered an orange juice and sat down in a corner where I could people-watch. The place was jammers with men in ill-fitting suits and women in acrylic trousers and shapeless blouses: the uniform of middle managers, secretaries and struggling junior professionals. They all seemed to be frowning and having the same conversation; the most-repeated phrases were 'mortgage arrears', 'living out in the sticks', 'can't afford a decent three-bed semi with a garden', 'soaring cost of childcare', and 'need a new car'.

This was the Lower Middle Class purgatory that my parents had escaped from when I was a little girl. And yet here I was, on the fringes of it, facing a future in it – if I *did* manage to get another office job. Even if John rescued mem, he could still abandon me the way Daddy had left Mummy, Daryus and me... Would John go back to Veronique? Or run off with someone else?

I freshened myself up in the Ladies' and scurried over to the bus stop, my jacket pulled over my head because it was raining again and it was too windy to use my umbrella. Out here on the bleak dual carriageway, the rain was driving – even if the motorists weren't. I tried not to catch their eyes as they sat in their metal prisons, whiling away the rush hour by listening to radio talk shows.

A doubledecker came trundling down the bus lane. Feeling gung-ho, I climbed aboard asked the driver to tell me when we got to the Flyin Brick, and sat down beside a shaven headed yob type who was cutting the seat with a pen-knife; he looked less dangerous than the girls at the back, who were punching and kicking each other. An old man in a dirty anorak and trackie bottoms sat serenely in front of them, as if everything was just dandy in his world; maybe he had spent his whole life in this hell and it had driven him, literally, demented.

The Flyin Brick was one of those 'superpubs' that had popped up all over Ireland during the nineties, and it was still doing well, judging by the quality of the cars outside. I wondered if people from my neighbourhood came here to have discreet affairs or do dodgy business deals; I kept an eye out for men in pin-striped suits passing around brown envelopes, but everywhere I looked the men seemed to be in casuals and the women wore everything from leisure suits to cocktail dresses.

If you didn't listen to the accents or look at the labels on their clothes, they were the same crowd you'd find in any pub, even back home in Belgowan. After all, Fanny Anchorbottom often went to the pub with her beer gut hanging over the waistband of her designer jeans. And the Ladies Who Lunch often wore yoga pants when they popped in for a spritzer on the way home from the gym.

What was different, though, was the way people were smiling – with their whole faces. And laughing without that hollow 'haw-haw-haw' or tight-throated squeal.

So this was the other Dublin – and it wasn't so scary.

'Hi Chloe.' I turned around and there was Brenda, looking like an off-duty Rubens. Her hair was in waves and she was slightly flushed under her dewy make-up.

'Brenda, you look fabulous!' I said, knowing that if I said this to one of my ex-friend in Belgowan, they'd think I was being sarcastic.

'Tanks. De girls are over dere. Go on over to dem. I'm gerrin dis round.' As she sashayed off to the bar, her cocktail dress swishing, I wished I had dressed up.

'I luv your belly top, Chloe', Tina said, but they were all smirking.

It struck me then that everyone was a snob of some kind: my ex-colleagues; my brother and his middle-class punk revival band who sang about being homeless but still lived with their parents; Daryus's girlfriend who no longer socialised with the refugees who'd come over to Ireland with her hidden in the backs of lorries; that taxi driver who had warned me about this pub; the pub's patrons who drove cars they probably couldn't afford – and there I was, being snobby again; for all I knew those people had paid in full for their shiny new cars.

'Would youse look at yer man in the Merc', Beverley was murmuring. 'He must be a major drug dealer to have a car like dat.'

'Yer woman wirrim must be on the mickey money.' Tina said, then explained to me: 'It's what you get for havin kids. All dem ones have to do is find some fella and gerrup de spout and they get a free Council house.'

Natalie chipped in. 'Yer wan looks like a foreigner – prob'ly can't even speak English.'

'You couldn't read or write until you dun dat literacy course last year', Tina laughed.

Natalie blushed and I felt compelled to defend her. 'That's so cool. Adults find it harder than children to pick up literacy skills. And you got a job out of it.'

But she giggled: 'You couldn't hold onto the job wirall your education.'

Nothing was harder to stomach than an underdog biting the hand that had fed it, but I let it go; it was Brenda's hen night, after all. I turned to her. 'When is the party starting?'

'When you buy your round, ya stingy fecker.'

I was relieved when a muscle-bound, nearly-naked guy with a spotty back arrived and gyrated in front of Brenda. She went pink. 'Ah, Jayzus, tanks girls. I didn't know youse had hired a stripper!'

'We didn't.' Sharon winked at the rest of us. 'Simon here just fancies the knickers off ya!'

Simon exposed himself to Brenda, grinned as the girls groped him, then skipped off, hopping into his thong as he left.

'He wasn't wurt de hundred yo-yos we paid for him', Beverley grumbled.

'You should have got him arrested for indecent exposure', I said and for some reason they all thought that was hilarious.

We were all 'rat-arsed' (as Natalie put it) by the time the pub closed, and I realised I was going to have to persuade a cab company to bring me home. I supposed I could get them to stop at a cash-dispensing machine on the way back.

'Shorry to disturb you, but could you call me a taxi?' I asked the barman.

'All right, luv.' He pointed at me. 'You're a taxi.'

'Ha ha – very original.'

'So are you. You won't get a taxi coming out here.'

So there was nothing for it but to stay in one of my new best friends' houses. I didn't fancy sleeping on Brenda's couch with the lovebirds upstairs practising for their wedding night (I imagined they'd make quite a lot of noise based on her drunken description of their lovemaking antics). Sandra, Natalie and Beverley also had full houses. So I jumped at Tina's offer. 'I've gorra sphare room – coz me Ma's done a runner again.'

'Again?' Beverley shrieked. 'Wheresh he gone?'

'She fucked off wit shome bloke she merrat a weddin. Probilly de groom – yooush all know whash me Ma's like.'

I didn't, but this was not the time to ask. I humbly accepted Tina's offer and staggered across the dual carriageway to the tiny terraced house she shared with her grandparents, her four sisters, her little niece and, occasionally, her mother.

'Jaysus, luvvie, you're de colour of boiled shit!' I was relieved Tina's granny was pointing at her; I don't think I could have handled insults in my drunken condition. 'Were you in dat pub till dis hour?'

I thought she was drunk like us; then I realised she was taking her false teeth from a tumbler. So this was the granny who wouldn't lower herself to dress like Mrs Anchorbottom.

She pinched my arm. 'You're awful skinny, luvvie. Jaysus, dere's no meat on you!' I was half-afraid she'd put in a cage and fatten me up for the Sunday roast.

Tina's granddad appeared from the gloom of the lounge and gave me a warm smile that made up for the old witch's welcome. 'Come in, pet, and watch de telly wit us.' There was a comforting smell of cigarette smoke off his little den; it reminded me of my Daddy, who used to smoke until Mummy made him give it up.

He rolled his eyes as a 30-something woman followed us in and stood in front of the TV. 'Are you smokin again? Filty bleedin habit!' she screeched.

She rounded on me. 'I hope you don't object to him smokin.'

'Not at all.'

'Better bleedin not! We can do what we want in our own house. Who asked you to stay here anyway?'

Tina, standing behind her, pulled a face and used her fingers to spell 'T'. So this was Tracey, her most annoying sister.

'Are you shewer you're not one o dem foreigners?' Tracey persisted.

'I'm from Dublin like you.'

'Not wit dat accent you're not.' She narrowed her eyes and pointed her finger at me. 'I know what yewse are like, yewse privileged people. I dun a course in sociology wit de Commewnity Awareness Group.'

'Oh? That must have been interesting.'

'Too right it was. Tawt me a lot about how d'udder half tinks.' She leaned forward and tapped her nose. 'Yewse are al lookin down your noses at us.'

I felt like telling her she was getting up mine, but decided it was too dangerous; I might be forced to defend myself and end up in prison for mugging a poor underprivileged single Mummy (I could imagine the psychoanalysis in *Sins On Sunday*: '...Poor little rich girl lost her inheritance and then lost her head...').

We sat in uneasy silence, pretending to watch the western, until the granny came out of the kitchen with mugs of tea. 'Dis'll sober youse up.' I didn't drink mine because there was a toothbrush in it – anyway, it was after midnight.

Tina mouthed 'A' at me and twirled her finger at her temple, but her granny rounded on her. 'It's yourselves dat haves bleedin Alzheimer's – from all dat bleedin drink!'

Tina took the mugs away, explaining to her granny: 'We have to get some sleep coz we've work in the morning – well, I have.'

Tracey shot me a sly grin. 'On de scratcher, are ya? Bleedin middle-class sponger.'

Tina and I ignored her and tramped upstairs, hanging on to each other for support. The bedroom was half the size of mine, and the Elvis duvet cover looked a bit manky, but I fell asleep almost immediately, my head reeling with arguments against snobbery and inverted snobbery. My father's desertion had plunged me into a very hostile world indeed.

I met another of Tina's sisters the next morning. 'Hey, Barbara, here's someone who's as skinny as yerself', Tina said by way of introduction.

Barbara, who looked about seventeen, flashed a nervous smile. She had a real beach bod, and clearly knew it as she was wearing a belly-top *sans* belly, and hipster leggings.

'You're not goin to school dressed like dat?' Tracey said. 'People will tink we're starvin you.'

'You look like sometin off an ad for famine relief', Tina added as Barbara helped herself to a hearty breakfast of fried eggs and bacon. I wondered if she deliberately chose fattening food to show her family she wasn't anorexic (and if they'd blame 'too much exercise' when she finally got a heart attack).

I felt like playing Fairy Godmother to this real Cinderella. 'Don't listen to them, Barbara. People are always telling me I'm too thin too.'

She smiled timidly while the Ugly Sisters glared at me.

I tried to change the subject. 'So, Barbara, are you the youngest?'

Her granny answered for her. 'De shakins of de bag, dat's what she is' Then she pointed to the strips of bacon I'd left on my plate. 'Do yewse not eat rashers out your way?'

'Chloe's a vegetarian', Tina explained.

'Humph! No wonder dere's no meat on you.'

After I'd finished my fried eggs (and tactfully pushed away the slipper Tina's granny had placed on my plate), I thanked them for their hospitality (they looked at me as if I'd spoken in another language – Tracey clearly still thought I was a 'foreigner') and walked with Tina to the bus. We parted in the city centre as she went to work and I wandered off in the opposite direction, feeling lost.

A crowded canvas

The rain had stopped and the drenched streets smelt of cars, damp clothes, deodorant and that familiar beery smell wafting across from the Guinness Brewery. I went into a crowded café crowded and ordered a latte with a croissant. It felt good to be free for the day, while the people around me were grabbing a quick breakfast on the way to work. The barista was dealing efficiently with an enormous queue of cranky office workers, all barking demands for different kinds of coffee.

I had an hour to kill before the National Gallery opened, so I read a newspaper someone had left behind. I had been avoiding the papers lately, afraid I'd see my Daddy's face smiling out at me in a tuxedo in an old photo with Mummy, or in a grainy still from the TV exposé, raising that champagne flute with little Lexus hugging his leg, Carmel beside him. Today, there was just a small article in a gossip column about him; he had his new family had left the Island of Santa Moneta and had been spotted on another island, where they were 'living it up' among the 'celebrity tax dodgers'.

I dumped the newspaper in a bin and walked to the National Gallery. The morning crowd was made up of serious art buffs, standing well back from the larger paintings to see the way the artists probably intended.

But my eyes were drawn to a woman who looked like she belonged at one of those swingers' parties they were always writing exposés about in *Sins On Sunday*. Her red mini-skirt had a slit up to her hip, showing off black fishnet stockings and suspenders, and a red bra was clearly visible under her black lace blouse. The blingy earrings peeping out from under her vivid red bob and the rigid set of her bony shoulders looked vaguely familiar and, when she moved on to the next painting, I saw her in profile and realised that it was Eleanor Fitzwalton. I should have known, of course; only a woman that old and ugly could get away with wearing an outfit like that and not be pestered by sleazy men waving wads of banknotes.

I tried to make a swift, silent exit, but she spotted me and trilled: 'Chloe! Yoo-hoo!' I waved and dashed out the door, hoping she wouldn't follow me. I didn't stop running until I reached the railway station, and was relieved when I could see no sign of her as I got onto the train. Well, that was the end of my National Gallery visits, I decided.

By the time I had eaten a sandwich at home, lied to Mummy that the Fitzwalton sisters had given me the day off again, I was ready to paint all those annoying people out of my life, and replace them with people I wanted.

I was charged-up with the urge to get started that I could hardly wait to open the lids of the paint-pots. I inhaled the scent of the paint; it was oil-based and quite expensive, a luxury for an unemployed, unrecognised artist.

Feverishly, I mixed colours, trying to get a skin tone that would do justice to Eleanor Fitzwalton – not her heavy make-up, not even her physical skin, but what she would look like if her skin reflected what I could only describe as her crazy annoyingness. In the end, I settled for vivid green; I was *fauve*-ing her – and not in a nice way. Green was also the perfect colour for a woman who claimed to be a 'rabid Irish patriot'. I looked around for a canvas and couldn't find one. So I painted the new, true Eleanor beside the shrouded one I had previously done. Somehow, she seemed less of a nuisance when I painted her honestly.

The next morning, I got up very early leaving Mummy to snore off her hangover; I couldn't cope with another tearful breakfast and I didn't have a good excuse for wearing shorts and a cropped top to "work".

I wore a bikini underneath, planning to spend the morning on the local beach. It was a beautiful day and I saw quite a few people who looked as though they were skipping work; you could tell because they were furtively looking around as they got out of their cars, and there wasn't a single phone ringing. I watched in amusement as a man in a business suit stripped off to boxer shorts, walked towards the water's edge, then went pale as the proverbial ghost when another man recognised him.

'Hi Jim!'

'Eh – oh, hello Derek. Day off. Lovely and sunny, isn't it? Nice to have a day off so unexpectedly. And yourself?'

'Oh, I just switched the mobile off – if anyone at the office asks, I'm stuck in traffic down the country.'

The colour returned to Jim's cheeks and he laughed. 'Might as well, Derek. The auld weather is so unpredictable, we might never get a day as good as this for the rest of the year – we might as well enjoy it. Sure, why not?'

'Why not, indeed – oh, fuck! Here's my wife!'

'Derek? Derek! What are you doing here?'

'We've both been told to take a day off', Jim cut in, but red-faced Derek was opening his car and pulling out a pair of black trousers and a white shirt. His wife fished a tie out of the boot and silently handed it to him.

They reminded me of my parents. Maybe that was why Daddy had left. I wondered if Veronique had made John feel like that. She looked like a right bossy-boots – a dominatrix, even – with her strong feature and sharp suits. But then I reminded myself that she had dumped him – hardly the action of a controlling wife, was it? Or was using reverse psychology? I had read in one of Mummy's magazines that the best way to win back an errant partner was to pretend not to care. I promised myself I'd never resort to such trickery.

I went home around eleven, when I knew Mummy would be out at her belly-dancing class. I washed the salt water off my skin, topped up my fake tan and threw on an old summer frock so it wouldn't matter if the tan smeared it. Then I made a hair appointment for that afternoon.

Mummy came home just as I was running out the door. 'Chloe, what are you doing home so early?'

'Eleanor and Francesca are sick.'

Her eyes narrowed. 'Where are you going now?'

'To Kay and Shay's.' Well, I wouldn't be able to ide a new hairstyle.

'Why don't you let Helen do your hair? You should be saving up – to invest in your future.'

'Mummy, I have to look presentable for work. And I'm investing in my future.' That had been Mummy's mantra back in the days when we used to socialise with the Anchorbottoms at parties full of bankers' sons. Now I was investing in a different kind of future; I wanted John to have no excuse to go back to Veronique.

A grown-up image was a good start.

Kay Duffy and her husband, Shay, were Belgowan's most inspiring success story. Kay had spent the first seven years of her life in a Council house at the back of the main street, at a time when it was just an ordinary Dublin suburb. Then, around the time the place became affluent, her father got a job, so the family were forced to leave the subsidised house and could only afford to live in the outer suburbs. But, through hard work and determination, Kay became a top hairstylist and now, at twenty-five, she was trimming the locks of the rich and famous in her super-cool salon, right in the heart of her old village.

Her husband, Shay, had an accent even thicker than hers, having been born and reared in one of Dublin' poorest inner-city neighbourhoods, but these days his friends included Hollywood hellraisers and he had beautiful actresses swooning at him in the mirror – and, yes, they were the kind of female movie stars who did NOT insist on being called 'actors'; these sirens well aware that sexism did more for them than feminism. So Shay was the envy of every straight man in the village. I often wondered how Kay coped with it; I'd be jealous.

What I liked most about Kay and Shay was the fact that they were the most united couple I had ever met. They were totally in love with each other – not in that soppy way Mummy and Daddy used to be on occasions such as her birthday or Valentine's Day, but in a way that didn't need cards or flowers or declarations of undying love.

'C'mere, Shay, give me a hand with sweeping the hairs off the floor.'

'Hang on a mo – I'm just goin out to get de groceries and a packet of fags. Want anytin in de shops?'

'Yeah – a bleedin Fworrovski necklace.'

'Ha-bleedin-ha. You'll have to do sometin to deserve it.' He blew her a kiss, winked at me and sauntered off, whistling a happy tune.

Kay put away the brush and turned to me, smiling. 'We had a trainee doing the Cinderella bit, but she thought Shay was her Prince Charming, so I fired her', she said candidly. 'So, Chloe, is it just the highlights again or do you want something cut off?'

'I don't want an actual cut', I said and she nodded, looking disapprovingly at my split ends but not saying what was obviously on the tip of her tongue; dealing with egocentric celebs had taught Kay to give the clients exactly what they asked for.

'So, just the highlights, then – and if you change your mind about a trim…' She grinned and waved her scissors.

'Well, actually, I wanted my hair up – in a sophisticated bun.'

'An up-style? No probs – and it'll hide the split ends. So, what's the big occasion? I'm only asking because I might have a few ideas. And I'm nosey', she confessed with a laugh.

'I'm just going to dinner – but the guy who's taking me out is kind of formal. He'll most likely be wearing a very expensive suit.'

Kay gave me a knowing look. 'An older bloke.'

Against my will, I found myself reddening and beaming; the last time I'd felt like that, I was 11 and had got my first Valentine card from a boy in school. 'Yes. He's thirty-one.'

'That is old! You're only – well, you had your debs last year, didn't you? So you can't be more than nineteen.'

I shrugged, smiled and nodded.

'Be careful, Chloe. I know what those older men are like – I see them in here all the time, getting strange things done with their hair. It's the mid-life crisis.' She stopped, as if he realised she had breached the courtesy boundary between hairstylist and client, and began to rectify the damage. 'I mean, thirty-one isn't old, Chloe, but you're a lot younger so you want to watch out he's not just taking advantage of your innocence. Myself and Shay are the same age – isn't that right, love?'

Shay, coming in the door with a six-pack of beer and a cigarette in his mouth, nodded.

'I was just warning Chloe to mind herself – she's going out with some aul fella and he wants he to wear her hair up.'

'Jayz. You'd want to watch dat, Chloe – he sounds like a bleedin control-freak.'

'He didn't actually tell me to put it up. I just feel he'd like me to look more mature.'

Kay and Shay swapped concerned looks. She ruffled my hair. 'All we're saying is that you should be on your guard. If you feel he's controlling you, get out of that relationship right away.'

I must have rolled my eyes, because she added: 'I know – it sounds like I've been watching too much *Oprah*, but I learned that from Dr Fincklestein.' She showed me a copy of *Popular Psychology* magazine with a picture of a wild-haired, bearded gent on the front cover. 'That picture was taken before we sorted his bonce. He's a top head-shrink that comes in here for us to work on his head.

Two hours later, I had a head full of highlights and an 'upstyle' that was fit for the Oscars – or maybe Cannes; it was very Catherine Deneuve-ly. I gazed in the mirror and felt I was looking at someone whose lover wore pin-striped suits and was getting divorced from a sexy Frenchwoman.

'You look like what's-her-face de prima ballerina', Shay said.

'Except she's a good ten years older', Kay added. 'Just keep your make-up classic and wear plenty of powder; then you'll look old enough to be going out with a thirty-one-year-old bloke.' She sighed. 'Oh, Chloe, what are we going to do with you? You could have any fella you wanted.'

'If you're really into older blokes, why don't you go for de jackpot and go out wit Steve Oldman?' Shay sniggered.

I cringed; the lead singer of Jurassic Rox had livened up the Active Retirement Group since he'd moved into a mansion on the cliffs. He'd introduced electric guitars to the sing-alongs and his harem of groupies turned up at bingo.

'Come back to us for a younger style as soon as you're finished with the cradle-snatcher', Kay said as I got up to leave.

I paid with my credit card, wondering if I should leave a tip and then deciding not to because (a) Kay and Shay, as the proprietors, might find that patronising and (b) I had no money.

My card was maxed-out and I was tempted to cancel the date. But I told myself not to be silly: John wasn't the kind of man who'd ask a girl to split the bill. I had left my gauche student days behind and John certainly wasn't anything like Brenda's fiancé, Clint, who let her pay for everything.

I kept out of Mummy's way as I waited for John to pick me up; she was in one of her quarrelsome moods. I had eventually told her the reason for the new hairstyle and dress – well, I could hardly hide them. She was full of questions, each one laden down with the assumption that I had no right to leave her on her own for the evening. I felt as if I was at the top of a see-saw, and this heavy person was sitting at the other end, glaring at me and demanding I use a counterweight.

'So this John has left his wife after only three years? He didn't stay with her long, did he?'

I had decided to tell her the truth because lies are such a burden; they always drag you down sooner or later. But Mummy could twist even the simplest truth into a noose around my neck. I wondered if she'd prefer it if John had been married for nineteen years, like Dad – though I didn't dare say it.

Now I stood in the attic, gazing out the window onto the street, trying not to fiddle with my hair. I looked at my watch; another fifteen minutes to go. Normally, I couldn't stand people who arrived early for social occasions; they always made me feel guilty for not being ready – and even guiltier for locking myself in the bathroom just so I could examine myself one last time in the mirror. But this time I wanted John to be early – I was terrified Mummy would hatch a plan to spoil everything.

She was pacing around the back garden below. I could hear her on the phone to Helen. 'Yes, she's leaving me alone in the house...going out with her boyfriend...divorced man...very insensitive after what happened to me, her own mother...completely heartless....'

He arrived about five minutes early. I recognised the BMW the moment it pulled up outside the low wall at the end of the front lawn. My heart turned over as I saw that familiar head. Even from above, it looked all grown-up and masterful; he'd take care of me, I was certain. I was glad he'd left the top of the car down; now I could watch him as he sat there, glancing at his watch every so often and pretending to read a map. At exactly eight, he looked at his watch, stretched his arms back and took off his jacket, flinging it over the back seat.

I scurried down the attic ladder and dashed down the stairs, three steps at a time, getting to the door just as he rang the bell. 'Oh, you were quick', he laughed, a surprised smile on his face. He was looking up at my hair; then his gaze lit on my eyes, then moved down to appreciate my dress. I heard the phone click beside me; Mummy had hung up the cordless extension and was obviously on her way in from the garden.

'Do you want to meet my Mummy before we go?' I said, trying to make it sound as if Mummy would welcome him warmly – and would be delighted to let her daughter go on a date with an older man who was getting divorced.

'Of course. I brought her something.' He handed me a bottle of wine: *Vermentina di Sardegna*. From the little I knew about wine, I knew this was good stuff. I hoped Mummy wouldn't embarrass me by saying she was 'giving up filthy alcohol', the way she had done, drunkenly, at Christmas when Carmel Delahanty had come to the house with a bottle of wine (and Lexus).

But Helen must have advised her to be tactful, because she came out to the door in hostess mode. 'You must be John', she said, throwing her head back, flashing her teeth and extending her freshly manicured hands.

John smiled like a schoolboy. 'Very pleased to meet you at last, Mrs O'Doolahan. Chloe has told me so much about you.'

Mummy fluttered her hand to her throat and went all pink, like a mother of the bride who'd just been mistaken for the bride's sister. 'Oh, I hope she hasn't been saying anything bad about me. You must think I'm this terrible gorgon –'

'On the contrary, Mrs O'Doolahan –'

'Oh, call me Bee, please.' She wagged her finger at him. 'Don't start making me feel old. My husband did enough of that.'

Then there was an awkward silence –I used it as an opportunity to leave. 'Mummy, we'd better go because John has booked a table for half eight.'

He grabbed my hand and leaned down to kiss Mummy on first one cheek, then the other.

'At least you didn't kiss her hand', I said as we got into the car and Mummy waved from the doorway.

He laughed. 'That's sort of dying out even in France; mostly old men do it.' He grabbed my hand and kissed it, his eyes full of mirth.

'You *are* an old man – compared to me', I said, beginning to relax.

'Well, I must say you're looking very grown-up yourself.'

I laughed. 'I was just being considerate; I thought you'd feel old if I dressed my age.'

He laughed. 'Ouch! I'm only thirty-one, you know – hardly an old lecher.' He shifted the gearstick and I found myself admiring his muscular forearm, which was tanned and had just the right amount of hair. He smiled at me. 'If I'd known you were going to dress like that, I would have worn something more formal myself. But I'm tired of wearing a suit all day at work.'

I looked at his jeans and navy shirt with grey pin-stripes, and laughed. 'Are all your clothes pin-striped?' He guffawed. 'I bet you wear pin-striped pyjamas.' 'Hey! How did you know about those?' 'And T-shirts, and....' I stopped myself; I didn't want him to think I was vulgar.

'You were going to say boxer-shorts.' He grinned, instantly putting me at ease again. 'Actually, I was going to say Y-socks.' 'Y-socks? What are those?' He was laughing and shaking his head. 'Well, if you don't know, I'm not going to tell you.'

He put his hand over mine, then drew it to his lips and kissed it. 'Put your seatbelt on; the guards are up ahead.'

I hastily strapped myself in just as we pulled in behind a car that reminded me of my father's old car, the one he had traded in for a flashy new Merc when we moved into the nicer part of Dublin; it was the same make and colour. I felt a knot in the pit of my stomach, even though I could clearly see that the driver was not Daddy.

John squeezed my hand. 'What's the matter, Chloe? You're not wanted by the guards, are you?'

'No. It's just that that car reminds me of my father's old car.'

'Oh.' He squeezed my hand again and looked at me with soft eyes. 'It must be terrible for you.'

The *garda* looked carefully at the tax disc on John's windscreen, then nodded and waved us on.

I smiled. 'John, why do you have such a fast car and drive it so slowly?' 'Well, I don't need to show off; I might be an older man to you, but I'm not ready to go through my mid-life crisis just yet. And there is this silly old thing called the law.'

He parked right outside the restaurant. 'Aren't you afraid of getting a ticket?' I asked. 'I'd rather pay the fine than hunt for a parking space around here.' He grabbed my hand. 'Dublin is a great city – if you've got money.'

The restaurant was the sort of place I imagined even Poo Anchorbottom would boast about having eaten in. Daddy had once dined with business contacts there and later grumbled to Mummy about the bill.

'I hope you like French food', John was saying. 'They do lovely Provençal-style seafood here.' I didn't answer; I was looking at the huge lobster lumbering along at the bottom of a fish tank, like an astronaut. John obviously misread my silence, because he murmured in my ear: 'I'm sorry, I forgot you were vegetarian.' 'Oh, I'm not really vegetarian.

I eat seafood.' I'd never liked the label 'vegetarian' anyway; it conjured up images of myself devouring a hedge. 'I guess I'm a hypocrite.' He laughed. 'Isn't everyone?'

The Maitre D' showed us to a table in a corner, but John shook his head and pulled out a chair for me in the centre. The Maitre D' shrugged and said: 'I'll send someone over with the wine list.' John sat down opposite me and grinned. 'Why should we skulk in the corner like illicit lovers?' I laughed. 'Well, it's not as if you're married or anything.'

I let him choose the wine and watched in amusement as he first sniffed it, then sloshed it round his mouth like a pro and said: 'We'll have it.'

I put my hand gently on his arm (actually, I'd been dying to touch it). 'John, I don't think I should drink any wine.'

'Why not? You're not driving – you can drink more than I'm going to.'

'No, I mean I don't want to drink because I'm not used to it and it makes me drunk.'

He laughed, and took my hand in both his. 'OK. I don't want to have to rescue you again the way I did the last time I caught you drunk. Barry lost a tooth from that punch I gave him.'

He gestured to the waiter to come over again. 'I'll have an orange juice', I said. 'Freshly-squeezed', John added. 'Oh, and could you bring us some bottled water?' He turned to me. 'I hate the way they automatically assume everyone wants a big jug of tap-water with ice cubes floating in it.'

We looked at the menu. I wasn't hungry; my stomach was fluttering and I wanted to swoon every time I looked into John's eyes. 'Can I just have the dessert?' I asked.

He laughed. 'The food is very good here – aren't you hungry?' I shook my head, breaking off a piece of bread and chewing it slowly. 'At least have the main course, and then see if you've got room for dessert. I'll do the same; I'm not very hungry myself.'

The quality of the cuisine soon convinced us that we were very hungry indeed. We ended up ordering the starter – *after* the main course, which made the waiter laugh but apparently didn't impress their celebrity chef because he came to the door of the kitchen and stood, glowering at us, arms folded.

'He'll probably spit on it', I laughed.

'If I taste so much as a hint of saliva on my seafood pancake, I'll sue him.'

'John Wrightman! Is it yourself?' We looked up and saw a guy about John's age, with a receding hairline and a harmless-looking face.

John stood up, grinning. 'Killer! I haven't seen you for, what, five years?' He turned to me. 'This is Chloe. Chloe, meet my old uni buddy, Killer.'

'My real name's Kilian – but you can call me Killer.' He leaned down to shake my hand awkwardly, like a teenage boy meeting the new headmistress for the first time. 'Nice to meet you, Chloe. Don't get up on my account.'

I let that go; Killer was the kind of guy who'd never been taught manners. His collar was limp and his skin was flaky.

'Have a seat, Killer.' John pulled out a chair. Killer sat down, between us – and immediately turned towards John. 'So, are you still at the old law thing?'

John laughed. 'Well, I can't see myself throwing all that education and experience down the drain. Are you still at the journalism?'

'Yeah – what else? We can't all give up our careers to marry a woman in another country.' He looked round at me. 'So, you must be the unfortunate woman. I have to say, you're younger-looking than I thought you'd be.'

I blushed, more from irritation than embarrassment. I wanted to prod Killer with my fork between his dishwater coloured eyes. He turned back to John. 'Put years on you, did she? These foreign women know how to wear a man out.'

John laughed. 'Oh, Chloe's not foreign. And she's not my wife. I'm getting divorced.'

Now I felt angry with John. He seemed to be enjoying having this oaf at our table.

'I might be needing a divorce myself – I just have to get married first. Here she is – my ball and chain.'

A thirty-ish woman was striding over to us. She was tall-ish, slim-ish with brownish black hair tumbling around her shoulders. 'Kilian, I've paid the bill and I've been sitting at that table feeling like an eedjit while you chat with your friends. Are we going or what?' Her accent was lower middle-class, which explained the self-conscious way she had applied her make-up (she had apparently aimed for the no-make-up look).

'Gina, this is a friend of mine from college, John Wrightman.' I saw her smile at John and he smiled casually back. I was suddenly glad she was so plain; I don't think I could have coped with the arrival of a beautiful woman at our table. 'And this is Chloe, his, eh –'

'Girlfriend', I said with a sweet smile.

'Why don't you two join us?' John said, smiling from Killer to Gina and back again.

'Yeah, why not?' Killer said, as Gina pulled out a chair for herself and sat opposite him. Now there were two people between John and me, I found myself thinking.

'Gina, what'll you have to drink?'

'Oh, that looks nice', she said, picking up the wine bottle in her manicured claws. I noticed her hands were wrinkled and there was a discreet diamond solitaire on her ring finger.

'Another bottle of that', John said to the waiter.

Gina picked up my half-full glass of orange juice. 'You're a cheap date, aren't you?' she laughed. I looked at John but he was guffawing at something Killer had murmured in his ear. Killer turned to the waiter. 'I'll have a beer', he said. The waiter scribbled it down and left us.

John and Killer were chatting about guys they used to go to college with; Killer was filling John in on what they were doing for a living, where they had bought a house and who they were married to.

Gina took off her black lacy shawl and draped it over the back of her chair, and I noticed she was wearing a very low-cut black dress. I suddenly felt a bit prissy in my high-necked number – and at the same time I wondered if vivid red was a bit loud. Still, I consoled myself by observing that her shoulders were rather flabby, and her upper arms were like sides of ham.

She was eyeing me the way I'd grown used to at all those society parties, as if she was looking for faults – real ones. I preferred the more generalised 'you're too skinny' gaze of my ex-colleagues.

I decided to play her at her own game; I was, after all, no longer a bashful girl trying to keep in with my parents' friends and their nasty daughters. So I returned the gaze, running it from her slightly lined forehead down to her plunging neckline...and, to my amusement, I discovered she was wearing what looked like toupee tape – in her cleavage! I had seen that on one of Mummy's friends, a woman who wasn't brave enough (or maybe, as the gossips claimed, rich enough) to have her boobs lifted.

'They're called breasts', she said loudly, staring hard at my chest. 'Not that you'd know.' John and Killer looked over at her, an amused look on each of their faces. 'What are you girls talking about breasts for?' Killer laughed. 'Trying to torture us?'

I ignored him, looked directly into Gina's eyes, and forced myself to grin as I said: 'Ah, I thought they were just loose skin.' She stiffened, so I turned the knife in. 'My own are up here.' I ran my hands over them and saw her go puce.

'Hey, girls, I love a good catfight but I don't want to get thrown out', Killer was saying.

Gina suddenly scraped her chair back, angrily grabbed her shawl and handbag and stalked over to him, clutching at his arm. 'I want to leave – now!'

John was looking confused but I thought I detected the hint of a smile. Killer was scratching the side of his neck and glancing nervously around at the other tables.

'I said, I want to go!'

Killer looked up at her. 'Off you go, then.'

'Oh!' She belted him with her handbag (it was Prada, I noticed; too good for her) and stalked off. He shrugged. 'She'll be back.' Before we could answer, she appeared behind him. I felt my eyes widen and my mouth open to warn him, but it was too late; she had poured a glass of something fizzy over him. A woman at the table behind was saying: 'Waiter! Waiter! Get me another bottle this instant!'

But Killer was laughing. 'Ah, women; where would we be without them? In the loonybin, probably.' He got up. 'Another dramatic end to a lovely evening.' He patted John on the shoulder. 'We must go for a pint. Give me a ring.'

John laughed. 'I can't; you're already engaged.'

Gina glared at me and, for a minute, I was worried that she'd hurl the glass at me, but Killer had grabbed it. She snarled at me: 'Red really isn't your colour, you know – not with your rosy cheeks. And you shouldn't wear your hair up; it draws attention to your fat nose.'

My nose wasn't fat, I thought. Childish, maybe – most people said it was cute. But not fat. I looked at Gina's and she waited for my riposte; her nose was probably her best feature. 'You must save a fortune on handkerchiefs with that little pinched snot. It's so tiny, it makes the rest of your face look like a football.'

She swelled up and I flinched as her claws come towards my eyes but Killer was covering her in a strait-jacket embrace. He looked at John and chortled. 'Bye folks.' He shook my hand in both of his this time. 'Chloe, it was fun meeting you. We must get herself and yourself together again – for a bit of mudwrestling. Wait for me, Gina; I'm coming.'

'Not tonight, you're not!' she said and stormed off ahead of him. He ran after her.

'I'm glad they've gone', I said, taking a piece of crab out of my seafood pancake. It had gone cold so I put it back on the plate. 'I was just going to get up from the table myself only she beat me to it.'

John folded his arms and looked at me with a bemused smile. 'You really don't get on with other women, do you?'

I shrugged. 'Can we order dessert?'

He signalled to the waiter. 'We'd like a dessert menu.' I noticed that the waiter was smirking. I turned to him. 'I hope we entertained you.' He sniggered. 'You did. Thanks. It makes up for having a shitty job.' He swaggered away and I looked at John; I caught him stifling a grin.

'You know, sometimes you remind me of Veronique.'

I felt suddenly very tired and, when my dessert arrived, I just picked at it. John paid by credit card. 'I'm not leaving a tip', he added. 'I just want you to know that you did the waiter out of a tip – and probably a job.'

'I'm sure he won't mind', I said casually. 'He said it was a shitty job, didn't he?'

He opened the car door for me, took the parking ticket off the windscreen, stuffed it into his jacket pocket and threw it onto the back seat. I noticed his face was slightly creased in the orange glare of a streetlight.

'So, what's the hippest pub in town these days?'

'Oh, there are so many cool places now, it's hard to decide', I said. 'Anyway, I don't want to go to any of my favourite places.'

'Why not?' His voice was sharp.

'Because all my ex-friends go there – the crowd I used to go to art college with, my neighbours. Since Daddy went bankrupt, they've been so horrible to me – so cold.'

'You have a way of making enemies, haven't you, Chloe?'

I looked at him, holding back the tears that were pricking my eyelids. 'It's not my fault. And I didn't start a fight with your friend's fiancée.' A tear broke loose and I felt it burn a trail down the cheek nearest John. He wiped it with a finger, then licked it.

He put the key in the ignition, then hesitated, staring ahead. 'OK, why don't we go to a really rotten pub – somewhere so awful we're unlikely to bump into any of your ex-friends or my current ones.' He smiled at me. 'I know just the place. It's five minutes' walk from here. We'd better leave the car here.'

'Is it a dangerous place?' I asked as we got out of the car.

'No, but I doubt the traffic warden will do the same car twice.' He reached back for his jacket, took the crumpled ticket out of his pocket and put it under the wiper.

Ten minutes later, we were still looking for that pub and I was feeling cold and tired – and my feet were hurting in those strappy stiletto sandals. 'John, it's closing time. They're not going to let us in any pub now.'

'They will in this place.'

'Are you sure it's around here?'

'Somewhere in this neighbourhood. It's just that they've changed some of the shopfronts since I was here before.'

'Maybe you should ask a cop where it is.'

'Thank you for the advice. I will.' I realised John was quite drunk; he had been knocking back beers with Killer – and he'd drunk a whole bottle of wine. 'Hey, *garda*!'

I watched in a mixture of fear and amusement as two policemen came over, the tall one looking at me with interest, the other suspiciously at John. 'Can we do anytin to help yewse?' the small, tough-looking one said.

'We're looking for a rough pub.'

'A common pub', I added, laughing.

The small cop sniggered. 'Yewse must mean Skanger's. It's not a pub dese days – dey've turd-dend it into a club. It stays open till four. Do yewse see dat alley? Go down dere and turd-en left.'

'Thanks, *garda*.'

'Been donkeys' years since yewse were on de tear in de city, right?'

'Yeah', John said.

'Speak for yourself', I Mumbled, vaguely offended at the cop's assumption that I was as old as John.

'Well, it's changed. We even have Dublin cops now.' He laughed and nodded towards his tall, silent colleague. 'PJ here is goin to be booted back to de cuntery as soon as we find a local lad to replace him.'

They walked away, laughing.

Skanger's was a dark basement full of sullen looking guys and girls in their twenties, mostly wearing T-shirts and tracksuit bottoms. They lounged against the mirrored walls or danced to remixed grunge, and barely looked at us as we entered. It was like stepping into a Knuttel print. The air was thick with sweat. 'It's a pity smoking was ever banned in public places', I said to John. 'It used to mask the other smells.'

We went over to the bar and a Jean Claude Van Damme lookalike in a tight white T-shirt growled: 'What do yewse wanh?'

'A bit of courtesy would be nice', John said. Luckily, the guy hadn't heard him; he put his hand to his ear. John ordered two orange juices. 'I need to sober up before I drive you home', he explained.

'I'm surprised that walk in the cold didn't clear the alcohol out of your system', I said.

'Ah, it wasn't that cold', he laughed. 'Are you really freezing?'

I nodded.

He put his jacket over my shoulders and led me to a corner couch. A girl in cropped trackies and a basketball top came over with our orange juices. 'Here yewse are – and before yewse ask, it's not freshly squeezed.' She walked off, sniggering.

I was suddenly overcome by a fit of the sniggers myself. I looked at John and saw he was cracking up too. 'I'm sorry, Chloe. This is probably the least romantic date you've ever had.'

'Actually, I've had worse', I said and told him about my debs ball.
He looked suitably sympathetic when I told him about Emmabelle McCowan snogging my escort.

'Horrible things are always happening to you', he said. He took my
left hand and kissed the fingertips. 'You need a manicure. You've got such beautiful fingers, it's a shame to neglect them.' He kissed my ring finger. 'Someone ought to put a ring on that.'

I waited for him to say something more romantic – I didn't actually expect him to propose on our first date (that was the kind of thing serial killers did in those tabloid papers my parents used to buy before we went upmarket) but the mention of the ring had sounded promising. But he just smiled and then he put his hand under my jaw and pulled my face close, and kissed me deeply.

At first, I let him do all the kissing; I was still thinking about the ring mention. Then I felt something surge inside my chest and I kissed him back, fully, wishing we could stay like that forever. He pulled me snug against him, his hands under his jacket, which still rested on my shoulders. I wrapped my arms around his neck and pressed my body into his. I found myself climbing onto his lap to get even closer. He groaned and rolled me over onto his other side, into the corner of the couch. His torso was on top of me and I could feel the sweat of his chest through his T-shirt and my dress. I let the jacket fall off and lay back on it, breathing through my nose as John kissed me hungrily. I felt his excitement; he certainly wasn't drunk now.

'Sorry, but yewse'll have to go somewhere else if yewse want to do dat.'

We sat up and saw a pock-marked man with grey hair and a wrestler's build standing over us. He squeezed John's shoulder and walked off.

We finished our orange juice quickly and left, John putting his jacket over my shoulders.

'I haven't been thrown out of a nightclub for snogging since I was a teenager', he laughed. 'Where to, now?'

'I'm hungry.' I knew I was being unreasonable but I felt I had to share my feelings with him.

'I was just thinking the same thing. There's an all-night American-style diner around here.'

'How do you know it's still here?'

'I went there with Barry a few weeks ago.'

'Oh.'

'Don't look like that. We didn't go to any lap dancing clubs.'

'Good. You wouldn't like them anyway – I met one of the dancers and she wasn't much to look at.'

'How do you know that?'

'My brother's living with her.'

'Your younger brother?'

'Yes; the only one I've got. He's eighteen.'

'Oh. Well, at least he's over the age of consent.'

'Mummy thinks he's still a baby. She thinks I should look after him.'

'Ah, I think the lap dancer will do that. Lucky little fecker.' He laughed and I joined in.

The all-night diner looked like the kind of place I imagined lorry drivers would go, to chat up haggard old waitresses and pick up drifter girls – like in American road movies. It was small, greasy-smelling and furnished in red plastic. But, instead of country'n'western music, there was a mellow, jazzy-blues kind of song playing softly in the background and there was no waitress, just a heavy-set bald man with a pointy black beard standing behind the counter. He was a cubist figure, his whole body made up of blocks. He had huge biker biceps and a surly expression.

'He looks like the devil', John whispered to me as we sat down in a seat near the window.

I laughed and shrugged. 'Well, then he won't throw us out if we misbehave.'

'No, but he might get jealous and keep us here.'

Stifling a giggle, I forced myself to concentrate on the menu, then I looked up and saw John's eyes laughing over the top of his. 'Come on, Chloe, choose something so I can order before he gets cross.'

We ordered French fries and a Cajun salad which warmed me up and gave me a pleasantly full feeling in my stomach. 'You eat a lot for such a slim girl', John said.

'Oh, don't you start about my weight.'

'I'm not criticising you, just making a detached observation. And, by the way, I think you've got a gorgeous body – what I can see of it.'

I found myself blushing. 'This sauce is really hot.'

'So are you. Sorry, I just had to say it.'

I suppose the old me would have cringed, but I just smiled. 'The music is really cool.'

But John was distracted by two guys in tracksuits who had just come in. 'Hey, that's one of my clients', he murmured. 'Oh no, he's seen me – oh, hello there.' He raised his hand in a reluctant wave.

The guys came over, bags of French fries in their hands. They stood in front of our table in their own cloud; a stench of fresh alcohol, stale sweat and something that I didn't want to think about while I was eating. 'How'ya Jonno', the one with a shaven blond head said. He looked about my age – except for his eyes, which had an ancient depth, like eyes you'd expect to find in a Mummy.... I should have been uneasy, but there was something comical about the situation. 'Is dis your bird?'

I looked at John and was amused to see he was colouring. 'Eh, yes, actually, she is.'

'I'm Chloe', I said, smiling because it covered the fact that I wanted to laugh.

'It's a pleasure meetin you, Chloe', John's client said. 'I'm Skoby – known in legal circles as Rich Lawless – and dis is me mate, Rob Wheeler.'

'I like your names', I said.

John was sitting with his arms folded, head cocked, looking at Skoby with the expression of a cross but tolerant parent. Skoby seemed to get the message quickly. 'We'll leave yewse in peace', he said. 'Bye Chloe. Your dress is lovely. I nicked one just like it for my bird.' They walked out, laughing and jostling each other.

John let out a sigh of relief. 'That Skoby is a dangerous little bastard', he said.

'He seemed OK.'

'He's in and out of prison like a yo-yo.'

'Was he disadvantaged?'

'What do you mean?'

'Well, that's what your uncle always says when he's defending people like him in the district court.'

'Oh. Underprivileged, you mean.'

'Whatever.'

'Actually, Chloe, Skoby is wealthier than you and I will ever dream of being. He runs a very profitable drug-dealing business and is clever enough not to damage his own health – he's teetotal, too, and a vegetarian. And he spends four hours in the gym every day. Oh, and he's got a degree in law.'

'You're joking.'

John shook his head and I realised he was serious. 'He's had plenty of time to study in jail.'

The city was rousing itself from a hangover by the time we found the car. We must have walked miles. 'I can't believe I actually managed to get lost with someone whose sense of direction is worse than my own', John laughed as we got in, shivering. 'At least I've sobered up.'

We cuddled, then two patches of fluorescent green flashed at the end of the street. 'Cops', I said. John sighed. 'We'd better get out of here before they update my parking ticket. Do you realise it's Saturday?'

He drove me home against the flow of rush-hour traffic. I pitied the grey-faced drivers on the other side of the dual carriageway; the upwardly mobile worked even on weekends. When we got to my house, he killed the engine and its growl was replaced by birdsong. The air smelled of summer and salt from the sea.

'It's going to be another scorcher', John said.

I snuggled into his arms, rolling back his shirtsleeves to enjoy the masculine smell of his forearms.

'Would you like to go for a swim this afternoon?'

'Yes.'

'Good. I'll pick you up around two, OK?'

I smiled and he kissed me, gently, then added: 'We can go to the beach in my part, if you like – it's on the other side of the city, where I come from.'

I'd forgotten that there were pretty beaches on the north side of Dublin. Now I looked forward to a sort of adventure; a beautiful day with John on his own territory.

Mummy was standing in the hall when I came in, a harsh look on her face. I guessed what she was going to say before she said it, but I had to listen anyway. 'Where have you been all night?'

I tried to look apologetic; the last thing I needed was a row, now, when I wanted to be in a happy mood for my afternoon with John. 'I'm sorry I couldn't call, but it was late and I didn't want to wake you up –'

'Chloe, I asked you where you were. Restaurants don't stay open all night.'

'We went to a diner afterwards.'

'Straight from the restaurant to a diner. You must be turning into an eataholic.' She looked me up and down. 'Helen thought you were too thin the other day.'

'That's because she's fat. Mummy, I'm telling the truth about the diner; we couldn't finish our meal because John's friend and some woman arrived and they kept talking and the woman was fighting with me.' I held in tears as I remembered my ordeal. 'And by the time they had left, our food was cold.'

'Hmm.' She folded her arms and looked at me with narrowed eyes. 'So you just went to this diner and spent the rest of the night there – you must have eaten very slowly.'

'Oh, we did.'

'Where is it? The diner, I mean.'

'Ah...I don't know. I can't remember the name of the street. We got lost and some cops told us where to find it.'

She pointed her finger at me and growled: 'I know when you're lying. I know by your face what you've done. You've slept with that man, haven't you?'

'No –'

'Don't lie to me! You slept with a married man!'

'He's getting divorced!'

'Ah, divorce....' Her eyes were filling with tears and I felt sorry for her.

'It's not like you and Dad', I said. 'His wife is leaving him. And I didn't sleep with him. Look at my eyes.' I hoped they had circles underneath but doubted it; I felt quite lively. I deliberately leaned against the telephone table, trying to look as if I could barely stand up. 'I'm exhausted, Mummy. I haven't slept all night.'

'I bet you haven't! You little sss –'

I felt a tear escape. My mother was about to call me a slut. But at least she hadn't said it. 'I didn't sleep – I didn't lie down with him, Mummy.' I blushed; how could I reassure my mother I hadn't had sex? I was too embarrassed to say 'made love' – and anyway I didn't want to cheapen the words by using them in a silly quarrel with my mother. 'I'm telling the truth.'

Her shoulders suddenly slumped and she sighed. 'Chloe, I shouldn't have to worry about you; you are an adult, after all. You're nineteen, you know.'

'Yes, I know', I said, wiping the tears away. 'Mummy, just trust me. I can look after myself.'

'No you can't. You're still living at home. And you've got no sense of responsibility – your little brother might as well be an only child, for all you worry about him.'

Now I was seriously fed up. 'So you want me to worry? Mummy, would you be happy if I sat and fretted all day about Daryus and Daddy and yourself?'

'Well, someone ought to care about us', she said, her voice breaking into a sob. She disappeared into the kitchen, slamming the door behind her.

I took a deep breath, then exhaled, the way I'd learned from Mummy's yoga books. Then I ran upstairs and got under the shower, keeping my head under the water to drown out the sound of Mummy's angry footsteps in the kitchen below. I waited until I heard the front door slam and the car drive away before I emerged to dry my hair, find something to wear for the afternoon, and take a catnap. I still wasn't tired, but I knew I would be later if I didn't lie down and shut my eyes.

Rathnamara was as picturesque as people said. Its tiny fishing harbour was as busy as Belgowan's and had the same mixed flotilla of rusty trawlers and elegant yachts. John's apartment was the top half of a two-storey house on a hill overlooking Dublin Bay, and he had a marvellous view from his bedroom in the attic.

The shelves were stuffed with books. 'Have you read all of these?' 'Yes.' 'Well, why do you hang onto them?' He looked puzzled. 'People always keep books – to read over and over.' I had never understood people who did that; life was too short, wasn't it? And John didn't seem like the kind who needed to show off that he had read all the modern classics. His collection of well-thumbed paperbacks proved that; they were mostly thrillers – escapist stuff.

'You should give them to Oxfam – make room for new fantasies.'

He smiled. 'Is that what you do?'

'I used to, when I could afford to buy new books. These days, I have to use the public library.'

He laughed. 'Poor Chloe. What kind of books to you read, anyway?'

'Oh....' I thought for a minute. 'You know something? I used to like reading blockbusters about rich, glamorous women who lost their fortunes and had to work as models. Now I prefer horror – because the characters are having a worse life than mine.'

He laughed. 'That can't be true.'

'Prove it.'

He took my face in his hands, rubbed his nose against mine, then coloured just a little and sat down on the black leather sofa. 'What do you think of my place?'

'It's like my studio, only with the sea right below', I said, removing my sundress and walking over to the window; I knew John would appreciate my silhouette against the light. I was wearing my skimpiest bikini, one I had bought in a chic boutique in the south of France the previous summer but had never been bold enough to wear. It was red with spaghetti-thin straps, and I had Immac-ed my bikini-line specially so I could wear the thong bottoms.

'You're not going on a public beach like that', he said, his voice thick and deep.

'Watch me', I said and darted past him down the stairs. He followed me, laughing, down the stone steps cut into the rocks and across the shingle. I ran into the waves, gasping as the cold water reached first my tummy, then my chest. 'Ooh, this is lovely!' I shrieked as a frothy wave covered me. John appeared in front of me, smiling, his hair plastered to his forehead so he looked as if he had a dorky fringe. 'You look like a mermaid', he said. 'Are you sure you weren't born in the sea?'

We swam parallel to the beach, our faces in the water, occasionally holding our breath and diving under. I tried to look at his blurry underwater-self, but the water was cloudy. I felt his hands on my waist, then his body against mine and then his salty mouth exploring mine.

Eventually, he took my hand and led me into the shallows, and a wave lifted us to our feet. 'Wait', I said. 'I need to fix something.' I found myself blushing. 'My bottoms.'

He laughed and walked onto the beach, leaving me to fix my thong back in place. He lay back on the beach, watching me moonwalk out of the water. 'You are a Venus.' 'Flattery', I said, laughing. He shook his head. 'False modesty doesn't become you.' He held out his hand and looked into my eyes as I came close. 'My fantasy woman.' 'But I'm real. Touch me.' He grasped my hand, kissed it, then pulled me down beside him.

We lay there on the warm sand, feeling the sun dry our pleasantly tired bodies. 'My little Venus', he said. 'Are you sure you're not Italian? You certainly talk like one.' He nuzzled my nose. 'So you've been chatted up by Italian guys too?' 'Of course.' I smiled; I no longer missed my exchange-student friends. 'John, will you always give me compliments? Even if I grow old and fat?' 'Yes – even if you get to look more like Venus the planet than the Botticelli painting.'

I stroked his cheek; it felt rough, like the skin of a trapped tope I had once stroked, back in Belgowan, before the fisherman had freed it from his net. John uttered a soft, low moan, then kissed me hard on the lips for what seemed like forever. Then we spent another eternity lying side by side, gazing into each other's eyes.

'Chloe, I really want to make love to you.' He suddenly leapt to his feet, pulling me up by the hand. 'But not here.' He led me up the steps and I felt my whole body flutter inside.

As we reached the lawn of the house, a man came out of the ground-floor apartment. 'Oh, shit', John said. 'It's my landlord – I owe him a month's rent.'

'Why don't you pay him?'

'Oh, I will – when Uncle Patrick pays me.'

The landlord, whose name was Mike, came up to the apartment and stomped around, frowning and rubbing at imaginary scratches. 'I'll have to charge you for wear and tear', he said.

'That furniture was already well-worn', John snapped. He was standing in his sopping wet pink-and-white floral-print swimming trunks. 'Now, if you'll excuse me, I need to wash the sand off so I can sit down.'

I had simply thrown my dress over my bikini – not that Mike was looking at me. He was more interested in the furniture.

'He reminded me of an octopus', I said, half an hour later as we sat in a little seafood bar at the harbour. We had gone there straight after Mike had retreated to his apartment downstairs; we hadn't felt like making love with him listening underneath, and his unwelcome visit had cast a shadow over the place. 'Lying in ambush below, in his lair, until he saw us, and then running his tentacles all over your apartment.' I giggled. 'And you looked so funny standing there in your wet shorts.' John guffawed and poured me a beer.

He opened a scallop. 'Have one of these. You look as if you came out of one – or maybe an oyster.' 'Thanks', I said, eating it off his knife.

'Someone ought to buy you a string of pearls.' 'The same someone who you said ought to give me a ring?' 'Yes. I wonder who he'll be.' His eyes were full of warmth and mirth, and I felt my cheeks burning.

In the car, as he was driving me home, I picked up his left hand and fingered his wedding ring. 'Why do you still wear this if you're getting divorced?'

'I can't get it off. I'll have a jeweller cut it.' He sighed. 'But first I've got to find a better landlord.'

'Why don't you buy a place instead of renting?'

'Well, maybe when my divorce comes through, I can afford a house in Dublin. I'm renegotiating the terms with Veronique. I realise now that I was stupid to offer her everything.'

I looked at him, trying to remember what he had left her – the chateau, the horses and dogs, the paintings. 'Do you think she'll let you change your mind at this stage?' He shrugged.

'She will if I tell her I could end up homeless. She's still got a heart.'

'Why won't your uncle pay you your salary?' 'Two reasons: he's a miser – and he doesn't want me to get divorced at all. He'd be happier if I stayed dependent on Veronique. But I'm sick of being her househusband.'

'Don't you have a job in France?' 'Only a nominal one – in her father's law firm. Veronique is one of my bosses, along with the rest of her family.'

'That must be awful. What about your parents?'

'They're not wealthy at all. They live in a three-bedroomed semi-detached house – way down the country: Longford.' I had heard of it but couldn't visualise any place in Ireland outside Dublin.

'Do you have any brothers or sisters?' I realised I still knew very little about this man I loved.

'Just a brother. He's only twenty-six but he's already settled down with a mortgage, a wife and two kids. He's an accountant like my father.'

'So you're the black sheep?'

'Baaa.' He grinned. 'And I don't want to be the Prodigal Son too. My father is always saying I should be more responsible.'

'So is my mother – and my Aunty Helen. It's an awful burden, being the eldest, isn't it? I get blamed for the way my brother turned out.'

John laughed. 'The young lad with the lap dancer. Well, I suppose my brother will never make me responsible for his downfall. I can't imagine him ever doing anything wrong.'

'He might run off with his clients' money and leave his wife and kids with nothing. My father ran away with his investors' funds – and he was the most responsible, reliable person you ever could meet.'

'Poor little Chloe', he said, with feeling. 'Life really has been hard on you.'

'Yes.' I kissed the fine lines at the corner of his eye. 'And on you.' I continued to kiss around his temple, enjoying the coarseness of his hair and the faint scent of some sporty, masculine shampoo – sandalwood and citrus mixed with something peppery. I drew back to look at his hairline. I was relieved when I couldn't find any white hairs; I didn't know how I'd handle being in love with a grey man.

He squeezed my hand. 'Chloe, let me concentrate on the road, hmm?'

He dropped me off at my gate, telling me he had to drive down the country to his parents' house that evening, and would be spending Sunday there, but would call me during the week.

I felt lost as he drove away. I walked slowly up the drive and entered the house quietly, not feeling like talking to anyone. I slipped up to my room, threw my light rucksack on the bed and looked at myself in the mirror. My hair was tangled, the salt water having enhanced the drying effect of the highlights. It looked sexy, I supposed, but I couldn't get a brush through it. I went downstairs to put on the hot water tank and find some of Mummy's conditioner for coloured hair.

'What did you do to your hair? You look like a sea-witch', Aunty Helen said, waving her cigarette at me. She was sitting at the kitchen table with Mummy, and I noticed with dismay that Mummy was smoking too; she'd given that up.

'You look like a fag hag, Aunty Helen', I said. 'And Mummy, you'll get wrinkles around your lips if you start smoking again.'

'Apologise to Helen this minute!'

I blew Aunty Helen a raspberry and went to the cupboard to find the conditioner.

That night, I painted John coming out of the sea, his body shimmering with water. There was very little space left on the crowded canvas, so I put him up in the sky, except now it looked like water, and this image of John was an island, with no friends, no family, no Veronique...and, of course, I left his ring finger bare. I worked quickly, using watercolours, heavily diluted; the effect was very fluid.

When I had finished him, I called his mobile, just once, but it was switched off. I didn't want to leave a message in case he'd think I was obsessive (he'd told me Gina was always leaving messages for Killer, demanding to know where he was and who he was with).

Then I wondered if he might not be at his parents' at all. What if he had gone out 'on the razz' with Killer and Gina, as Killer had been suggesting? I was sure Killer'd be happy to have me along, but Gina wouldn't, and she seemed to have plenty of control over her fiancé – who was John's best friend from college. Maybe John wanted to spend an evening with friends his own age.

I looked at the painting again, and, on impulse, painted Killer and Gina on either side of John. Then I painted them again, just above his head, the second versions almost identical to the first.

By the time I had finished, there were lots of little Tonies and Ginas, all around John, swamping him. I cried and went to bed.

I tried to forget about John on Sunday; it was a day of rest, and I needed to recharge myself, so I went to Mass with Mummy.

Daryus wasn't there. 'I suppose he's with his lap dancer', Mummy snorted as we came out of the church afterwards. 'Her name's Mira', I wanted to say, but I decided silence was easier, and kept walking towards the car.

Then I looked back and saw Mummy was trying to get away from one of our neighbours, who was clutching her by the sleeve. It was old Mrs O'Toole, the local postmistress – the nosiest woman in Belgowan. I stayed beside the car, eavesdropping; it was easy, because Mrs O'Toole had an inbuilt megaphone.

'And what's your Chloe doing with herself these days?' she was asking.

'Oh, working as a secretary.'

'Funny, but I saw her on the beach the other day – Friday was it, or Thursday?'

'Mummy!' I yelled. 'Are you coming or what?'

She seemed reluctant to leave now. Mrs O'Toole was a skilled scandalmonger; first she fished for information, using little bits of gossip as bait – then she sold it to the whole neighbourhood. She was always being invited for quiet lunches in the pub by the likes of Poo Anchorbottom, the Chamber of Commerce and our local politicians. She enjoyed round-the-clock police protection, never had to buy her own drink, and chatted with her dead husband every Tuesday night courtesy of a medium who relied on her for background information when meeting new clients.

Mummy only came away when Mrs O'Toole spotted someone else she knew and latched onto them (or maybe she had realised Mummy was just looking for gossip rather than imparting it).

'Well, Chloe, we're the talk of Belgowan as usual', Mummy said once we were in the car. 'Mrs O'Toole knows all about Daryus and that lap dancer.'

'Mummy, why do you care what the neighbours think? They're not worth impressing – they never were.'

'I care when they tell me things about my family that worry me.' She sighed. 'Mrs O'Toole told me she'd seen you around quite a lot during the week.'

'I know. I heard her – nosey old cow.'

'Eavesdropping is not very nice, Chloe.'

'Neither is spreading scandal.'

'She was telling me something she thought I needed to know. You seem to be getting a lot of days off work'.

'Well, the Fitzwalton sisters are very sick.'

'I hope they pay you for those days. It's not going to be easy managing on what's left of my savings – and I'm certainly not fit to find a job in my emotional state.'

It rained in the afternoon, but I didn't feel like staying in and painting – didn't even want to look at John or any of the others on my canvas. I needed to take a break from intense passions.

So I went to the gym and just lounged in the jacuzzi, which I had all to myself (most people had family things to do on Sundays, I supposed). It was an open, unisex jacuzzi at the side of the swimming pool, so I suppose I was tempting trouble in my skimpy bikini, but I wanted to take the hex off it; I didn't want to think of it as something I had only worn with John, because, if he left me, I'd always think of it as a souvenir of a lost love.

I opened my eyes when I smelt expensive massage oils and heard male voices murmuring in some foreign language. They were Japanese; probably businessmen staying in the five-star hotel attached to the gym. I inwardly cursed them for spoiling my tranquillity but smiled politely as I got out of the steaming bubbles; it was amusing to see their oriental composure vanish as their jaws dropped.

When I got home, Mummy was lying on the couch, watching an English soap. 'You took my bay-bee! And then you murdered his faw-ver!' some woman was screaming at another.

I sighed and went up to my room to read a novel – one of Daryus's sci-fi sagas with lots of monsters and absolutely nothing that reminded me of anything in my own life.

The next morning, I dressed in a long summer dress with capped sleeves and went out early; I wanted Mummy to think I was going to work. I switched my mobile on as soon as I was out of the house. I hoped John would call and ask me to meet him in town, but he hadn't by the time I got to the railway station.

There was no point in going into the city centre if I wasn't going to be meeting John. I couldn't afford to go shopping – and I certainly wasn't going to the National Gallery; Eleanor and Francesca had ruined it for me.

Instead, I decided to visit a little gallery run by struggling artists. They held a new exhibition every week, according to the 'What's On' column in the local paper.

Actually, the exhibition was awful. I could see why the sculptor and painter were unemployed. Still, I felt guilty for not being able to buy something; artists needed all the help they could get. And maybe I wasn't being fair to them, looking at their works while I was in a bad humour.

Why hadn't John called? I was still asking myself the same question late in the afternoon, as I sat on a wall along the seaside promenade, eating an ice-cream.

Then I got a text message that made me smile: 'Meet U 4 drinks 2morrow at 8? Finn McCool's.'

I texted him back: 'OK. C U'.
Then I went home to find a shorter dress.

Finn McCool's was one of Dublin's most fashionable pubs. The decor changed every week in harmony with the interior decor magazines, the background music was always on the latest hit list and everyone seemed to wear the same perfume. The clientele was twenty-thirty-something – though the doormen made exceptions for geriatric rock stars, TV personalities and rich businessmen like my Daddy (though somehow I doubted he'd ever brought Carmel Delahanty here).

I had avoided the pub since Daddy's bankruptcy scandal, because I'd been afraid of bumping into the sons and daughters of his high-profile creditors. Now I realised I was going to be bumping into people all night; the place was packed. I looked around for John, then saw him leaning against the bar, a pint of beer in his hand, talking to someone I'd seen before – Killer! And there was Gina, grinning at something with a group of similar women – all thirtyish, carrying ostentatious designer handbags, smelling of expensive perfume (like the stuff I borrowed from Mummy).

I stood in the doorway, waiting for John to see me. Killer nudged him and he turned, smiling. I weaved through the crowd, dodging the splashes from over-full glasses, and ignored Gina as she pretended to smile at me, her eyes hard as pin-pricks.

'What are you having?' Killer asked me. 'Not an orange juice again, I hope.'

'Why not?' I asked.

'You'll have to come off the wagon sometime.'

John laughed and gestured with his head towards Gina and her coven. 'I thought you liked wagons.' Then, to me: 'Is "wagon" still slang for "old cow"?'

'Yes', I said, looking at Gina, who was throwing her head back in an exaggerated manner, pretending to laugh with her friends while scrutinising me out of the corner of her eye. 'But I can think of better words for that one.'

Killer chuckled. 'Ah, go on have a real drink. I'm dying to see a good drunken catfight.'

John put his arm around my waist and said: 'Killer's got a morbid fear of people who don't drink, because he's terrified they'll remember the next day what he did the night before – right, Killer?'

'Ah, go way with you.' He pretended to punch John in the stomach.

'And he's old enough to remember the dry dancehalls', John added.

'Would you get up the yard! Those were in my father's time. He still has nightmares about them – why do you think he raised me to be an alcoholic?'

It was like being at the 'afters' of a family wedding, wishing the older relatives would just leave the disco... Over-thirties, alcohol and loud music made a caustic cocktail.

Killer ordered an orange juice for me, the barman cocked an eyebrow and Killer said: 'She's a recovering alcoholic.'

'Wrong place for her then, isn't it?' the barman laughed and sauntered off, shaking his head.

'You'll be waiting all night for an orange juice in here', Killer said. 'Are you sure you won't have a beer?'

'Do I look like a beer drinker?'

John chuckled. 'She drank beer with oysters yesterday.'

'I only drink it with oysters', I said, realising that I sounded drunk even though I was the only completely sober person there.

'So what do you drink?' Killer asked me. He seemed to be obsessed with getting me drunk; that harmless face hid a leering soul.

'Well, it depends on what I'm eating', I said, remembering how I used to come here with my ex-friends and sit on the VIP balcony, snacking on pieces of fruit, olives and pretzels in between alcopops and exotic juices. I looked up and saw some girls and guys who looked familiar – but I couldn't tell from this distance...anyway, people always seemed to look homogenous in these places, like co-habiting species of animals gathering around a watering hole on the African planes. Those were the giraffes over there – tall and spotty. And there was a beautiful cheetah with her tongue down a married TV presenter's throat...and some lion cubs were tussling playfully in a corner, their prey a bottle of expensive champagne...and those long-legged antelopes were being stalked by a pack of wolves in sheeps' clothing – the kind that was tailor-made in Savile Row, London.

'Would you look at the gams on that one', Killer said as a very tall girl walked by in a micro-mini. I was sure I'd seen her on the cover of glossy magazines; she was probably a visiting supermodel, over for a fund-raising fashion show. Killer sighed and sang: 'If I were a rich man...'

'Or a young man', I laughed as the model sat down on the lap of a guy about her own age – my age, too. He looked like a soccer player – he probably was. I wondered what I was doing there, with two thirty-something men, listening to one of them talk about the 'beautiful young things' while the other, my boyfriend, just squeezed my hand and smiled at me as if I was an ugly little sister who needed a morale boost.

'Well, John, are you going to introduce your better half to us?' a farmer type with a country accent said. He was about thirty, too; maybe they all said things like 'better half' for girlfriend and 'gams' for legs. The group of men he was with raised their beer glasses and grinned.

'Chloe, are you just going to pout at my friends or will you be a nice girl and say hello?' John laughed.

'Ah, leave the auld pout alone', the farmery guy said. 'It's very sexy. Chloe, you're gorgeous. Here, let me get you something stronger to drink – a nice beer'll fatten you up. You're awful thin.'

I got fed up saying 'No, thanks' every time they tried to ply me with alcohol, so in the end I just said: 'Fuck off.'

Instead of looking shocked, as I thought older men would, they laughed.

It turned out they had played rugby at college with John and Killer. Most of them were from the country and they all had family farms – of one kind or the other.

'You've met the girls, Chloe?' the farmery guy said.

'She's met Gina, anyway', Killer chortled. 'They had a right shindig in a restaurant. I thought they were going to start tearing each other's clothes off.'

'Ah, don't exaggerate, Killer', John cut in, but the other men were more interested in Killer's version of the story.

One of them turned to me: 'Well, Chloe, I'll have to introduce you to my better half or she'll get jealous – she'll think you're flirting with me.'

'I doubt it', I said.

'Ha-ha. Caoimhe! Come here and meet John's better half. She's nearly as gorgeous as yourself.' He put his arms around my shoulders and murmured into my ear: 'You know I'm only humouring her.'

'She looks as if she needs to be humoured', I said, pulling away from his drunken embrace. He smelt of beer and stale sweat and his hands were clammy.

Caoimhe looked like the kind of woman I'd seen in the gym, pedalling furiously on the exercise bike with a snarl on her face. She was wearing a very feminine floral dress which would have looked so much nicer on me (in a smaller size, of course). She pumped my hands up and down and tiptoed up to kiss my cheek; I didn't bend down.

'Ooh', she said, pinching my waist.

'Haieeehh! That hurt!'

'Sorry. I didn't realise you hadn't even got an inch to pinch.' Her avid little green eyes narrowed and the pupils shrank to pinhead size. 'I can see you've never had to give birth or sit up all night with a crying baby.'

'What are you talking about?'

She gestured to my torso. 'Your body. Your skin. I'm giving you a compliment – don't you get it?'

'Thanks', I said.

'No probs.' She smiled, icily. 'Anyway, your time will come. You'll know what it feels like to be twenty-nine.'

'Do you remember?' I said.

She smirked and wagged her finger at me. 'Witty, aren't you? Gina told us all about you. Come over and talk to the rest of the girls.

'What girls?' I snapped as she dragged me by the arm over to the centre of the group. 'I've heard about circling your wagons but this is a bit much.'

'Girls, this is Chloe, who needs a good feed.'

They all laughed, a cacophony of cackles, sniggers and self-conscious guffaws.

'Pleased to meet you, Chloe', an enormous blonde said. 'I'm anorexic too – only I forgot to vomit!'

I ignored her and glanced over at Gina, who was glowering at me with her eyes, but trying to appear as if she was smiling; her lips were drawn back in a rictus grimace and I noticed she'd applied lipstick all the way up to her nostrils. 'Oh, Chloe and I understand each other', she said, her voice sounding just a little drunk. 'We're very alike.'

'No we're not', I said.

'Oh, but we are. We're both competitive –'

'I'm not', I interrupted. 'What or whom have I got to compete with?'

She flapped her claws in my face and continued talking, glaring at me: 'We're both passionate, we're femme fatales, we'd fight tooth and nail to hang onto our man –'

'I wouldn't', I said. 'If he wanted to leave me, I wouldn't try to stop him.'

Caoimhe cut in: 'Very argumentative, aren't you? I suppose that goes with being skinny – you're all nerves. You need to calm down.'

I'd had enough experience as a misfit in school to know that I was supposed to burst into tears at this point, and then one of the group would stop cackling with the others to comfort me, and they would all apologise insincerely, postponing the taunting session for another day. But I wasn't going to let them see me cry – I wasn't! I blinked back the tears, and wished I was at home, painting – or alone with John. I looked over at him but he was chatting with the men.

'Why don't you all fuck off?' I said quietly.

Gina let out a high-pitched cackle. 'Oh, leave her alone, Caoimhe. She'll tear your eyes out if you get on the wrong side of her.' She stroked my arm. 'You see, Chloe, you really are like me! It's a Latin thing – maybe you've got some *Latina* blood.'

'Gina's half-Brazilian', Caoimhe said to me. 'That's where she gets her dark good looks from.'

'She's dark alright', I said, wondering if she realised that a lot of Brazilians were blonde and they all knew how to pluck their eyebrows.

'I'd love to be blonde, like you', Gina was saying. 'Then I wouldn't have to spend so much time waxing all those awful unwanted hairs – they grow all over me. I'm just so hairy.'

'You'd still be hairy', I said. 'Only you'd look like a yeti.'

The group giggled and Gina coughed her beer back into the glass.

'Why don't you get it all waxed off?' Caoimhe said to her. 'Or you could get it lasered – '

'I'm not hairy, you bitch!' Gina snarled at her. 'I was only trying to be friendly with Chloe, wasn't I, Chloe? It was just girltalk.' She said it all in one word: 'Girltalk'. It sounded like a corny name for a girl band.

'I've got cellulite', another woman chipped in.

'And I've got tree-trunk legs – look!' This one lifted up her skirt, drawing gapes from some nearby men, who immediately lost interest.

Caoimhe turned to me. 'So what's your problem, Chloe?'

The others chorused: 'Yeah, what faults have you got?'

'Bad personality', I said and they laughed – but I didn't.

I looked over towards John, and realised he was grinning. Then his face softened and he shoved the leering lads away and elbowed his way through the women to pull me into his arms. 'Come on, stay over here where I can look after you.'

'Ah, she's shy', Killer said. 'She's only a kid.'

'I'm not. I'm nineteen', I said, blinking back tears, wanting to leave but afraid John would let me go; he seemed very fond of his friends.

'She's a bit young for you, John', Killer was saying. 'You should go for a mature woman – they know how to take a bit of slagging.'

'It's called bullying', I cut in. 'I studied it in school – oh, I forgot, in your day it was acceptable.'

'Oooh, that hurt', Killer chortled. 'But, seriously, Chloe, you'll have to grow up a bit if you want to hang onto a guy like John. All the girls are mad about him – even my Gina says he's a fine thing.'

I forced myself to laugh, to swallow my indignation. I looked up at John but he was talking to another man, ignoring me. He and the other man were having a lighthearted argument about the merit of one make of car over another. I yawned.

'You have to learn to fit in with our crowd', Killer was whining into my ear. 'We're all part of a team – it's like in work. What do you do for a living, Chloe?'

'I'm unemployed.'

'Oh. Well, you must be studying, or something.'

'No.'

'I'm sure we could find you a job. One of the girls could –'

'No! I don't want to work with people I can't stand.'

'But you're so young. You must have some ambition....'

I tugged at John's sleeve and murmured in his ear. 'I'm bored. I want to go home.'

One of the rugby-farmery men started to sing drunkenly: 'Tell me the way to go home, I'm tired and I wanta go ta bed....' The other men joined in, laughing and banging their beer glasses on the counter.

'John, please', I said.

He looked embarrassed. 'Ah, Chloe, don't be a sour-puss. We were going to go on to a club.'

'John, I'm not dancing with these people.'

Killer leaned over my shoulder. 'Who said anything about dancing? We're going there to drink and admire the talent. We're too old to make eedgits of ourselves on the dancefloor in front of the young things.'

'I know where we can get a great gander', the farmer cut in. 'I know a club that's full of gorgeous young things in mini-skirts, hot pants – the lot.'

'Why don't we all go to a lap dancing club?' Killer suggested.

The others sniggered and glanced nervously over their shoulders.

'We'd have to sneak out and leave the girls behind', Killer said. 'But Chloe can come with us.' He stroked my arm; I flinched.

'Her brother lives with a lap dancer', John said, squeezing my shoulders proudly.

The others chortled and made various 'fworr' sounds, and Killer leered at me, putting his glasses on for a better look: 'I hope you'll get us a free pass.'

'Girls don't give passes to men in glasses', I said. 'Come on, John.'

John put his jacket on and shrugged at the others. As we left, I heard Caoimhe crying to Gina: 'But I'm not a "Working Mummy". I'm a "Yummy Mummy".' She mimed quotation marks with her fingers, the way I'd seen people do in re-runs of nineties soaps; this was the *Friends* generation and it wasn't ageing gracefully.

I clutched John's arm. 'I don't want to be a Yummy Mummy. She isn't yummy at all.'

We came out onto the cold street and said nothing to each other as we walked to the car. The shrill voices echoed around the nearly empty street. A group of guys and girls my own age were staggering along the opposite path, laughing about something; they might have been drunk but they were probably just happy. I caught a whiff of cheap perfume from one of the girls; it smelled young.

I realised John was walking briskly, and I ran to catch up. 'John?'

'What?'

'Why aren't you holding my hand?'

'That's what your problem is, Chloe. You need someone to hold your hand all the time. You're too immature.'

'You're angry.' I felt tears well up.

'I'm not angry – just pissed off.'

'You're pissed.'

'No; I'm completely sober, Chloe. More sober than you are, ever – God knows what you'd be like if you drank.'

It started to rain. 'Now it's going to piss', he said, sounding like a grumpy old man. 'Just as well I left the canopy on the car.' He got in and opened the door from the inside. I hesitated; I felt like running down the street to the taxi rank.

He rolled down the window. 'Chloe, are you going to get into the bloody car?'

'No.'

'Stop crying! That won't work anymore. I've had it up to here with this little girl act.'

I began to walk down the cobbled street, glad I was wearing flat sandals, even if they were soaking wet. I heard him call my name, so I walked faster, then broke into a run. I breathed in the scent of Dublin – the fermented hops from the brewery, the urine from a wall, the smell of wet blankets and old sweat from a man curled up in a doorway, and the River Liffey just ahead. It all smelled nicer in the rain.

I didn't know where I was going, only that my life was all about crossing the river, back and forth. Maybe my luck would turn if I went over to the other side again.

'Chloe! Come back. Chloe, don't do it.'

I stopped in front of the river. 'Do what?'

'I – I thought you were going to jump in the river.'

'What?' I couldn't believe what he'd just said.

He ran up to me and put his arms around me, his chin on my head. 'I was afraid you were going to commit suicide.'

'Why?' I was puzzled now, and wished I wasn't enjoying his embrace.

'I was a bit too hard on you. I thought you might take it badly and –'

'Kill myself because you and your friends treated me badly?' I was angry now. On a sudden impulse, I drew back and slapped his cheek. He looked up at the sky in apparent shock, then down at me, his eyes blazing with something that looked like lust but could have been anger. I raised my knee half-heartedly towards his crotch, wanting to knee him the way I'd seen a girl do in a film, but somehow I couldn't bring myself to do it.

He walked a few paces away and sat down on a bench, his knees apart, elbows on them, head between his hands, staring at the pavement. I walked slowly over to him, wondering if he was aware I was coming back to him. He looked up.

'John, I'm sorry I didn't get on well with your friends.'

'It wasn't your fault.'

'I know. But I'm sorry for you.'

'So am I – for us. Chloe, it's just not working out.'

I felt my blood freeze and my legs suddenly gave way. I found myself sitting on the pavement, looking up at him, crying.

'Come on', he said, getting up. 'You'll catch cold. I'll drive you home.'

'I'll get a taxi.'

'Don't be ridiculous. I brought you out and I'll take you home.'

I cried silently as he drove out of the city, towards Belgowan. He stared ahead, obeying all the traffic lights. I was dismayed to see that they turned green just as he was slowing for the amber. It seemed everything was against us.

When we reached the coast road that led to my street, he slowed down and pulled in beside the low wall overlooking the cliff. He reached across me into the glove compartment. He wasn't doing it so he could brush his arm against me, I realised, because he quickly grabbed a box of tissues out and handed it to me. 'Blow your nose. And wipe your eyes carefully – I don't want your mother thinking I made you cry.'

'But you did.'

'Oh, don't give me a guilt-trip. I behaved like a gentleman – that's all I've done since I've known you.'

'Why did you force me to mix with those horrible people?' My voice sounded hoarse to my own ears, and felt weak. I wasn't crying now because I was too tired.

He sighed and said nothing for a while. I waited for him to speak. Eventually, he put his hands at the top of the steering wheel, turned to face me and lay his cheek on his arms. He had dark circles under his eyes, like bruises, and I wanted to reach over and kiss them better. 'Chloe, I'm very tired, as I'm sure you are, but we need to talk about this. I don't want to leave you...'

I felt my blood rise...

'...thinking I'm a bastard.'

The blood drained from my cheeks and pooled in my stomach.

'Chloe, can I ask you something?'

I nodded.

'Who do you hang around with?' I didn't answer, not knowing what to say or what he was getting at, so he clarified: 'You must have a gang of girls your own age – a best friend, you know, like other girls, other women.'

I sighed. 'I used to have lots of best friends. But ever since my Daddy went bankrupt –'

He was shaking his head. 'No, Chloe. Don't use your father's bankruptcy as an excuse. You never really had a close female friend, did you?'

I thought for a minute. 'I did, a few years ago.'

'In school?'

'Yes.'

'Where is she now?'

'Oh, we drifted apart. She's in college now, studying something boring –'

He sat up and pointed his finger in the air, the way I'd seen Mr Wrightman Senior do when he was pontificating. Like uncle, like nephew; I wondered if John would grow stout and cranky with age. 'You see, Chloe, this is what I mean. You're such a snob.'

'Me? A snob?' I felt my cheeks flush. 'I'm a *victim* of snobbery – and inverted snobbery. Everywhere I go, people attack me because I'm too posh, or not posh enough, or too young, or too pretty.'

'Everyone's against Chloe. Poor Chloe', he said. 'Do you realise you sound paranoid?'

'Maybe everyone really is against me', I said, beginning to laugh because it was funny when I looked at it objectively.

'Chloe, have you ever heard the term "frienemy"?'

'Yes. I read about it on the internet. It's a false friend, who is really an enemy, who stabs you in the back and smiles at you when you turn round.'

'Do you believe frienemies are common?'

'They are if they have the wrong accent', I sniggered, nervously, feeling as if I was whistling in the dark.

'Don't be flippant, Chloe. I'm trying to figure out how tolerant you are of other people.'

'Well, I certainly wouldn't want a frienemy.'

'That's what I was afraid of hearing. You see, you don't compromise on anything – you want the perfect friend, the perfect lover.' He reddened as he said 'lover' and I found myself blushing all over. He cast his eyes ahead, into the dark, looking out to sea across the curve of the coast. 'Chloe, every single one of those women you met tonight was a frienemy of the others. I've heard them talk behind each other's back, seen them flirt with each other's boyfriend at every opportunity. When two of them go to the Ladies', they go to bitch about another –'

'How do you know that?'

'Everyone knows it. It's common knowledge that women go to the toilet to gossip and slag off other women.'

'I mean, how do you know that those women – your friends' wives and girlfriends – flirt with each other's men? You said yourself you hadn't seen the guys – apart from Killer – since school.'

He looked at me sheepishly. 'I was with them on Saturday night.'

'You told me you were going to your parents'.'

'I lied.'

I shivered, feeling very much alone. 'I never thought you'd lie to me, John. I trusted you.'

'I know.' He put his head in his hands again. 'I'm sorry.'

'I'm the most trusting woman you'll ever meet – and the most loyal.' My voice was squeaky and shaking; I felt angry with it, wishing it would go all calm and well-modulated, like a movie star's. 'I'll never be a frienemy to anyone, man or woman, because I don't believe in pretending to like someone and secretly hating them. When I turn against a person, I don't stick around long enough to stab them in the back – I just avoid them.'

He turned to face me again, a look of sheer curiosity on his face. 'What do you do if you're forced to mix with someone you despise?'

'Like tonight?'

'Good answer.' He chuckled. 'You've got a cutting tongue for someone so young and innocent looking.'

'I don't mean to be cutting. I don't like hurting people – but I have to do something when they keep attacking me.'

'Yeah. I can understand that.' He sighed. 'I'd do the same in your situation. It's just that – why can't women have simple, honest-to-goodness camaraderie, the way men do? Hmmm?'

'Because we're not men. You sound like Henry Higgins.' I laughed, feeling a little less sad.

He smiled. 'And you're my Eliza Doolittle.' He paused. 'Well, OK, men don't make the most sensitive friends –'

' – unless they're artistic or gay.'

He laughed. 'Killer and the rest of the lads certainly aren't – well, not that I'm aware. But at least I know they go for a drink with me because they enjoy my company, not because they want to appear friendly in front of other people.'

'John, can I ask you a hypothetical question?'

'Sure.'

'If you discovered all your friends were frienemies, would you still hang around with them?'

'No, of course n –'

'Oh, John, you need to learn to compromise....' I laughed.

'*Touché.*'

'Some people hang onto their frienemies because they're terrified of being alone, and of what other people will think of them for being friendless.'

'Yes. Sad, isn't it?'

'I'd love to have a true friend – who wouldn't? – but they're not easy to find.' I stopped and thought for a moment, grateful that John was staying silent with me; we were the classic example of people who had reached the same wavelength, and I had never felt closer to anyone...never less alone. If only I could find a female friend so understanding. 'What I need is a gay man to be my best friend.'

'Maybe you will have one when you're in your thirties, still single – and still unable to make friends with other women. A gay man is a thirty-something single girl's chicest accessory.'

'I hope I won't be single in my thirties. I want a gay man friend now – in case I ever need a substitute for a bridesmaid.' I blushed at my own reference to things weddingy, but John was squeezing my hand and chuckling. 'A bridesman. Well, I'll find out if any of my men friends have gay tendencies and pass them on to you.'

I laughed. 'No more rugger buggers, please – and no farmers.'

'And no women. That narrows down the field a lot, doesn't it?' But he was still laughing.

'Does Veronique have a best friend?' I asked suddenly.

He hesitated. 'Not really. She's got a few female acquaintances but they're not close. Other lawyers, clients, family friends. They meet up for business lunches and fundraisers. They don't cry on each other's shoulder or watch chick flicks together.' He shrugged. 'But Frenchwomen are usually more interested in the opposite sex – apart from lesbians and bi-sexuals of course...and she's not – as far as I know.'

'I bet her female acquaintances don't even want to know her now.'

'That's what she said! How did you know?'

I shrugged. 'Mummy's friends stopped inviting her to dinner parties as soon as Daddy left. They obviously think she's going to jump on their husbands.'

He shook his head. 'I've just realised how little I know about women. You're so much more complicated than men – all this business of pretending to be simple when you're actually scheming foxes.' He laughed. 'Or acting all mysterious and femme fatale-ish, the way Janet does –'

'That's the way drag queens go on', I laughed. 'Janet should pretend she's really a guy and she'd get a lot more attention.'

He guffawed. 'That's a bit below the belt, Chloe!'

'Sorry, but she's been so horrible to me.'

'Horrible to me', he mimicked, sounding like a lousy drag queen. 'You really are just a kid, aren't you?' He was looking at me with affection, as if I was a child. Then he sighed and gave me a searching look. 'I'm not trying to patronise you. What I mean is you're childlike, not simply childish. Do you know the difference?'

'I think so.'

'You're childlike, the way you look at everything and everyone with the eyes of a baby who's seeing the world for the first time. And sometimes you're all petulant and childish. Most of the time, you're both. And then sometimes you seem to be hundreds of years old – I'm not talking about the hairstyle or the clothes, but what comes out of your head.'

I looked at him, realising he was beginning to understand me in his own, rather arbitrary way. I admired him for being able to understand a woman of my age despite being a man – and an older one at that. But I didn't want to patronise him by telling him.

'Chloe, tell me what you're thinking right now. Let me inside your head.'

'Oh, I feel confused, a lot of the time – and even my confusion isn't clearcut. Sometimes I'm certain I'm one person, then I find I'm not that person at all; I'm something totally different or partly different or I'm a complete stranger to myself.'

He nodded, seeming to understand.

'John, do you ever feel as if you're a misfit?'

'Of course – I always have done. That's why I went to live in France.'

I laughed. 'I suppose being a foreigner is a good excuse for not fitting into a role in your family or circle of friends.'

He grinned. 'Yes. You have far more freedom to be yourself –'

'Your complete self.'

'Not a link in the social circle, a cog in the wheel.'

'I know exactly how you feel, John.'

'I know you do.'

'I've never really felt at home – anywhere. Not in my old neighbourhood or my new one.'

'What about your brother? Is it as difficult for him?'

'Daryus wants to be a misfit – it's part of being a punk.'

'I remember punk the first time around', John laughed. 'I wanted spiky hair for my First Holy Communion.'

'That's the way I think of Daryus. He'll always be Mummy's little boy who can't look out for himself. Why do you think he's living with an older woman?'

John smiled ruefully. 'I lived with an older woman – I married her. But I certainly never regarded Veronique as a mother figure. In fact, I'd find that a complete turn-off, and so would she.'

'No one likes to be cast in an unflattering role.'

He nodded. 'But some of us just put up with it to hang on to the people we love.'

He had his hand on the back of my seat, I noticed. And we were facing each other, our cheeks on the headrests.

'John?'

'Mmm?' His eyes were soft, warm and, it seemed, just a little lustful.

'Do I look as if I've been crying?'

'A little. Your mascara is all down your cheeks.' He took a tissue, licked it and wiped my face, gently. Then he threw the tissue on the floor and took my cheeks in his hands. 'I'm sorry I wasn't more understanding, Chloe.'

'Is it still over between us?'

'Only if you want it to be.'

I just looked at him, wanting him to say some magic words.

'You've got me, Chloe. You can do whatever you like to me; you decide when to end it, when to re-start it. I can't resist you.'

'Why can't you resist me?'

'Because – because I think I'm in love with you.'

I didn't really believe him, but I put my arms around his neck and kissed him. We stayed like that, enjoying the kiss, for a long time, then drew back – I don't remember which of us pulled gently away first – and he drew me snug against him so my cheek rested on his shirt. I listened to his heartbeat, and soon it blended with the more familiar dull rumble of the waves that always lulled me to sleep in my bed.

When I awoke, the sun was painting the sea red, just beyond the cobweb shadow of the cliff. John stretched his arms back over the seat, yawned and smiled sleepily at me. 'Do you realise that we've slept together?'

I laughed.

'What are you going to tell your mother?'

I shrugged. 'I can say that we went to an all-night party.'

'With your new best friends?'

'With my frienemies.'

He left me at my gate and drove off to catch up with the rush-hour traffic; he had to be in court to defend a man who had flashed in a public park. 'What are you going to tell the judge?' I laughed. 'Oh, that the poor sad bastard was drunk – and lonely. He was just looking for a bit of attention – like those women in the pub.'

As I came in the door, Mummy was waiting for me, her face granite-like. 'I've been at an all-night party', I said, forcing myself to smile. 'John introduced me to all his frienemi – friends.'

'Your breakfast is on the table. Won't you be late for work?' She looked me up and down. 'Oh, don't answer. I don't believe you've got a job at all – unless you're on the game.'

I burst into tears and ran up the stairs. How could my mother say such a thing? I knew she didn't believe I was a prostitute – she knew I was with John, after all, and I'd introduced him – but it was the fact that she wanted to hurt me that I couldn't bear. I lay face-down on the quilt and sobbed. After a while, I heard her slam the front door and drive away.

She was probably going to see her solicitor; she always wore a severe trouser-suit and business-like make-up for meetings with him, as if she was trying to convince him that she was a client who deserved to be taken very seriously – and she was paranoid that he might think she was flirting with him if she wore a skirt. Mummy had always spoken scornfully of jilted wives who used every trick to get a good divorce deal. In fact, she had sneered at divorced and separated women in general – even Aunty Helen's ears would have burned if she'd heard the way Mummy had talked about her to Dad after Uncle Con left. 'She's turning into an old floozie', Mummy used to say. 'Going around with cleavage on display, as if that will get her a new man.'

With the house to myself, I felt calmer. I got up from the bed and took off my dress. It smelt slightly of John's aftershave and sweat, mingled with my eau de toilette. I wouldn't wash it until I'd got his scent on some other garment. I held it to my nose and breathed it, remembering how it had felt to sleep in his arms. I had never imagined sleeping in a car would be so pleasant.

I took a shower and rubbed body lotion all over, to keep my fake tan from peeling off. Then I looked at my body in the mirror. I took my hair out of the shower cap and it cascaded long and golden on my shoulders. I wondered what kind of plant I would be if I was a still life. Something sweet-smelling and dewy with a long stem...a daffodil with bright yellow petals.

I smiled, wondering why I had ever felt poor; now it no longer mattered that I would never be able to afford expensive clothes or a set of tooth veneers like my wealthy ex-friends. I no longer cared about silencing their taunts, or those of women like Caoimhe and

Gina whose sole aim seemed to be to look for other women's faults to draw attention away from their own – which were faultlines, great gaping chasms, destroying everything around them, leaving only wounds and simmering, melted rock.... And yet, something beautiful always grew in wounded ground; those women's cruelty had given birth to a kernel of understanding between John and me.

I climbed the attic stairs to put some still life into my painting; it definitely needed plants.

I painted an orchid first, wilting just slightly. I imagined it would begin to smell foul after a while. As I mixed oils to show the beautiful imperfections in the stalk and the moist petals with their drying tips, I noticed they were forming the face of my mother. It was probably just coincidence, but then I realised I had put Daryus beside her – his punky hair looked like one of those spiky plants from South America Mummy kept in the conservatory. Mira appeared as a red geranium; bold, brash and not very pretty when you looked at her closely – but you could see her appeal. They didn't actually have faces, but I had worked their features into the foliage, the colouring, the light and shade....

I dotted putrid-looking mushrooms and toadstools around the grass, and found they reminded of Caoimhe, Gina and the other over-ripe 'girls' I'd met the previous night. They were poisonous, with white undersides and sticky brown heads. Killer was a particularly obnoxious-looking puff-ball mushroom, shooting spores in all directions the way he had been spitting as he spoke. The other men were brown fungus, sticking in between the roots of a noble oak.

I paused, admiring my handiwork, not sure I liked it but knowing it meant something. I wanted to go on; I had a strong sense of another plant – could even smell its sap, which was sweet as liquid amber and yet tangy as damp, chopped pine; fleshy like a fresh orchid but with the delicate simplicity of cherry blossom. It was impossible to paint the petals because they seemed to be hidden in the bark of a strong but supple beech tree which was still smooth and just beginning to thicken to the shape of a man's throat. I painted it in deep browns with flickers of green light where the sun reflected off some leaves, way above, out of view. It was just a trunk with no branches – nothing except a beautiful, large, green stamen. As I finished it, I knew it was John.

I felt the colour rush to my cheeks. I wanted to paint myself as a daffodil before the mood passed but I just couldn't.

Then something told me I'd have to paint Veronique first. I tried to depict her as ivy, fungus like that living on the beech tree that was really John, then an insect crawling in the fissures of John's bark...but I couldn't; it didn't look right, and it hurt me to paint anything ugly on John. I decided to forget about her and just paint some more trees – see who they turned into. I painted a little copse around John, not recognising any humanity in them; they were just plants.

Then she emerged – as a tall, elegant elm, her huge eyes appearing as shadows in the leaves. Veronique was the most beautiful tree in the picture.

When I had finished painting, I realised that I had painted the whole group – the mushroom people and my floral family included – in miniature, in a bottom corner.

I found myself adding things all day, in between tea breaks. I painted Janet from (ex) work as a thick, tough stem with lots of thorns and no petals. Barry was a worm, wriggling among the mushroom ladies (they'd be just his type). Mr Wrightman Senior was a grumpy-looking woodlouse-beetle hybrid. My ex-colleagues appeared as earwigs, Tina's grandparents a pair of old thorn-bushes, her beautiful sister a caterpillar who, in a just world, would turn into a social butterfly – but would more likely be eaten first. Skoby and Wheeler, I painted as two black tulips – I must have been thinking of the Dublin slang for a chancer: 'A right tulip'.

Aunty Helen was a thistle, her husband – my Uncle Con – a pile of compost incongruously left at her base ('Con-post', I supposed it would be called; she was still receiving creditor's letters addressed to him).

Poo Anchorbottom was a disgusting flesh-eating plant. Her daughter Fanny and all my other ex-friends in the neighbourhood were little nettles.

In front of these, I painted two little buttercups, casting a cheerful yellow light up: Kay and Shay, the happy hairdressers who got on well with even the most arrogant customers.

Eleanor and Francesca Fitzwalton emerged afresh; this time I discovered them posing as a couple of wallflowers. They had no wall to lean against, so they were leaning on each other. Eleanor was multi-coloured, gaudy; Francesca a uniform purple. The cats, Eblana and Anna Livia, were prowling in the long grass close by.

Daddy appeared towards the end, but he was just a silvery snail's trail disappearing off the edge of the canvas.

I heard Mummy come in but decided to linger in the attic; I didn't want her to know I was still home. I looked at my watch; it was nearly five. The miniature scene at the corner of my painting had taken a whole day – but that was probably because I had taken so many breaks, letting the inspiration well up before continuing.

As often before, I wondered what compelled me to paint. Maybe it was because I had given up keeping a diary when I was fourteen years old; Mummy had read it and scolded me for calling her 'my social-climbing Mummy'. I wondered what she would have discovered if I'd kept a diary now – it was just as well I was channelling my thoughts into painting. Even if she recognised the people, she would think I was just painting them in a meaningless, abstract way, wouldn't she? Surely she couldn't read my secret thoughts from my painting?

I went downstairs when I smelt cooking; she had made pasta, which I loved. The aroma of basil mingled irresistibly with tomato.

But then I saw she was adding chicken to it. 'Mummy, you know I don't meat.'

'Chicken isn't meat.'

'Tell that to the chicken.'

I grabbed my coat and went down to the chipper to buy myself a take-away meal – so I could eat as I walked down by the harbour, which was the safest place for a girl walking alone at night as there were always plenty of fitness-walkers taking advantage of the fresh air. They stared as I ate chips on the harbour wall, and I heard a woman say: 'That girl must be having a blow-out. You can do that every so often if you're on a strict diet.' Bloody cheek of her, I thought; I was nineteen, naturally slim and had never needed to diet.

At least it was a warm evening – and it wasn't raining. I watched the fishermen load lobster pots onto their trawlers. They seemed so carefree, whistling and bantering. Their camaraderie was as pungent, simple and solid as the smell of brine, engine oil and rotting fish; there was nothing misleading about it.

That night, I dreamt about being surrounded by mushroom-women with putrid, rubbery fingers that stroked my arms and legs, as if trying to rub away my skin. They were chasing me into the River Liffey. I heard Eleanor scold me: 'Use the Irish name, Chloe – 'Liffeh'. It's spelt "L.I.F.E.". Life. You mustn't forget your native language, your roots, where you came from...your life ...life...'

Impressionism

Mummy had gone out when I got up the next morning, so I had a leisurely fruit-and-cereal breakfast alone, enjoying every bite. I used to think genetically modified seedless grapes were a crime against nature until my painting went all surreal. I had changed my whole perspective on life, and now I was free to do things I used to balk at; I was no longer a snob of any kind.

John called me on my mobile and asked me to meet him at lunchtime, for a picnic. He picked me up at the railway station and drove along the river, then in through the gates of Dublin's huge Phoenix Park. The boulevard that went through it was lined with summer people –
girls in floral dresses, men in T-shirts or just jeans, children frolicking, people walking their dogs. All bathed in a hazy sunshine and the scent of freshly-cut grass.

We parked on the grass beside the polo grounds and watched a match; the ponies moved fluidly, whirling as they turned. The sun reflected their shiny gold and silver coats, as if they were a shoal of fish. I looked across at the pavilion, where a band was playing, competing with the commentator's loud speaker and the rumbling murmur of people laughing and chatting, the tinkle of glasses. I wondered if any of Daddy's creditors were over there, watching the match and sipping bubbly.

'It's great that you can watch polo for free, isn't it?' I said.

'Yeah', John laughed. 'Sometimes Dublin is a good place to be poor in.'

'Has your uncle paid you yet?'

'Not everything he owes me for all those hours. But he says I'm spending too much time on the cases.' He shrugged, suddenly looking fed up, and I was sorry I had cast a cloud over his day.

'Have you tried to get a job in another firm?'

He sighed. 'I dropped my CV into lots. Most of them sent me polite letters saying they didn't need a new solicitor. Two of them gave me interviews but looked at me in a funny way when I explained I had spent three years in France, working for my wife's firm – and still didn't speak French fluently. Well, I wasn't going to lie about that; they'd catch me out sooner or later.

'And anyway I suppose they didn't want to take me on when I wasn't sure how long I was going to stay in Dublin.'

He must have read my eyes. 'Don't worry, Chloe. I'm not about to go away just yet. Not for a long time.'

'If you go away, will you take me with you?'

He didn't answer, just sighed and stroked my back.

Encouraged by the softening of his eyes, I said: 'I'll ask Mummy if you can move in with us – as a lodger. It would be a lot cheaper than renting that apartment.'

'Can I share your room?'

I laughed. 'Only when Mummy's out.'

He dropped me back to the railway station, ignoring the horn blowing and catcalls of motorists behind him as he gave me a slow kiss.

When I got off the train, I went for a walk along the coast road, then sunbathed in the cove. I went home around six, planning to tell Mummy I had gone to work, but knowing she wouldn't believe me – especially when she saw my sunburnt face and shoulders.

She was on the couch when I went in, sitting up straight, a piece of paper in her hand.

'Mummy?'

She looked up coldly.

'Are you all right, Mummy?'

'Since when have you cared about my welfare, Chloe?'

'Mummy –'

'Sit down, Chloe.'

Obediently, I sat down in the armchair opposite. I felt a gnawing in the pit of my stomach, the kind I used to feel when she and Daddy argued.

'Chloe, I've been using my credit card to buy groceries.'

Yes, I thought, if you counted designer handbags as groceries.

But Mummy had on her self-righteous face. 'We can't afford to live here, Chloe, in this big house, in this affluent neighbourhood, with no income.' Her face looked pale and haggard. I had never seen Mummy look so old. 'You're unemployed, Chloe.'

I looked down. There was no point in pretending any more.

'And I'm not going out to work, Chloe – not at my age. I couldn't cope with being told what to do. And I'm not going to clean houses for Poo Anchorbottom and her friends!' She thumped her fist on the coffee table. 'That bitch offered me a job this morning – as a charlady!'

'You're right not to work for her, Mummy; she's always left her cleaning lady short and that's why she's looking for a new one –'

'I've got no intention of working for her whether she pays me or not! She only offered it to me to humiliate me; they're all gossiping about us in this village –'

'Mummy –'

'Chloe, will you listen to me!' Her voice was high-pitched and edgy, and I realised she had reached the nadir of a bad hangover. 'My solicitor says he can't track down your father's money – and he wants his own fees. I'll have to sell our home!' She burst into tears and put her head in her hands. She was rocking back and forth, and I realised she was in despair.

I went over and sat beside her, and put my hand gently on her head but she brushed it away. 'Mummy, I've got an idea. Mummy, stop crying. Mummy, please listen to me, at least.'

She looked up, her eyes tearful but still cold.

'Mummy, why don't we take in lodgers? I mean, we've got five bedrooms and there are only the two of us –'

'I'd never let anyone sleep in Daryus's room!' she snapped.

'I didn't mean we had to let out all the rooms.' My brother's room was a shrine to the Prodigal Son; his electric guitar, keyboard and expensive drum kit, his posters, an old rugby ball.... Mummy would never throw them out as long as she had a son.

'Anyway', she was saying, 'I've made up my mind. I'm selling the house.'

So that was that. Mummy had even been to an estate agent and got them to plonk a 'For Sale' sign on the front lawn. I had been too dreamy to notice it as I came in, but now I gazed at it from my attic.

I cried as I looked around at the studio I loved so much. Now I'd never paint a masterpiece in it. There'd be no money to have windows set into the gables of the attic in the three-bed semi we'd be moving to. It would be a small attic, anyway; suitable only for insulation and Mummy's marriage memorabilia which was presently in a corner of the bedroom.

'I'm making a fresh start', she had said. 'I'm not having your father's clothes in my bedroom in the new house. There'll be just you, me and Daryus.' She was still deluding herself that Daryus would come back.

She even knew where to look for our new house: Clonbollard, where that pub, the Ramblin Roundabout was – where the taxi-driver had dropped me on the way to Brenda's hen party. A lower-middle-class no-man's land half-way between the city and the crime-ridden outer suburb where Brenda and Tina lived.

I wondered if I'd ever turn into one of those people I'd seen in that pub on the dual carriageway; grey-faced wage-slaves spending their lives in the smog. The place was haunted with the curses of a million commuters.

And now I was going to be buried alive there – unless I escaped now. There was no time to lose, I told myself; if I reached the point where I was living in Clonbollard, I'd never find the energy to travel to work every day. I needed a job now – so I could find somewhere to live.

It would have to be a compromise: a room in someone's flat or house, sharing a bathroom, kitchen and living room. I might even have to share with frienemies.

Then I thought of John, and wondered if he'd like to share a flat with me. Somewhere smaller and cheaper, with no cranky landlord.

He said yes. I'd been half-afraid he wouldn't, so I didn't tell him until that evening, after he had fed me oysters in Belgowan's best seafood restaurant and had earned my trust by ignoring the pouty waitress who was being just too attentive.

We seemed to glide out of the restaurant, like the besotted-looking couple in a Chagall print I had on my bedroom wall.

He drove along the coast road and pulled in beside the low wall above the cliff, and kissed me long and tenderly. 'We can do this all the time when we live together', I said, ending the kiss so I could rest my cheek on his shoulder. 'Somewhere like this would be perfect, by the sea, where we can go for swims.... It will have to have big windows to let in as much natural light as possible – I need that for painting.'

We got out and walked until we found a path that led to a cove, and I led him down the stone steps onto the rocky shore. The air was humid, carrying the urine scent of wild flowers and the burnt skin smell of scrub grass that clung to the cliff edge, then the sepulchral odour of damp earth where the cliffs met the rocks, and the oily, salty perfume of wet sand, crushed shells and brine. Everything was perspiring, breathing, touching. I felt a delicious thrill as I took off my sandals and stood on the cool sand.

John gently pulled the straps of my dress down and kissed first one nipple, then the other.

'John, ohh! Keep doing that...'

'John, I – I'm not ready to make love yet – '

'Shhh. Don't spoil it. Enjoy.'

'But John – ohhh.... John, I've never – '

He stopped teasing me, put his hands lightly on my shoulders, and looked at me with puppy eyes. I found myself blushing. 'I've never done it before.'

'Didn't you have a boyfriend?' he asked, his voice tender. 'The boy who took you to your debs? The one who went off with another girl?'

I shook my head. 'I never let him make love to me.'

John smiled. 'Maybe that's why he left you.'

I shrugged. 'He would have left me anyway; he was a bit of a jock. He de-virginised lots of girls in my school.'

John guffawed. 'De-virginised.'

'Well, you could hardly call it deflowering, the way they described it afterwards.'

'So why did you go to your debs with him of all people?'

'I couldn't find a boy I really liked. The more interesting ones seemed to go for older girls – girls in university. I had to ask someone and he was available.'

'That's a bit mercenary, Chloe. I'm surprised at you.' But he was laughing. 'It's like something a guy would do – date someone they didn't like rather than have nobody.'

'It's like having friends you don't like rather than be alone', I pointed out. 'Like boring Killer and those farmery-rugby men you drink with.'

He chortled. '*Touché.*'

'And frienemies', I added. 'Like their silly girlfriends. I used to have friends like that, right through school. I used to try to imagine they were nice people – but it was like eating food you don't like because everyone else says it's good, you know?'

He nodded. 'So you were in that frame of mind when you went to your debs with a boy you didn't like.' He smiled, and kissed my fingertips. 'I'm glad you're choosier now; at least I know you really want me.'

'I do – passionately.' I put my arms around his neck and pressed my body against his. I opened the buttons of his shirt to feel his skin against mine.

'Chloe', he said gently, pulling the straps of my dress up onto my shoulders. 'I'm not going to deflower you tonight.'

'But you have to', I said, suddenly wishing I hadn't stopped him
earlier.

'I will, I promise – if you'll still have me.' He smiled. 'Just not yet.'

Mummy was watching a late film when I got in, but she switched it off. 'I'm going to bed', she yawned. 'I might as well enjoy sleeping in my nice big bedroom while I can.'

'Mummy, I've an idea for you', I said. 'You don't have to move to Clonbollard.'

She looked at me warily.

'You can get one of those chic one-bedroomed apartments here in

Belgowan – with a sea-view.'

'Where would you and Daryus sleep?'

I smiled, barely able to contain my happiness. 'I'm going to live with John. And, well, Daryus won't be coming back – he's happy with Mira. You can save a lot of money if you buy a studio flat. Maybe you could live in a nicer location than Clonbollard.'

Mummy burst into tears. 'How could you be so cruel, Chloe?'

'Mummy, I – I....' My voice trailed off as she sobbed. Did she expect me to live with her forever? In a single bed in a poky little house, in a place whose only attraction was the dual carriageway passing it by?

'My Daryus will come back. I know he will. My son is the only one I can rely on.' She sat up and looked at me through eyes that looked like pebbles at the water's edge. 'Your Daddy can stay away forever, as far as I'm concerned. And you....' She looked me up and down and I wished I wasn't wearing my pretty summer dress; it seemed to betray the fact that I was living a carefree life. 'You can go wherever you want, Chloe. You don't care about this family.'

I collapsed on the carpet in tears and when I looked up she was gone and she'd turned the lights off. I sat on the floor in the moonlight until the house got cold.

Then I went upstairs to my attic and tried to sort out the strange mixture of hope and despair that was coursing through me, like the frantic brushstrokes of a mad painter. I looked at my painting, realising for the first time how totally absurd it looked; a stream-of-consciousness picture, done haphazardly and with total disrespect for technique. I had even tried to mix oil and watercolours – on the canvas.

Maybe it was just as well I was leaving this place; maybe I'd leave the painting here too.

I went to my room and lay in bed, unable to sleep, crying every so often as I remembered the way my mother had looked at me when she'd said it didn't matter to her where I went. It was my family who didn't care about me, not the other way around.

But when dawn flooded through my curtains, promising another beautiful August day, the tears ebbed and I rose lightly, throwing on my summer dress and looking forward to a new life – with John.

I spent the morning answering 'Staff Required' ads on shop windows. I couldn't face any more recruitment agency ladies who wanted to know about my last job and qualifications, and anyway I now realised that I never wanted to work in an office again – it was bad enough having to work in a boring job without being forced to sit in a room with the same group of people every day. At least in a shop there would be lots of strangers flowing in and out.

This time, I did my job-hunting in a large town up the coast, halfway between Belgowan and the city centre. It had a harbour and some old Georgian houses that had been converted into flats which were largely occupied by students, unemployed people and those on low wages. John and I could rent a place cheaply here, and still afford to go out...

There was something very romantic about the idea of being a fast-food waitress or a sales assistant, working among immigrants and part-timers, laughing every time people asked me what a clever girl was doing in a dead-end job, or told me I was pretty enough to be a model. They'd pity me for my lack of prospects, thinking I envied them their daily struggle up the money mountain. And at the end of my shift I'd go home to my equally laid-back lover, the lawyer who had given up his career for his wife and lost her too. I was in love with the kind of man my Daddy used to call a 'loser'.

And I was truly happy for the first time in my life, because I was free. I no longer needed wealth, as Daddy did, or the envy of other people, as Mummy did. My old neighbours could sneer all they like as I served them a take-away meal or scanned their groceries at the check-out.

My optimism buoyed me up for two hours, as I left my phone number in various outlets, laughing when a supermarket manager asked me for my CV.

'I'll drop it in later – but it's probably irrelevant to the job.' He was looking for people to pack bags at the check-out.

'It's just a formality', he said. 'If you've no experience, we'll train you.'

Then the staff supervisor of a fast-food café offered me an impromptu interview. I smiled, feeling sure she'd hire me instantly; after all, I had a good attitude.

She handed me a form to fill out. I couldn't remember the exact grades I'd got in my final exams at school, so I left those spaces blank, thinking it was better not to look over-qualified anyway; many of John's criminal clients were disillusioned underachievers with IQs too high for their jobs. I didn't even mention that I'd been to art college; it would hardly help me shovel French fries into a paper bag.

The supervisor sat down with a clipboard clutched to her chest and took the page from me, glancing at it to make sure I'd filled in my name and address. She looked at me, her eyes roaming from my hair to my denim dress and up to my eyes. I noticed her hair was greasy, scraped back into a severe ponytail to reveal unplucked eyebrows and a spotty forehead, and her lips were tight. She couldn't have been much older than I was, but she wore a middle-aged frown.

'The person we're looking for has to be a team player', she said.

I smiled and nodded.

She pointed a chipped fingernail at me and I noticed her hands were red and rough. 'Do you get on with people?'

'Well, if they're nice to me, I do', I laughed, thinking she was one of these 'hard tickets' whose belligerence was just a form of horseplay – I'd learned a lot from working with Tina, Natalie and the others in the office, and this girl had a similar accent. It was probably a working-class thing.

But she looked genuinely angry as she stabbed her biro onto her clipboard, drawing a deep line across something. She looked up, her eyes like flint. 'Thank you for coming in. We'll call you.'

The supermarket manager called my mobile just as I was about to go for coffee (to boost my morale as well as my energy). His personnel officer wanted me to come in for an interview, he said.

'Can we do it now? I'm only across the road.'

The personnel officer was on a minimum wage too, judging by her ill-fitting cut acrylic business suit. I was sure she had a plastic handbag. But I forced myself to smile at her; she grimaced back, showing teeth that badly needed an orthodontist.

She left me alone to fill out a blockbuster of an application form. I laughed at the question: 'Have you got a criminal record? If so, please give details.' There was a large space under that and I wondered if I should mention that my boyfriend defended shoplifters. Another beauty was: 'Please give details of all infectious diseases you have had.' I was tempted to write 'intolerance and poveritis'.

As I waited for her to return, I looked around her office. There was a little pile of those application forms, each with a passport photo stapled to the front. I flicked through them. The other aspiring bag-packers all looked younger than me – except the foreign ones whose names looked funny in English and whose nationalities I'd only ever heard on news bulletins about wars. I was sure I'd have great fun working here in this cosmopolitan environment, learning the languages of people who'd escaped from terrible situations and still knew how to smile.

The woman entered and I hastily put my application form on top of the pile, blushing. 'I thought you'd want me to leave it here', I said.

'Give it to me', she snapped. 'I decide where everything goes in my own office.'

We sat in silence as she read my form. I wondered if she was reading slowly on purpose, then thought surely not, as she had the look of a person with a busy, high-stress job. I was glad I wasn't going in for her position.

'I notice you've got a lot of hobbies', she said. Out of boredom, I had filled in the space devoted to 'leisure activities'. She tapped her fingernail on the desk as she read them out: 'Painting, reading, swimming, working out in the gym –'

'Well, I'll probably have to give up the gym', I laughed. 'I can't afford to renew my membership.'

'…. You've got certificates in scuba diving, dinghy sailing and showjumping, you used to be a member of a tennis club, you like travelling, eating out. You really are a busy girl, aren't you? Like, *busy* busy!'

'Well, I think life is for living.'

'Mm-hmm.' She leaned her chin on her knuckles and stared at me with clinical interest. I supposed personnel officers found people very interesting.

I forced a smile. 'I just want a steady job with regular hours and a reasonable salary, so I can help my boyfriend with the rent and have some money left over to enjoy life.' I was suddenly proud of myself for having such a mature attitude.

She snorted. 'So, let me get this straight. You want this job to subsidise your – ahem – leisure time activities.' She said it as if it was something illegal – I might as well have said I wanted to use the shop as a base for drug dealing.

But I gave her the benefit of the doubt; maybe she was just playing hardball because it was part of her job to weed out insincere people. I looked her in the eye, knowing I had honesty on my side – and relieved that I was no longer expected to be ambitious. 'Yes', I said. 'I don't want a job I have to think about.' I saw her stiffen, so I clarified. 'I want something therapeutic, because I use my brain for the other things –painting, being with my boyfriend.' I laughed. 'Well, you know.' Surely she could understand that?

She suddenly smirked. 'Thank you for coming in, but you're really not what we're looking for. We want people who care about their work.'

She was laughing as she opened the door of her poky little office to let me out. I realised she had thought I was crazy – but surely she was even crazier if she believed anyone would actually care about a job packing groceries. But then I noticed the plaque on her door: 'Human resources', it said. How could I have expected any kind of humanity from someone whose job was to treat people as a commodity to be mined and exploited?

A glance at the check-outs convinced me that I was lucky not to have got the job. A supervisor in a nylon uniform was ticking off a woman about Mummy's age, wagging her finger and warning her: 'If you're late back from your coffee break ever again, I'm firing you.'

'But I was only ten minutes late.'

'The break *was* ten minutes! And don't back-answer me or I'll report you to the manager for insubordination!'

I went for one more McJob interview, holding back the tide of disillusionment until yet another minimum-wage manageress looked me up and down with beady eyes and asked me: 'Have you got any questions about the job?'

I smiled sweetly and returned her scrutiny. 'Would I have to wear that uniform?'

Then I went to the Job Centre and grabbed a handful of leaflets about various careers. Maybe I could find a middle-ground; a job with bosses who would treat me with respect because they'd assume I was doing it as part of a 'career path'; I could leave as soon as they started making unreasonable demands. I stuffed them into my backpack and went into a park which had a hill overlooking Dublin Bay. I sat on the grass, enjoying the afternoon sun, and flicked lazily through the leaflets.

'Be anything you want', they said in bold, brightly-coloured print. I supposed that was just career guidance-speak for 'The world is your oyster', which I'd heard many times from my schoolteachers, my lecturers in the art college, well-meaning people at parties, model agency scouts, strangers on the street who'd seen something in my face and felt compelled to tell me I was lucky.... Even my Daddy had said it, when I was a little girl. Maybe they all believed I was so fortunate – so privileged – that I didn't need any help, just a reminder to use those gifts I took for granted.

At least the career guidance leaflets gave some hard-nosed advice: how to open that oyster. I wondered which one I'd be better suited to. I liked them all, really. Be a fashion designer? A photographer? A veterinarian? A lawyer?

The courses were free for people on Social Welfare, according to the leaflets. I wondered what the people in the dole office would say if I gave my address. Surely they wouldn't believe me when I told them that Daddy really had left me with nothing. Maybe they'd even say I was ripping off the taxpayer, just as he had done when he'd run away and left the Revenue Commissioners fuming.

Well, I thought indignantly, I'd already had to live with the shame; I might as well live up to it.

Then I reminded myself that I wouldn't be living in the five-bedroomed mansion of rich parents, in Dublin's most exclusive neighbourhood. I'd be in a tiny flat with John, living the life of the underprivileged; I'd have the right to ask for help.

John could draw the dole, too; it would be better than begging his miser of an uncle to pay him the salary he was due. John and I would have a wonderful life together as State-supported students; he could study for another career – a more creative one.

Maybe we could both do an English language teachers' course. That only required a few months of training. Then we could fly away somewhere foreign – somewhere warm, where we could wear light clothes...a humble little fishing village in South America, say, where we could live cheaply on fruit, veg and fresh seafood. Even the poor people looked healthy in Latin America, with good teeth and golden skin, the girls all fine-boned and graceful like George Morton's wife – at least, that's how they always seemed to be in the 'off-the-beaten-track' travelogues I liked to watch on TV. And if John so much as glanced at one of those beauties, I could always switch my affections to one of the muscular men with moustaches and tight T-shirts who always seemed to be working the fishing nets in those same travelogues. But John would stay faithful to me, I knew – and the ambitious local beauties would lose interest in him as soon as they discovered the handsome foreigner was not a millionaire, coming to take them away from their simple poverty.

There would be no 'Ladies Who Lunch' or 'Yummy Mummies' in my new home; the mothers would treat their children like children, not fashion accessories, and anyway there wouldn't be any designer mother-and-baby shops. And the old women would be motherly in a warm, Latin way, like those Italian ladies who had comforted me in the National Gallery.

There would be no art gallery, of course, in our simple little South American fishing village. But I could paint to my heart's content (even outdoors, in the sun). Anyway, I'd make sure to choose a mainland place, with good rail connections, so we could visit a big city whenever we longed for some sophisticated culture – or just wanted to lose ourselves among the crowds, to enjoy being 'Nobodies'.

I was so tired of life in a small, isolated community. My neighbourhood in Belgowan was a kind of island – a fortress one, shut off to outsiders by the forbidding house prices. The whole of Ireland was an island, not just physically but culturally; no one understood you if you reserved the right to be vain about your appearance or didn't want to spend an evening with 'frienemies' – or even if you merely wanted to drink orange juice in a pub.

I gazed down the hill at the railway tracks leading into the city, then across the calm water at a boat ferrying day-trippers to one of Dublin Bay's little uninhabited islands; they were carrying picnic hampers. I wondered how my Daddy was finding life on his Caribbean island, a haven for pirates and now tax evaders. It was strange, the way Irish people sought out even smaller islands than their own, for holidays, daytrips – or great escapes.

My whole life seemed to have been divided into a series of islands lately; islands of acquaintances who never came into contact with each other...except on that canvas in my attic. It was only in my painting that I could imagine Tina from the office standing beside Poo Anchorbottom, or Aunty Helen chatting away with Skoby, or old Wrightman with Eleanor and Francesca Fitzwalton perched on each of his pin-striped knees.... In real life, they could only come into contact with each other as professional and client, employer and employee. I could imagine Tina's granny as Poo's cleaning lady but I couldn't see them going on holidays together. I could even, theoretically, imagine Janet with her arm around Brenda's Clint – but only if she was calming him down in court after he'd been arrested for overzealously evicting revellers from a night club and was threatening to flatten the judge's face for him...

Kay Duffy the hairdresser had told me she often wondered why her clients invited her to parties, only to introduce her as 'the darling girl who does my hair so beautifully'. Kay would never be in a position to snog Mr Anchorbottom (even if she wanted to) or wear a more expensive dress than his wife – but she did in my painting.

In real life, I was the only person I knew who seemed to be able to island-hop, getting deeply involved with everyone – one way or another. And yet each of these islands closed me in every time I landed. Maybe John had hit on the truth when he had flirtingly called me a mermaid; I felt happier floating around than walking on hard earth.

I left the park when it began to drizzle. I liked the feeling on my skin, but I didn't want to catch cold.

It would be so much nicer in South America.

John called me as I sat on the train, going home. I had been about to call him; I was bursting to tell him about my plans for us. But he had something to tell me first: 'Wear something smart; I'm taking you to a very nice restaurant, to celebrate', he said.

'Celebrate what?' I asked, thinking he was going to say something flirtatious or witty.
'I've got a new job.'

One of the solicitors' firms had offered him a position, he told me as he handfed me oysters. 'I still have to negotiate the contract, of course, but I know they'll pay me more than my uncle does. I can afford a luxury flat. We can live on restaurant food – and you won't have to work. How would you like to be a kept woman, Chloe?'

He grinned at me and I laughed. 'I'd love that', I said. 'But you'd have to let me imagine I was independent.'

'I could buy your paintings.'

'How do you know you'd like them?'

'I mightn't, but I'd pretend to. When are you going to show me them?'

Drawn from the heart

Mummy was going to stay overnight with Helen – to grumble about having to sell the house, I supposed – so I brought John home. 'She'd throw a fit if she knew you were going to sleep in my room', I said, as we came into the hall.

'Sleep?' He laughed. Then his eyes darkened and I felt myself melt into his arms. 'I'll be gentle, the first time we make love. I promise.'

'I know, John.' But I drew back from him; I was so afraid our lovemaking would be a disaster. After all, I'd had no experience. 'Let me show you my paintings first.'

I led him slowly up the stairs, stumbling on a pair of shoes. John caught me and laughed, picking up the shoes. 'These look fit for Cinderella', he said.

'They're Mummy's – and so are all those others.' I pointed to the Jimmy Choos and Manolos strewn all over the stairs.

'I knew it; your Mummy is Imelda Marcos.'

'She went wild on shoes after she ran out of handbags to buy – the designers can't produce them fast enough for her.'

'That bad, hmm? Your mother sounds depressed to me.' I looked around to where he was standing, on the step below me, and his eyes were serious. 'Chloe, is there any way you can get your Mummy to go for counselling?'

'She gets all the advice she wants from Aunty Helen – who's divorced.'

I saw him flinch so I walked up a few more stairs, saying lightly: 'Let's not talk about divorced or separated people now, John. It's too depressing – and anyway I can't do anything to help my Mummy.'

'Maybe not now, but she's going to turn to you sometime, Chloe.'

'I – I'll always be there for her. Of course I will. Now, do you want to see my paintings?'

He held my hips as I walked ahead of him onto the landing. 'Is that your room?'

'Yes. How did you guess?'

'The name on the door kind of gave me a clue.' He laughed and pushed me towards it. I'd forgotten my bedroom door had a ceramic plaque with 'Chloe's room' spelt in bougainvillea letters. Now it looked kitsch and a bit, well, childish.

'Well, can I go inside your room?'

'OK.' I suddenly felt shy as I opened the door and John walked in, inhaling deeply, looking out of place in my floral-print bedroom. 'I like the wallpaper. Pink really is your colour, isn't it?' He smiled, picking up Oscar, my big pink teddy, and playfully kissing his nose. He opened my rosewood wardrobe and let out a chuckle.

'What's so funny?'

'How can you find anything in here? It's stuffed!'

'Most of the clothes are last season's. I bought them in Italy and France.' I stopped, remembering my last shopping spree in Nice. 'Didn't Veronique have a full wardrobe?'

'Of course – actually, she had one of those walk-in ones. It's just that I reckoned she had built it up over years. You're only nineteen and you've collected all this.'

'You don't know very much about women, for someone who's been married. Actually, I throw out my old clothes every year – I give them to charity.'

'Good girl.' He laughed.

'I suppose I'll have to hang on to them from now on.'

He chortled. 'No. I won't have you complaining about lack of clothes. When you're my kept woman, I'll keep you in frocks – on one condition.' He lifted my chin with his finger. I smiled, knowing what he was going to say. 'You have to take them off for me.'

I wriggled away, suddenly feeling shy again – I didn't know why, but John brought out mixed feelings in me.

When I looked around at him again, he was fingering my mahogany dressing table and the matching chair with its pink cushion. He stood in front of my full-length mirror and smiled at me. 'Come here', he said, putting his hand out behind him. I took it and he drew my hand around to his hard, flat stomach. I looked over his shoulder at us in the mirror. He was looking at my bed. The pink duvet-cover was all rumpled because I hadn't ironed it; Mummy used to have a daily help who did that sort of thing but now we couldn't afford to pay her.

'Come on up to the attic and see my paintings', I said, leading him by the hand.

'I'm enjoying the view already', he said, and I remembered I was wearing a short dress. I scurried up and waited for him.

'It's not a masterpiece, but, well, it's my hobby.' There, I'd called it a hobby! I was turning into my Mummy. Maybe it was for the best that I was no longer taking my art seriously; if I had been really good, my art lecturers would have stopped calling me 'promising' and actually got me an exhibition. The college would have offered me a scholarship and I wouldn't be facing life as a kept woman – no matter how rosy that sounded, it wasn't the life I had dreamed of when I was a little girl...yet, now, it was all I wanted.

John was gazing at the painting on the easel with what looked like amusement. He stood back, then went close and leaned down to look at the miniature mushroom ladies. He chuckled. 'Amazing.'

'I was only messing.' I hoped he didn't think I was crazy.

'That looks like Killer's awful girlfriend – what's her name?'

'Gina.' I found myself laughing.

'It's funny, she *does* remind me of a mushroom – one of those sickly-sweet-smelling ones that are supposed to be poisonous. And who's the bum sticking out of a flowerpot?'

'Oh, that's one of Mummy's friends – ex-friends.'

He raised his finger in the air. 'It's that Poo lady, isn't it? The socialite you and the girls were laughing about in the office – I tore that page out of the magazine, you know. I kept it as a souvenir of you.'

'I'm glad you recognised her bum', I said, trying to sound stage-jealous.

'Oh, I've never seen it but I can imagine it. Don't tell me she flashes her buttocks as well?'

'No, but she will as soon as she gets them lifted. She's such a show-off, she'll probably join the ladies' rugby team and moon out of the windows of coaches.'

He recognised the Fitzwalton sisters immediately. 'But Chloe why did you put my uncle in between them?' I shrugged; I really didn't know. 'And there he is again – with his arm around another old lady.'

'That's Tina's granny – Tina from the office.'

'Ah.' He looked round at me and smiled. 'How do you come up with these ideas?'

I shrugged again. 'I don't decide what to paint; I just feel compelled to put these people together, turn them into things they're not, distort them a bit. I don't know why.'

'But don't you see, you're not distorting them, really? That worm is Berry to the core – the man *is* a worm. And Janet there – she is a thorny old stem with no petals. And there's my uncle again – as some kind of beetle.'

'I'm amazed you recognise the faces. I mean, I didn't deliberately make the shadows of the branches into facial features. I didn't even set out to paint those people – it just happened.'

'When you were feeling sad, or angry, or confused, right?'

'Yes. So you really understand.' Well, he didn't look as if he was taking the mickey; he was scrutinising the painting from different angles, moving back and forward, side to side, standing up and lowering himself to his knees.

'You see, Chloe, I can see the faces from certain angles and distances.' He let out a little gasp. 'That's Veronique, isn't it? As a tree?'

I felt embarrassed. 'Yes, but John, it's only figurative –'

'Don't apologise. I'm sure she'd love it. She is like a tree, you know – a supple tree like this one, strong, able to bend in the wind....'

'What do you think of Clint?' I was anxious to get off the subject of Veronique.

'Clint?'

I pointed to a large beetle-like figure; its head looked like a motorbike helmet. 'Brenda's boyfriend – Brenda from the office?'

'Oh, Brenda the receptionist. She married that guy, you know. She's just back from her honeymoon.'

I suddenly felt guilty about having deliberately missed the wedding. Brenda and the other girls hadn't been so bad – their teasing hadn't been half as cruel as John's friends' girlfriends'.

John was still looking at the painting. 'And that's your dog, I suppose: Scarlet O'Hara?'

'Oh, yes.'

'You just painted her as she was – she was an Irish setter, wasn't she?'

'Yes. I – well, I see her exactly as she looked. She was a dog – a bitch – well, I mean she was my best friend.' I felt guilty for laughing about her, but told myself Scarlet wouldn't mind. Putting her in the painting wasn't as good as having her with me, but it was the next best thing.

'You've captured the essence of people in this, haven't you?'

'Well, I suppose I've captured the impression they leave on me.'

'Not just on you – on me, too.' He gazed from one figure to the other. 'But I don't see you in it.'

'Oh, I don't know why, but I've never felt the urge to paint myself. Maybe I can't.'

'Maybe you're in every one of these people – well, your representations of them.'

'You're saying I cannibalised them?' I laughed. 'The artist as parasite –'

'As a kind of vampire.' He chortled. 'Aren't you worried about where all this will end?'

'Maybe I'll turn into something really hideous – like those personnel people who call their job "Human Resources".'

'Yuck. I'd prefer you as a vampire.'

'John', I said suddenly, 'do you believe in ghosts?'

He cupped his hand over his mouth as if to hide a guffaw. 'Well, I keep an open mind on the supernatural.'

'You know the way you can watch someone in a film, even if the actor is dead?'

'Ye-es.' He was smiling at me now, as if he thought I was telling him a joke and he was waiting for the punchline.

'So you agree that a person's image can be left behind for us to see, even after the person is dead?'

He laughed. 'Yes, of course. But, Chloe, we're talking about an image, captured on celluloid, video, a computer microchip –'

'Or the air – the natural atmosphere – or the walls of a house. Maybe there are photographic chemicals floating around that occur naturally, and we haven't discovered them yet.'

'Mm-hmm.' He was still grinning.

'And not just image – sound, too, or scents, or even thoughts....' I realised he was shaking with laughter. 'John, you don't have to believe it. It's just a theory I have. Maybe I'm wrong. But, look, why can't it be true?'

He was still laughing, but he stood up straight. 'Sorry, Chloe. I'm sure your theory is very good.'

'John, have you ever seen a Renaissance painting and wondered if those eyes gazing at you are the ghost –'

'Of the person who sat for it? Oh, so my passport photograph is my ghost too...and my wedding photographs....' He was laughing again.

'Not necessarily the ghost of an actual person – maybe the artist just captured something of himself in the painting, and it's the ghost of a thought, a feeling. I mean, you've seen the Caravaggio painting in the National Gallery, haven't you? *The Taking of Christ?*'

He nodded.

'Well, he seems to have captured his own fear and indignation in that – Caravaggio knew exactly what it felt like to be arrested. He captured the ghost of his fear in the way the soldiers' hands are grabbing Jesus, in the movement of their shoulders, their torsos, you know? I imagine the police who arrested Caravaggio also kicked his shins; I know it, actually – by the expression on the faces of the soldiers in the painting.'

John nodded, smiling, as if humouring a babbling toddler or a much-loved aunt with Alzheimer's. But I was determined to make him understand. 'John, those soldiers' faces are the ghost of Caravaggio's indignation – at have being arrested himself.'

'Why was he arrested?' John sniggered. 'He must have done something bad. Didn't he murder someone? I heard he painted with his victim's blood.'

'He was a bit of a thug, I suppose.'

'Like some of my clients! Skoby, for instance – maybe he'll paint a masterpiece someday.' He chuckled and kissed my forehead (patronisingly I thought). 'Chloe, what a funny creature you are. You've got a wild imagination.'

124

'Well, you liked my imagination when you were looking at my painting', I said, feeling hurt.

'Oh, I did. And I do see your point about ghosts and all that – well, I haven't got a better theory.' He sniggered. 'So would you say Caravaggio was in a moral frame of mind when he painted *The Taking of Christ*?'

'Now you sound as if you're cross-examining a witness', I laughed. 'Actually, I still think it's a moral painting, even if Caravaggio was just using it as a medium for his own bitterness at having been arrested.'

'OK, explain this theory and I'll try to get it. How can a moral painting be painted with, eh, base intentions?'

'Well, the act of painting it obviously made him think about the greater injustice that was done to Jesus. It must have done – Jesus looks so abandoned in it. I *know* Caravaggio felt that loneliness.'

John nodded, still smiling but no longer laughing.

'And also it shows that good always triumphs over evil in the end.'

'Go on.' His tone of voice wasn't ironic.

'Well, the act of painting brought out his moral side. How else could he have created something so – so *good*? And it survived long after the bad things had happened to him – and to Jesus, of course.' I was aware that I sounded a bit childish, yet John was looking at me with a serious expression now. 'It survived for hundreds of years, John. The way a plant survives even if you kill it – it just rots into the ground and reincarnates itself. Just the way an act of cruelty brings out the kindness in people who witness it. And understanding is born of puzzlement – the more you think about something that you find incomprehensible, the more you learn.'

'And the more mysterious someone is, the more you want to know about them', John said, kissing my hand.

'But only if they're mysterious in an interesting way', I said. 'I mean, not like those crazy women – those girlfriends of your friends.'

He laughed. 'Oh, I couldn't be interested in them if I tried. Not even Gina, the femme fatale.'

'The *faux* femme fatale.' I suddenly felt silly and childish; why had I even mentioned John's friends' girlfriends? Now he might think I was jealous – even though I wasn't.

'Where am I in all of this?' John was asking now, looking at the painting again.

'Well, if you don't recognise yourself, I'm not going to tell you', I said.

But he really didn't, and eventually I pointed out his many manifestations in oils and watercolours. He chuckled when he realised I had painted him as a beech tree. 'You gave me a stamen, too! And it's huge! I hope I don't disappoint you tonight.' He drew me into his arms and kissed my lips, looked at me with amused and yet lustful eyes, then gave me another little peck, and then he took my face in his hands and pressed his mouth against mine, and gave me a deep kiss that made my legs go from under me. We fell on the floor, laughing, and resumed the kiss.

We rolled and knocked over one of my older paintings, which I'd framed and then left, propped against a table-leg; forgotten. 'Oh, that's something I did a few months ago', I said, getting up to put it on top of the table. It was an oil painting of my parents and Daryus; I had done it before Daddy left, and never had a chance to show it to him.

'It's totally different to the other one, isn't it?'

'I fancied myself as a classical artist – well, neo-classical.'

'It's excellent. And so is this.' He gazed at another small picture of my beloved Scarlet, scampering on a hill, looking like a dog in a nineteenth-century hunting print. 'Chloe, you seem to have artistic schizophrenia.' He chuckled.

'I don't know what brought it on', I laughed. 'I just stopped painting for a while and then, when I went back to it – oh!' I stopped laughing, because I remembered the period when I didn't want to paint. I felt a tear roll down my cheek.

'Chloe, what's the matter?' His voice was tender, his eyes melting.

'John, I stopped painting when Scarlet died – around the time Daddy left.'

He comforted me in his arms, leaning back against the table. Then he kissed the top of my head. 'We don't have to make love tonight, Chloe. I'll just hold you and we'll cuddle.'

'John.' I looked up at him and stroked his cheek, which felt rough; he needed a shave. 'I – I want to make love. Tonight. In my bed.'

He made love the way a sculptor moulds clay, teasing his subject out of the block of earth that traps it. He used my bed as a last, kneeding me onto it; then, when I could bear it no longer and realised that he couldn't either, he got up, fished a packet out of his trousers which he'd left on my chair, and took out a condom. I lay there, feeling very shy and at the same time bold, as he put it on. He looked up, bashful faced himself, and said in a voice that was intended to sound flippant but was deep and husky with lust: 'I'm sorry it's not green – the stamen in your painting, you know?'

I felt only pleasure. All my fear evaporated as I realised that those girls in school had been wrong; 'the first time' wasn't painful for every girl. 'John', I whimpered, wondering why I didn't feel the need to scream or moan the way women did in films. I was sure I sounded like a hungry puppy, not an excited lover, and yet the sensations coursing through my body were more intense than anything I had ever experienced. 'John-John-oh Johnnnn....I love you...John....'

'Veronique.'

I felt my heart curl up and weep. I tried not to whimper 'John' again but it came out anyway; my body was betraying me. I knew I should have let him feel guilty, showed some anger at the mention of her name...but I was full of John and I could feel only love....

And now he was looking at me as if he hadn't said her name. I felt my love swell and flood me, enveloping the two of us in a cocoon. Not even the ghost of Veronique in my bedroom could come between John and me.

Then he said: 'Oh, Chloe! I'm finished! Finished!' He stopped thrusting and suddenly all the hollowness inside me was filled.

'John! John!'

We seemed to collapse together, and our limbs went all loose. I felt the weight of his body but it was a pleasant burden. He was breathing heavily, his sweat running in rivers from the hairs on his chest onto me. He rolled to one side and we lay facing each other, his hand resting lightly on my waist. 'Chloe, that was amazing.' He drew me to him and kissed my lips, gently. His eyes were dark, the pupils seeming to fill the irises. 'Chloe.' He swallowed and smiled. He looked almost childlike now. 'Chloe, I think I love you.'

'I love you too, John.' Now why had I said that? I still wasn't sure what it was that I was feeling.

He looked down at my body. 'How beautiful you are.' He caressed my hip. 'Your skin is so soft.' He kissed my neck. 'I'm sorry I said Veronique. It was just a reflex action. I really was thinking of you.'

We woke up lazily, his chest against my back, my buttocks snug against him. The sun was streaming in through the petal-printed curtains. I felt him stir and I stretched back my arms, luxuriously. I turned round to face him; he had closed his eyes again but the lids were flickering and his lips were smiling just a little. I was sure he was pretending to be asleep – which was fine by me, as I wanted to look at him in private. I felt as if I was admiring a painting. He looked sweet, loveable, his hair ruffled and damp with sweat, a definite shadow on the lower part of his face now. I traced his fine, straight nose – almost too pretty to be a man's – and the strong line of his jaw. He reminded me of a picture from a storybook I still kept from when I was a little girl – the prince who had rescued the Little Mermaid. Only he was a grown-up version. Tiny flecks of sunlight dappled his face, like the markings on a particularly pretty fish I had seen while diving in the Caribbean. His rather long eyelashes fluttered and he opened his dark eyes, smiling at me.

'Would you like breakfast in bed?' I asked him.
'Are you trying to make me feel like an oldfashioned man?'
'No – just a kept man.'
He laughed. 'Will you wear an apron?'
'If that turns you on.'
'With nothing else?'
'OK.'

I found some stale croissants in the bread basket, debated whether to heat them up, then decided to put them out in the garden for the birds. I didn't finish breaking them into crumbs: I had just stepped out when I realised I was wearing only an apron.

'I'm sure the neighbours saw me', I said, as I handed him a bowl of cornflakes. 'They're an elderly couple, very strait-laced.'

He laughed. 'They'll have plenty to gossip about at the Neighbourhood Watch meetings.'

After we'd finished our spartan breakfast (Mummy hadn't even got in coffee) we made love again, tenderly, then I glanced at the clock. 'It's half eleven, John. Mummy will be home from Aunty Helen's any minute.'

John was going out the door just as Mummy came in. 'John just dropped in for coffee', I said.

'Hello, Mrs O'Doolahan', he said with a bashful smile. 'I was just visiting Chloe.'

'I know you were', she said tartly. Then she laughed. 'Nice of you to bring coffee. I keep forgetting to buy it. Oh, get away with you!'

She went in, leaving me to kiss John goodbye. 'Your Mummy is really nice', he said. 'Look after her.'

'I wish I could clone myself and leave the copy with her, so I could be free.'

He laughed. 'When we get that flat, we must have her over for meals.'

'But not all the time.'

'Chloe, she's your Mummy! Don't you want to mix with your own family?'

'Right now, I just want to be with you.'

'You will be with me – all the time.' He kissed me again, then got into his car.

Daubed in oils

John had already resigned from Wrightman, Wrightman & Wrightman, and was due to sign the contract with his new employers the following week. But he still had some cases to resolve. 'I'll be glad to be rid of these clients', he told me as we had lunch in a very expensive city centre restaurant. 'I'm sick of drafting wills for old farts who'll probably outlive their grandchildren, they're so tenacious. And Skoby has absolutely no sense of shame – it's embarrassing, pleading leniency for a guy who thinks of prison as a Chamber of Commerce.'

'What did your uncle say when you said you were leaving?'

'He huffed and puffed and cleared his throat, threatened to cut me out of his will – the usual. But he's asked me to a party next Friday. It's his silver wedding anniversary.'

'Are you going to go?'

'Yeah. I can't let down Aunty Maeve. I suppose that's why he had to invite me – I'm still her favourite nephew, anyway.' He leaned over and took my hand. 'I want you to come with me.'

'Are you sure? I mean, he's not going to be happy if the person he fired just a few weeks ago turns up at a family gathering.'

'I don't care about his happiness. He was horrible to you. Anyway, he won't be nasty to you in front of Aunty Maeve. And I'm sure she'll love you. She thought the world of ....' His voice trailed off and he looked embarrassed. 'Oh, shit, Chloe, I didn't mean it to sound like that.'

'It's OK. She liked Veronique, right?'

'Yeah.'

'And she won't approve of you bringing Veronique's replacement to visit.'

'You make yourself sound like a new car.' He laughed and kissed my knuckles. 'Look, I know this is going to be a big family scandal, but I have to knock it on the head. Veronique and I are getting divorced, it's our decision, and I'm going to be with you. My family will have to accept it. And the best way to make that clear is to introduce you to everyone together.'

'Will anyone from the office be there?'

'Well, Janet will be there – she's my second cousin, on Aunty Maeve's side of the family. And Barry– sorry about that, but his father was Uncle Patrick's favourite brother, which is the only reason Barry has a partnership in the firm. Sandra and Brenda and the others certainly aren't invited!' He laughed and mimicked their accent: 'Give us a borrill of dat bubbilly stuff, Mr Wrightman – or can we call you Patrick?'

'John, I didn't know you were a snob.'

'Well, talk about the pot calling the kettle blackarse! You were a right little snob yourself, only a few weeks ago. Anyway, if I were a snob, why would I have taken a job defending gougers like Skoby?'

'To feel superior?' But I found myself laughing with him.

129

'I won't be defending anyone in my new job; it's exclusively litigation. No-win-no-fee stuff – hey, I might even come across Skoby if he has a nasty fall staggering out of his local pub, or slips on a patch of grease in the chipper, gets manhandled by an over-enthusiastic nightclub bouncer, that sort of thing.'

'You might end up prosecuting Brenda's husband, then.'

'Clint? Ah, no. If I come up against him, I'll pass the case onto someone else. He looks as if he could do some GBH.'

The Wrightmans lived in a large farmhouse in the countryside north of Dublin. It had a long, curved drive with stud-railing on either side. I could smell the creosote on the wood in the humid heat of the summer evening, and I couldn't suppress a squeal as an exquisite thoroughbred colt paced our car along the fence, followed by a graceful broodmare. I noticed other thoroughbreds across the paddock. John stopped the car and I leapt over the door; horseriding was one of the things I missed most about my old life. The foal whickered and nuzzled my outstretched hand, then gobbled my fingers, trying to bite them with his gums. His mother butted him away gently, keeping a wary eye on me. I patted her and she seemed mollified.

'Your people are wealthier than my Daddy was', I said. 'I didn't know your uncle made so much from writing a few pensioners' wills and house contracts.'

John smiled. 'Aunty Maeve is the one with the money. Her family own a lot of land.'

We got back in the car and drove up to the gravel patch in front of the house, where a collection of Mercs and BMWs sat like wealthy parents at a school awards ceremony; among them, John's sports car looked like the mini-skirted mum in that old country'n'western song Daddy used to play in the car in his salesman days.

The front door was open and I heard the roar of dignified laughter. I felt a quiver in my tummy; it reminded me of evenings with the Anchorbottoms. Any moment now, I thought, a girl my age with a bland, well-bred, well-fed face will walk carefully down the steps in an expensive frock and bray: 'Chloeeee, you poor thing, you look absolutely freeee-zing in that little dress.' There was always a Fanny Anchorbottom at parties like this – and a posse of tight-faced mothers on hand to manoeuvre me away from the most eligible man.

John was squeezing my waist. 'You look amazing. Don't be nervous. I'm sure Aunty Maeve will love you – and if she doesn't, she's no longer my favourite aunt.'

Just then a petite lady with short blond hair and a knee-length black dress appeared in the doorway. 'John, how lovely to see you', she said. Her voice was like rich honey; this was a lady who had never felt the need to coo or bray.

'Aunty Maeve', John said, bending down to kiss her on both cheeks. 'This is my girlfriend, Chloe.'

She flinched just slightly at the mention of the word girlfriend, but recovered her composure enough to put on a charming smile and draw me down by the hands to plant a scented kiss on my left cheek. 'Do come in, Chloe. You look as if you walked straight off the cover of a magazine.'

I looked back at John, he winked and I let Maeve lead me by the hand into a large drawingroom with a crystal chandelier in the middle, blue-and-gold Regency-style furniture and some abstract paintings that looked as if they belonged in offices (I reckoned Mr Wrightman had got them off his tax). The room was spacious enough not to be overpowered by the vivid red walls and abundance of people in black. There were lots of subtle perfumes and well-modulated voices reeling off the names of the top ten restaurants, the latest art-house movies and those books which had recently been reviewed in the boring broadsheets; people whose minds only knew what was fashionable to know.

Maeve led me around the room, as if showing a prize filly at auction, murmuring introductions before passing on to the next grouplet. They all appeared to be clones; the men mostly pin-striped, the women like a flock of crows in dresses designed to blend in at any social occasion. They ran their eyes over me before turning back to their friends to murmur something about jobs or houses or where their children were going to school (the children all seemed to have currently fashionable names and to play either rugby or tennis).

I gave a start as I came face-to-face with Mummy's solicitor, whom I'd only met once, in his office, shortly after Dad had left. Now he was looking embarrassed and Mumbling: 'So the job didn't work out, after all? Pity. I just put in a good word for you with Patrick to keep your Mummy off the breadline. And now you're going out with John? So you did well out of it, after all.' I thought he was a bit oafish but found it hard to believe he was the grasping ogre my mother had painted him, until I realised he was murmuring to his wife: '...Donach O'Doolahan's daughter. Mother still owes me the fees...'

The wife turned to me with a scrunched-up smile that made her look like a glove-puppet, and whinnied: 'Oh, you poor thing. It must be soooo embarrassing for you, being reminded of the scandal every time you go out. I wouldn't be able to cope – I'd hide my face.'

'I would, too – if I had face like yours', I couldn't resist saying, and Maeve gave an embarrassed laugh and propelled me towards another group. 'John's parents, Amanda and John Senior', she murmured. 'This is Chloe – you know, John's new, eh....' She finished with an awkward laugh.

John's Dad, who looked like a slimmer version of his brother, and an older, bald version of John, smiled weakly and nodded. His wife stood up straighter and pursed her lips.

Now I remembered something John had told me about his parents: 'They're the best argument for divorce I've ever seen. They should have left each other years ago. He's a dog man, she loves cats and they disagree on everything. Mummy goes on holidays with her sisters to forget she's married to him and he's spending his retirement in the pub.'

Poor man, I thought, living a half-life with a woman who squirmed every time his sleeve touched her arm.

Maeve took my wrist. 'And this is John's brother, Gavin, and his wife, Heather.' The prim-looking couple sniffed and picked my hand up as if it was an ornament they had decided not to buy, after all.

We seemed to have met everyone in the room, and now Maeve was removing my shawl and murmuring: 'John's ex is here. She's staying with us. I thought you should know in case you got a shock.'

Aware that my face had turned puce, I tried to sound nonchalant. 'Oh, Veronique. It's all right; I used to work with her.'

Maeve's eyes and mouth opened. 'Ah.' She looked me up and down, and I was suddenly aware that my red dress was very short and my shoulders very bare. She smiled tightly. 'You seem so young to be practising law. You can't be more than...?' I let her wait a second, realising that she was one of those women who had got cattiness down to a fine art. 'Nineteen', I said at last. 'I was just a trainee secretary.'

Old Wrightman suddenly appeared beside us. 'Miss O'Doolahan – well, I suppose I should call you Chloe now.'

'Only if I can call you Patrick', I laughed, thinking how much easier it was to cope with an embarrassing situation once the knives were unsheathed.

He 'hurumphed' and walked away, his hands behind his back.

His wife took my wrist. 'Come and meet the family, Chloe. I'm sure you'll get on very well with them.'

'Oh, I'll fit in – somehow', I laughed. I looked around for John, saw he was talking to a man in a corner, and shrugged: I could manage this situation on my own.

'Nora', Maeve was saying, 'this is your cousin John's new, eh, girlfriend. Chloe; my daughter Nora – oh, and her husband, Tom.' Tom was just nodding, smiling and heading off in the direction of a group of men.

Nora had inherited her father's stockiness and broad forehead, but her hair was cut in a chic brown crop. She looked up at me with the bovine expression of someone who's never doubted her place in society or her role in the family. She was well over thirty, and her dress was identical to her mother's. 'Pleased to meet you', she said primly, holding our her hand. I noticed the fingers were short and cigarette-shaped but well-manicured, with an expensive-looking diamond ring on her wedding finger – the kind of ring that required fingers like mine, I found myself thinking.

'I'll let Nora introduce you around', Maeve said, slinking off with my shawl dangling from her fingertips.

'So you're John's cousin', I said, suddenly feeling awkward; people like Nora always left me speechless because I knew they were completely without humour.

'Yes', she smiled blandly. 'Let me get you a drink. Red or white?'

'Oh, eh, white', I said, and she took a glass off a passing tray. 'This is John's girlfriend', she said to the woman with the tray, who gave a double take and then smirked. 'Pleased to meet you. I'm Caitlin, Nora's younger sister.'

'Chloe', I replied, returning Caitlin's top-to-toe gaze. She was just as plain-faced as Nora, and even blockier, but she held herself as if she was petite like her mother: a Sassu sculpture pretending to be a Hummel ornament.

Caitlin reached out to clutch a passing woman. 'Eithne, come and meet Chloe – John's girlfriend.'

Eithne was different yet again, a plump, sandy-haired version of her sisters, with an undeniably ugly face but one that that smiled a lot. She too wore a cookie-cutter cocktail dress. 'I'm Nora and Caitlin's younger sister', she said, with a minxy grin. 'The beauty of the family.'

'You haven't seen Iseult yet', Caitlin cut in and Nora laughed nervously. 'Far prettier than any of us – but she doesn't know it.'

'Iseult's the rebel of the family', Eithne said. 'Well, I suppose John is now. You must be still in your teens.'

'Barely.' I forced myself to giggle, feeling silly and girly even as I did it in the presence of these dullards. 'I'm nineteen – just twelve years younger than John.'

Caitlin and Eithne exchanged a smirk; Nora just continued to look bovine.

'Oh, there she is now', Caitlin said as a girl with waist-length brown hair strode into the room, followed by a big man with a shoulder-grazing, grey mop and matching beard. He looked like a Viking and was probably old enough to have come over on the first longboat. He had the muscular arms of people who spend a lot of time hanging onto throbbing handlebars, and, like Iseult, was dressed in black leather. I watched them take off their jackets to reveal matching sleeveless black T-shirts with the gory logo of a death metal band sprayed across them in red and white. He revealed tattooed arms which would have been shocking if they hadn't been so predictable, and a furze of grey hairs bristled over the neckline of his T-shirt.

'You're right, she is pretty', I said. Well, she probably could be if she sorted out her acne and got liposuction in a few strategic places, I supposed. But I liked her for the way she made the room go silent.

Maeve rushed over to her, looking agitated. 'Iseult, dear, I thought you were still out in Spain, was it? Wherever you're teaching English to those dreadful foreigners.' She haw-hawed and looked around the room as if she expected people to think she'd said something hilarious.

'Hi Mummy', Iseult said, taking out her chewing-gum to kiss her mother on the cheek, then putting it back in. 'I came back because I missed Gunner.' She grinned and leaned against the hulk's shoulder.

'How's it goin, Maeve?' he said.

'Oh, eh, hello, hello. We've met before, I think....'

'Course we have. Well, I'll interdewse meself again: me name's Gunner.' He opened his mouth wide to let out a whiskey laugh (and a gust of foul breath, judging by Maeve's cringe), took her tiny hand in his huge one and pumped it up and down. 'Love the place. Not my taste in furniture, mind you. Got anytin to drink?' He answered the question himself, grabbing a glass of red wine from the sideboard and slurping it. 'Grand stuff. Iseult, get us a few sausages. I'm starvin.'

Maeve flitted off, looking stone-faced, while Iseult grabbed a tray of cocktail sausages from Nora's husband and the little groups of people bunched together again, murmuring among themselves. Gunner wasn't bothered; he seemed to be enjoying himself, pretending not to appreciate the art (I could see he was just being an inverted snob when he compared a priceless abstract to 'a bad heroin trip').

Mr Wrightman Senior lumbered over and hugged his daughter (he reminded me of the solid, careworn father in De Chirico's *Prodigal Son*) and ignored Gunner – who was busy scoffing sausages.

I was about to go and find John, when I saw a familiar silhouette in the doorway.

The tight black dress hugged Veronique's lean frame, instantly making all the other women in black look ungainly and frumpy. It was cut to mid-thigh, straight across; hers were legs that didn't need the flattery of a flirty, diagonal hem or a slit. She wore black fishnets which would have looked tarty on most women, and shoes with thick ankle straps that only the longest legs could carry off. Her shoulders were bare, pale and looked as delicate as a Capodimonte figurine's. Something glittered around her neck – and on her left hand.

I saw John go up to her, take her shoulders lightly in his hands and kiss her on both cheeks. Then he put his hand around her waist and brought her over to me, a gentle smile on his face.

'Hello, Chloe', she said, and I noticed her eyes were very carefully made-up, no longer smudged, sultry and French-looking as I remembered them.

'Veronique.' I found myself blushing, wishing the evening was over.

'John's told me about ze two of you', she said softly. 'I'm very appy.'

I didn't know how to reply, so I just smiled.

'I'll leave you two alone', John said and rushed off. Bastard, I thought.

'So', Veronique said with a bright smile, 'you are not working for my orrible honkle-in-lav. E fired you, *vrai*?'

'Very *vrai*', I laughed, grateful to her for putting me at ease – and even more guilty at having taken her husband, even though it was she who had left him....

'But I am sure you are appier now. You were not suited to zat kind of work. John tells me you're an artist.'

'Well, I'm not a very successful one.' I laughed.

'Maybe when you are dead', she laughed, then grabbed my arm. 'Oh, I don't mean to say it zat way. It sounds like ze – ow you say –
ze Freudian fall.'

'Freudian slip', John said, returning with a tray full of canapés. 'You haven't seen Chloe's Freudian painting. Talk about Dorian Gray!' He chortled.

Suddenly, the evening had become lighthearted, a friendly fencing match between the wife and the wife-to-be.

Iseult and Gunner came over and introduced themselves, she with a shriek of 'So here's the girl my cousin's crazy about – sorry, Veronique!', he with a chesty chuckle and an impromptu burst of song – a Brendan Behan number about life in a Dublin prison, tailored specially for John, Veronique and me: 'The auld triangle, goes jingle jah-ang-ill....'

John stopped him with a slap on his beefy shoulder (I was sure he'd picked that up from his farmer friend; I'd seen people in the country do that to tractors). 'Are you all right, Gunner?'

'Couldn't be better, Jonno.'

'How's the bike?'

'Strugglin, Jonno, strugglin. I oughtteh put it out of its misery – send it to de knacker's yard, y'know? But I can't bear to part wit a ting dat's travelled all over de cuntery wit me.'

'Come on, I'll introduce you to some of the lads. They're all weekend bikers.'

Gunner's face broke into a piratical grin as John led him off. A group of be-pinstriped men backed off, then extended their fingertips when they realised John was determined to introduce Gunner. 'John tells me you've got a Harley. Shaggin great machine, what? Bleedin bitchin!'

Iseult was beaming. 'John's so good at making everyone feel at home. I made sure he was invited for lunch the first time I brought Gunner to meet Mummy and Dad.'

'What does Gunner do?' I heard an elderly woman ask Nora. 'Oh, he's a lorry driver', she replied. 'Really!' the other woman snorted. 'Yes', Nora said. Unsatisfied with her response, the old gossip-hound snorted again, raised her eyebrows and followed her nose in search of a bite.

Veronique and I sat on a windowledge; Iseult on a piano stool nearby, firing questions at us. I didn't mind, and I was sure Veronique didn't; anything to keep the vultures out of our circle. 'So, Chloe, you've worked with Janet', Iseult was saying. 'Yes, as a secretary.' 'That must be awful! She's an absolute cow.'

'Here she is, now', Veronique murmured and we looked over at the door. 'With her little boy.'

Janet was clutching a child in her arms. He looked about twice as big as my half-brother – far too old to be carried, but Janet had the biceps for it. She was wearing a long, silk, ivy-green dress split to the thigh. She looked all right – apart from the butch arms.

'She loves her child', I heard one of the older women cooing to another. 'She's such a good mother.'

'For a butch woman', Iseult murmured to Veronique and me and I felt as guilty for laughing as Veronique obviously did; she too was hiding behind her hands.

'I didn't know Janet had a child', I said.

Iseult snorted with laughter. 'I can see you're thinking: "Who on earth could the father be?" Well, it's Barry – look at him.'

And there was Barry, taking the child from Janet, lifting him playfully above his head.

'Barry was still living with his wife when he was bonking Janet. But she wasn't ashamed; when you're as ugly as she is, you take any man you can get. She even called the kid "Barry".'

I didn't know where to look – at the happy non-family, at Iseult, at my lover across the room...or his wife beside me. 'Is Barry's wife here?'

Iseult spluttered into her wine glass. 'No-o-oh! She wouldn't stand in the same room as the woman who shagged her husband. Can you imagine the humiliation?'

I felt Veronique stiffen beside me, so I gabbled to Iseult: 'Still, I suppose Barry mustn't have loved his wife. I mean, he left her', I said. I wished I could swallow the words as soon as they were out of my mouth.

Iseult laughed. 'Oh, no, Chloe, you've got it all wrong; she left him. Because of Janet. That's why everyone thinks Janet is a sexy temptress – and she plays up to it, the cow.'

Janet was dragging the child back from Barry now, that habitual frown back on her face. 'You're frightening my baby, Barry. Poor darling.' She leaned down, examining the child's chubby cheeks for signs of damage.

Then, to my amazement – and the obvious amusement of everyone else in the room, she sat heavily down on the chaise longue with the child on her lap, pulled down the top of her dress and began to feed him. Iseult cringed. 'The little monster is nearly four!'

'They look like a profane depiction of the Madonna and Child', I said, realising that I had drunk too much wine – and no longer caring: Janet had been nasty enough to me when I was working in that office.

Iseult roared with laughter and I saw a few of her relatives frown at her before resuming their conversation. Veronique was laughing softly, her head down. 'Veronique', I whispered and she looked up at me before bursting into a fit of silent laughter again.

'Are you not having anything to eat?' one of the women cut in, shoving a tray of devils-on-horseback under my chin as if she was about to guillotine me.

'Oh, no thanks.'

'On a diet, are we?'

I debated whether to tell her I didn't eat meat, then decided I hadn't got the energy for a quiz about my eating habits, so I just smiled and said: 'No, I just don't feel hungry. But thank you.'

She hurumphed and did the same to Veronique, who shook her head and gasped out 'No zank you'; she was still laughing.

'I'll have some – cheers', Iseult said, grabbing a handful and stuffing them into her mouth.

Janet was working the room now, with her 'baby'. 'She's probably going to ask us for money', Iseult mumbled through a mouthful of bacon.

Most of the women were cooing over Barry Junior. 'They do say a love child is always more beautiful than others', an old crone said to two younger women, who rolled their eyes.

'I think it's disgusting', another, obviously tipsy woman said. 'Flaunting the child as if an extra-marital affair was something to be proud of. The tart!'

'She brought that child to take the attention away from my little Gregory.'

'No, it's my Ellen she's competing with. She's the same age as Barry Junior. I'm sure she had him the same time because she wanted to outshine me at the christening.'

'You're all just jealous', the crone sneered.

'I think you mean envious', another woman chipped in. 'But you can't blame us for being just a teensy bit resentful of Janet. I mean, she's got a lover, a career *and* a child. And a nanny to care for him so she can spend lots of time at the beautician's and the gym.' The woman speaking had jowls, ratty teeth and a carefully-hidden figure in a froth of black lace.

Iseult looked at Veronique and me, then sniggered, splattering her wine on the carpet. 'What is it about women like Janet that makes other women pretend to envy her? It's as if they're trying to draw attention away from the fact that they envy someone else.'

We laughed, and I guessed she was referring to Veronique – after all, she was easily the most glamorous woman in the room. But Veronique was looking at me and saying: 'You seem to bring out ze cat in ozair women, Chloe. Even I was envious when I met you first.'

'But you've no reason to be', I said.

'Ah, maybe when I was your age, *non*, but now – look at zese wrinkles.' She indicated her eyes. If there were any wrinkles, I couldn't see them.

'Where are the rest of the children?' one of the envious mothers said. 'We ought to bring them in to play with Barry Junior.'

'I'll go get them', another smirked.

'This will be fun', Iseult murmured as the gaggle of mothers scurried out of the room, squawking loudly about their 'darlings'. They were all talking to the children in third-person babytalk: 'Come to Mummy, sweetie-bun...What's Mummy's ickle-lickle munchkin got in his handy-wandies?'

'Yuck', I said. 'If I ever have children, I'm never going to insult them by speaking to them like that.'

Seconds later, a sweaty-faced girl in a pink tracksuit came in with a bawling baby in her arms. 'I don't think you should have woken him – I'll never get him asleep again after this', she was saying.

'Are you telling me what I can or cannot do with my own child?' the woman with the rat's teeth snapped.

Soon, the room was awash with children of all ages, shrieking, giggling and running in and out everyone's legs. It was like a fertility ritual. I saw some of the men frown, but the women were beaming as if they'd got bananas wedged sideways between their teeth.

A little boy raced up to me and halted, soldier-like, his thumb in his mouth.

'Hello', I said, finding myself smiling despite the fact that he looked similar to my awful little half-brother. I hoped I wasn't getting broody like those silly women.

'My Mummy's a Yummy Mummy', he said.

'Oh? And what's your name?'

'James', he said. 'I know your name.'

'Do you really?'

'It's Anorexia.'

I felt my face blanch and saw Iseult's shocked expression. Veronique put her hand on my wrist.

'Mummy told me to tell you she's a Yummy Mummy and you're not!' the kid said, with a cross little face. Then he smiled angelically. 'Bye. You're very pretty.'

Iseult looked as if she was going to explode. 'You see, I was right', she said. 'They've been slyly ogling you all night, pretending not to notice you. I know what they're like.'

'Are you OK, Chloe?' Veronique was saying, tears in her eyes. Now I felt terrible about taking her husband – even if she didn't want him.

'I suppose I should be used to it by now.'

'No, Chloe. No one should have to listen to that.'

Iseult was storming off into the middle of the group of mothers. I saw them look alarmed as she shoved two of them aside, singled out the one who was clutching little James like a shield, and roared: 'Have you no shame?'

'I – I don't know what you're talking about, Iseult.'

The other mothers were smirking

'Go over and apologise to Chloe right now.'

'It's not James's fault. He's only a child –'

'I'm not blaming the boy. But you – using your own child as a weapon against another woman just because she makes you feel old!'

James's mum was jerking her head back and glaring at Iseult like a crow fighting a losing battle to defend its position on a cable. Iseult backed her into the fireplace and screamed at her: 'Go over and apologise right now or you can fuck off out of my parents' house!'

'What seems to be the trouble?' Maeve asked, running into the room with a pale, crumpled face.

I saw John put his arms around his aunt's shoulders and lead her over to the chaise longue, where her husband and his father were sitting. The rest of the men seemed to have grouped behind the chaise longue, as if they needed a safety barrier while they enjoyed the catfight. Gunner was grinning as if a bikers' festival wet T-shirt contest was about to start. I noticed Janet was standing among the men, looking uncomfortable, her child clasped around her neck like a live foxfur stole. The children clutched their mothers' legs. Iseult looked every inch the Bogeywoman – but I felt honoured to have her on my side.

Some of the women broke free from the group and rushed over to me, and there was a cacophony of 'Chloe, I didn't say it!' and 'She was only joking, you know.'

I flinched as one of them grabbed my hands and focused on me with a scrunched-up forehead. 'Actually, we were all just admiring how pretty you looked. We're so happy for John.'

'Yes', another piped up. 'We're glad John has got himself a woman with plenty of childbearing years left.'

I felt Veronique get up from beside me. I looked up and she was stumbling away, one hand raised to her face. I pushed the Yummy Mummies away and elbowed my way through the crowd, following her into the hall, but she was disappearing up the stairs.

'Veronique, it's me, Chloe. Veronique!'

I heard John's voice roar in the room behind me: 'Nobody leaves this room.' A chorus of 'Keeping us prisoner!' and 'Who do you think you are?' followed, then old Wrightman's voice boomed: 'You can all go out the kitchen door if you like – but not the hall.'

I went upstairs and stood outside the door of the room Veronique had gone into. 'Veronique, they're not coming up. Will you just let me in?'

I heard a sob. I pushed the door and it opened. She was lying face-down on the bed, her left hand outstretched on the pillow, the diamond ring glittering.

'Veronique, that was the cruellest thing I've ever heard.' She didn't answer, just kept sobbing. I knew pity would never be enough to comfort her.

Then something came to me – it was as if I was painting the outline of a fantasy creature and suddenly it developed familiar features, the way the tree had turned into Veronique and the mushrooms into those women I'd met in the pub. I spoke in French, partly because I didn't want any potential eavesdroppers to hear (I was banking on the fact that English-speaking people rarely understood other languages) and partly because I felt that Veronique would listen to me more intently if I spoke in her language.

'Veronique, it's really you they envy. Can't you see that? They're all calling themselves "Yummy Mummies" because they think motherhood is the only thing you can't have. It's not aimed at me – it can't be. I'm only nineteen, remember? Women as vicious as that wouldn't stab with a blunt knife.'

She raised herself on her elbows and looked around at me, her mascara all smudged, her eyes puffy.

'Veronique, I saw the men looking at you – even the young women's husbands. You're older than them and yet you make them look like old housewives.'

She gave me a weak smile. 'You're so kind, Chloe, but –'

'Veronique, listen to me. I'm wise beyond my years.' (Well, I hoped I still was; Daddy always used to tell me that.) 'You remember the way they were going on about Janet – the career woman with a lover *and* a child, and all the free time she has to look after her beauty?' Veronique had to laugh at that. Encouraged, I continued: 'Well, you and Iseult were right: they were only acting envious of Janet because she's plain and unpleasant and they can reassure each other that this femme fatale is not such a threat after all. They can pout in their cars on the way home and ask their husbands: "Darling, do you find Janet attractive?" and their husbands will laugh and say: "Of course not!" and be grateful for having better-looking, more charming wives.'

'Yes', Veronique said. 'That's as I thought – and Iseult thought so too. But just now they were envying you.'

I shook my head. 'No. Well, maybe. But it was more directed at you, Veronique. I'm not really a threat to them. I'm not a glamorous foreigner, I'm not sophisticated, I'm only a kid in their eyes – a silly teenager. The only women who envy me are those my own age, or sometimes older single women whose boyfriends still act like teenagers.' I thought of John's friends and their thirty-something girlfriends trying to blend in among the young things in McCool's. 'But those women downstairs are wealthy, with secure marriages. The only thing missing in their lives is a bit of glamour. And then you come along, and you are everything they would like to be and never can be – no matter how much money they or their husbands earn, what they spend on clothes or at the gym. And you're cleverer – John tells me you are a brilliant lawyer in France.'

She smiled – the kind of smile that didn't quite reach her eyes but was still beautiful. No wonder the other woman hated her. But I felt privileged to be on her side; it was as if we were two Cinderellas against an army of Ugly Sisters.

'Veronique, they had to find your Achilles heel. And that was it: you're not a mother and it's probably too late to start a family.' I didn't like saying that, but it had already been said and anyway I had to make my point.

'Ah, how clever you are, Chloe. You are using their knife to butter my bread!' She was laughing now. She put her hand out. I took it and sat down on the side of the bed. 'Chloe, I am happy that my *Jean* has found you.'

'He still loves you, you know.' Now, why had I exposed my own Achilles heel?

She giggled. 'Poor *Jean*. If only he were French, he could manage this menage-a-trois more skilfully.'

I felt my blood freeze, but Veronique was going on: 'It's OK if you want to make love with him. I shouldn't have been so harsh with him, throwing him out of my bed because he looked at some silly girls. He can stay here in Ireland as long as he likes – and make love to you. I am just as happy to have a holiday from him; there is no shortage of men in France for me, men who are always looking for a woman to take to the restaurant, the beach, the bedroom.'

There was a knock at the door. 'Is it OK if I come in?'

'*Jean*! We are ere', Veronique said, her accent sounding foreign again, now that she had reverted to English.

I cast my gaze down as John entered, the familiar aftershave now making me swoon with revulsion.

'Ah, you look happier now, Veronique. I thought you might like to come downstairs; the others have left. There's just the immediate family now.'

It did seem quiet, I was thinking. My head felt light and there was a ringing in my ears.

'Chloe, I think we should leave, hmm?'

'Ooh, I am forgetting', Veronique squealed. 'Chloe, I ave somesing for you.' She was giggling and opening a wardrobe. 'First I give you my usband and now zis.'

She flung something onto my lap. My eyes were blurred, but they gradually came into focus. It was a blue dress, in some gauzy fabric. 'It will be perfect with your eyes. I find it is too young for me.'

'Next you'll be giving her your ring', John chuckled. 'Come on, Chloe: say goodnight to my ex-wife-to-be.'

I had heard him properly, hadn't I? John wouldn't have said that if he and Veronique were just using me as a surrogate lover, would he?

'Put it on now', Veronique said. 'It's OK; John will ide is eyes – unless ee's seen your body?'

So she didn't know we'd made love – and she was acting as if she'd never said the things she'd said just before he had entered... I was confused. I held the blue dress up to my face; it gave me a few moments to think. Had Veronique simply been in denial for a moment because she was still in shock? I decided this was the best theory; it was easier to cope with.

'Come on, Chloe, try it on', she was saying.

'I'll wait outside', John said. 'I can't imagine what you look like without clothes, but my imagination is running riot.' He laughed and went out.

'Well, go on, Chloe.'

'Veronique.' I looked into her eyes, which were sad again, the mirth having fallen away like a mask at the end of Mardi Gras. I decided to switch the conversation back to

French, now that we were alone; I wanted to be sure she understood. 'Are you and John going to get back together again?'

Tears welled up in her eyes. 'No!' she sobbed. 'I sent him away and now he has found you, and it's not his fault.'

I stroked her head but she pushed my hand away. 'Go, please. But put the dress on – otherwise he will think we are fighting.'

Relieved, but also embarrassed, and tired (as if all the colour had been drained out of the evening), I slipped out of my red dress and stepped into the blue one. I looked at Veronique in the mirror, but she wasn't looking at me; she wasn't even bothering to check out my figure to see if it was better than hers. Maybe she didn't care – or maybe she didn't want to know. She just lay on her side, gazing down at the duvet.

'It fits', I said, for something to say.

She raised herself on one elbow. 'It's beautiful on you.' She suddenly wrenched her wedding ring off her finger and thrust it at me. 'Here, take this too.' Her eyes were molten lava.

'No!' I backed out of the room, clutching my red dress in front of the blue one. 'Bye Veronique. Have a nice...life.'

John was grinning at me. 'Have you two been laughing about me?'

'Oh, John, why do you think everything's about you?'

He sang as he bundled me down the stairs: 'You're so vain, you probably think this song is about you, don't you? Don't you?'

My ex-boss and his wife were at the end of the stairs, looking sober. John kissed her on both cheeks, then clapped his uncle on the shoulder as I kissed Maeve. She held onto me for a moment. 'We must have you and John to dinner some time', she said. Her husband gave me an awkward kiss – it was more of a sandpapering, really. Then he cleared his throat and lumbered back into the sitting room.

As they closed the door, we walked to John's car. A woman got out of a Merc parked alongside; it was one of the Yummy Mummies. I could see her husband in the driving seat; the child was probably asleep in the back.

She minced towards us, her heels sticking in the gravel. 'I just wanted you both to know that I wasn't a part of that. And please tell Veronique when you see her again that –'

'Leave my wife alone', John said. 'And my girlfriend.'

I saw a little girl sit up in the back of the Merc. I felt like the Wicked Witch from a fairytale as the child's mother wailed and ran back to her car.

'So she gave you a hand-me down?' John was laughing as we drove away.

'She tried to give me her wedding ring too.'

'Ah, she was just messing. She'll keep it as a souvenir.'

I fingered his ring. 'Are you always going to wear this?'

'Always is a long time – ah, Chloe, stop sulking. How did I end up with two neurotic women in my life?'

'She seemed to think she could take you back whenever she wanted.'

'Well, she can't. I'm my own man. And anyway...' He squeezed my thigh. 'I'm crazy about you.'

'Just crazy?'

'OK, I'm in love with you. Chloe, I've already told you I love you. Can I not change the track occasionally?'

I put my hand over his, and manoeuvred it to the inside of my thigh. 'Chloe, stop that while I'm driving. We'll have plenty of time for that when we move into the apartment.'

'So you still want to live with me?'

'Of course. Nothing's changed. Do you still want to live with me?'

'Yes.'

'Good.' He took his hand away to change gears, then took my hand in his and kissed it. 'Enough romance; I'm hungry. Aunty Maeve always has those awful canapés. I'm sure she uses dogfood for paté. I noticed there weren't any vegetarian ones – or seafood. You must be starving.'

My tummy rumbled in reply. We laughed.

'That settles it. OK, right now, I feel like a big, greasy bag of chips. How about you?'

'Yes!' I said, feeling like a child.

He pulled into an Italian chipper. 'These are real chips – not those awful skinny cardboardy things you get in QuikBurger.'

We ate them parked outside. 'You do eat a lot for a slim girl.'

'I need the energy', I said. 'I burn it up.'

'You burn me up – sorry for being corny, but I haven't had a good look at you all night. You look really stunning in that.'

He pulled me into his arms and kissed me deeply. I inhaled his aftershave, and the cocktail of perfumes that clung to me: Veronique's from the dress, and the remnants of my own.

Two cops came over to separate some brawling lads, and John murmured: 'I'd love to stay and watch, but we're double-parked.'

'You'll have to pay all those other parking fines.'

'Veronique will pay them; she likes to support me.'

He drove me home and parked outside the house, the engine running. 'Let's go to a club tomorrow night – somewhere where no one knows us, where we can smile all night.'

'I'd like that.'

'Hey, what's this?' He guffawed as he fished a napkin from between the seats. I'd used my curry sauce and a chip to draw an Egyptian Mummy on it, bandages streaming behind it like banners as it marched towards a cowering little boy. I laughed. 'It's a Yummy Mummy.'

The house was in silence as I came in. I'd always felt three in the morning was the eeriest time. Now I hesitated at the end of the stairs; I could hear Mummy shifting in her bed, could hear the house sigh as its floorboards cooled in the night air. There was an emptiness in the place. Maybe I was just imagining it; after all, I had just come from John's warm embrace, his kiss....

I walked into the drawing room and stood at the big window, trying to make out the sea behind the trees; to tell which part of the flickering silver was moonlit water and which was cloudy night sky. But there was a mist and all the trees looked like brides sharing the same veil. The foghorn moaned and I shivered; it always reminded me of those stories I'd heard about shipwrecks, and I was sure there had been many on those rocks below the cliffs. I fancied I heard the porpoises too; I knew there was a school of them out there; I had glimpsed them from that trawler Daddy used to take me out in with his fishermen friends.

The 'For Sale' sign floated in the fog just in front of me, like a tombstone in an old horror movie. 'Get out', it seemed to say. 'You and your Mummy don't belong here.'

I grabbed Mummy's big cardigan from the armchair and sat down, hugging my knees, mourning the end of the long, unusually hot summer; it was the first of September.

My new life with John lay ahead of me like a warm blanket; I hoped it would last longer than the luxurious life I used to have. I smiled as I tried to imagine our new home. He'd said it would be an apartment, with a sea view, near the city but close to Belgowan so I could visit Mummy – then I reminded myself that Mummy would be living out in Clonbollard, in a semi-detached dogbox, lost out there in the smog.

And someone else would have my attic. Maybe it would be a child's bedroom. That would be fine with me. Little kids might be annoying, but they were fiercely loyal – unlike parents.

I ate some grapes from a bowl on the coffee table and tiptoed up the stairs, avoiding the creaky places, then up the ladder to the attic, to see my painting in its proper environment while I still could.

There was nothing on the easel. I stared, thinking my eyes were playing tricks on me – after all, I was tired and had been drinking wine all night. But there really was nothing there. The easel gaped at me, its empty mouth a cry, its crude wood a bereaved father, accusing me of letting our child be taken away.

I really was drunk, wasn't I? And helpless. If Mummy had destroyed it – and I was sure she had, since she thought my painting a waste of time – nothing would bring it back. Maybe she had put it in the recycling bin. I ran down the steps, trying not to wake her, and out to the kitchen to look; it was full of newspapers and cardboard, but no canvas.

Maybe Mummy had been offended by my depiction of her as a miniature weeping willow growing out of a wine-bottle – but would she have recognised herself? People never seemed to see themselves in caricatures, even when everyone else did.

It was too dark, cold and lonely in the house for me to sleep. Maybe a home knew when it was going to be abandoned, and reacted by closing in on itself, hiding its soul from its betrayers the way a proud, jilted lover spurns a 'Let's-still-be-friends' consolation prize – the way I imagined Veronique would have behaved if it had been John who'd asked for that divorce.

I turned on the radio with the volume low. But the music was irritating – why did all-night DJs play such dreary tracks, when they probably had an audience of night-shift workers desperately trying to keep awake, or insomniacs who had long given up on sleep and were just looking for something to distract them until dawn? I switched over to a local station that played repeats of all its mid-morning phone-in shows; Mummy always listened to them, because they were full of information about the neighbourhood.

I normally loathed that kind of thing and had convinced myself I would never become the kind of person who worried about broken footpaths, overgrown hedges, youths loitering around the off-licence and dogs fouling the grass verges. But now I wondered if I John and I would join a residents' association once we'd moved into our new home; did they have miniature versions of Poo Anchorbottom in chic apartment blocks? I hoped we wouldn't grow old like my parents, sucking up to the wealthy neighbours. Fat lot of good it had done Mummy, anyway.

If John and I ever had children, I vowed, I'd never force them to play with kids they didn't like, wear hand-me-down coats from rich neighbours' daughters or join rugby clubs like poor Daryus, who had always preferred soccer – and I'd never call myself a 'yummy mummy' or a 'stay-at-home mum' or a 'working mother'. I'd just be a good mother. I'd try to be as normal as possible.

Was it possible to be 'normal'? Maybe I could manage it if I unloaded all my crazy thoughts onto canvas and kept doing that until the well that produced them stopped filling up.

I sighed, switched off the radio and conjured up thoughts of John to fill the emptiness my stolen painting had left.

The fog had cleared when I woke; sunlight was streaming through the windows, and I realised I had left the curtains open. I blinked, focusing on something large and pink in front of me. Oscar, my teddy – no, it was Mummy, in a shocking pink tracksuit, the kind of thing she only wore when she was shopping in the cheap supermarket on the outskirts of Belgowan.

'Chloe. Chloe! Wake up, pet.'

'Have you joined some religious cult, Mummy?' I didn't know which was weirder: the clothes or the uncharacteristic bout of love-bombing.

'No, no, you silly girl. I'm going to help Poo Anchorbottom get the exhibition space ready.'

'What?'

'She needs hands-on help carrying all the paintings, the table for the canapés, a few chairs...'

So Mummy had found a job as Poo Anchorbottom's roadie. 'I hope she's paying you.'

'Of course not! It's voluntary, for one of her charities – the whales or starving children or something like that.' Mummy was breathing heavily, the way she did when she was impatient to tell me something. 'The point is, I showed her your painting – and she accepted it!'

'How charitable of her.' I wanted to throw up – and it wasn't just the hangover that was making my eyes throb and my throat feel as if someone had used a hairdryer inside it. 'Mummy, can I have a glass of water?'

She brought me a jug and glass from my dresser – she even poured it out for me. 'Thanks.' I gulped it down; it was lukewarm and a bit stagnant.

'Chloe, you're going to be a famous artist!'

'Mummy, I hardly think an exhibition in the Parish Resource Centre is going to turn me into the next Van Gogh.'

She wagged her finger at me. 'Chloe, sometimes I wonder at your lack of ambition. That's what's holding you back, you know.' She beamed. 'Poo never does anything half-hearted – you should know that by now, Chloe. She's inviting all the arts critics from the most important newspapers, and that photographer who does the diary section in *U Know Who* magazine, and some other influential people – dealers, arty types, you know.' She flapped her hand at me. 'Get up! You'll have to help out, since Poo is doing you such a big favour.'

I smiled lazily. 'Mummy, I'm sure Poo would be shocked if I offered to help out; I'm going to be a celebrity artist, remember?' I looked at my fingers. 'Anyway, I need to keep my hands soft for artistic work.'

She laughed. 'Oh, all right, Chloe. But I promised her you'd do something – you could help with the guest list. You can invite all your lecturers from the art college –'

'Mummy, I'm haven't kept in touch with anyone from college.'

'Well, now's your chance to get back in touch.'

Still, I found myself enjoying the prospect of having my art finally recognised. It couldn't be so awful if Poo was going to put it on display among works by prestigious local painters who had won awards and were frequently reviewed in the arts columns. And John had genuinely liked it.

I thought about putting him on the guest list, then changed my mind; I didn't want Poo to earmark him for Fanny. Not that he would be interested in a dumpling like that after being married to Veronique. But then my debs date had thrown me over for Emmabelle McCowan, a girl who made Fanny look like a supermodel.

In the end, I simply fished out my art college yearbook and copied everyone's contact details. Who else did I know who liked art? Surely an artist had to have some arty friends. The only ones I could think of were the Fitzwalton sisters. I had been feeling guilty about the way I had run out of their home – and worried about what I would say if I bumped into them when I inevitably gave in to temptation and visited the National Gallery again. So I put them on top of the list; their address looked impressive.

'I'm so glad you could help us, Chloe', Poo gushed as I handed her the list. She was wearing a more expensive version of Mummy's tracksuit but didn't seem to be doing any manual work, just supervising her acolytes. 'Your painting is quite...eh, fascinating.' She had put it in a dark corner at the back of the room. 'I'm sure some eccentric arty type will buy it.'

'What's the charity?' I asked, more out of boredom than genuine curiosity; I was waiting for Mummy to give me a lift home in the car because I still had a hangover and couldn't face walking up the hill in the heat.

'Oh, it's for a homeless shelter. Just think, Chloe; your painting could take some poor person off the street!'

I laughed as I got into the car with Mummy. 'Poo is one of Ireland's richest landladies. She could solve the homeless problem in five minutes by lowering the rent on some of her apartments.'

'Chloe, that's not a nice thing to say.' But Mummy was smiling. Then she sighed as we pulled into the drive. 'That "For Sale" sign is depressing me.'

Bold strokes

John wanted to take me to a club that night. He called in the afternoon to remind me. 'I'll pick you up late-ish. There's no point going on the razz before ten – and you're not going to want to sit in a restaurant in your clubbing clobber.'

I tried not to laugh at his self-conscious attempt to sound like a guy my age. 'Clubbing clobber' sounded like something a middle-aged fashion columnist would write, like 'groovy gear' or 'trendy togs'. 'John, are you sure we'll get in? I mean, the bouncers might say it's "members only" or full up.' I was trying to be tactful; I could hardly come right out and say they'd think he was too old, could I?

'Of course they'll let us in – as long as we're wearing the right duds. It's supposed to be a really happening place.'

I groaned.

'Chloe, what's wrong? Hey, you're laughing! What's so funny?'

'See you after ten, John. My house.'

How do you dress for a night in a cool club – with a boyfriend over thirty? Especially one who has lived abroad for years and looks like a foreign gentleman over on business? John's mannerisms, his way of walking, his clothes, even his skin, looked Continental – and, much as I found hand-kisses and well-fitting shirts attractive, I couldn't see how he was going to blend in Dublin's Saturday night hipsters.

I had pretended not to know where the 'happening places' were, but John had found out from someone at work. I hoped for my own sake it had been Barry; I'd rather look like jailbait in a room full of old men than bump into my old college friends on the dancefloor with John.

Not that I'd gone off John; my heart still curled and lay down every time I thought about his eyes, or his hands, or.... But he belonged strictly to my new grown-up life.

To be honest, I didn't even want to go to clubs any more. I was nearly twenty, after all, and would soon be living with my lover in a plush apartment – while most of my old friends were either still living with their parents or sharing rooms in the university zone.

Mummy sniffed when she saw what I was wearing for a night 'on the town', as she called it. 'John won't approve of you showing your navel.'

'How do you know what John thinks, Mummy? Anyway, you wear belly tops to your Oriental Dance lessons.'

'With wide-legged trousers, pet.'

'Oh yes; they're called harem trousers, aren't they? They're practically transparent and they hang lower down on your hips than these.' I felt quite conservative in my white hipster jeans; I had decided against a mini-skirt at the last minute.

'You need to dress more ladylike now, Chloe. After all, you're going to be well-known after the exhibition.'

'Mummy, please don't tell John about it. I – well, he'd be embarrassed.'

Naturally, she ambushed him at the front door as I was rushing to answer it. 'Chloe's going to be famous! Her painting is in an exhibition.'

I still didn't want to talk about it as we drove away. Eventually, John laughed and squeezed my hand. 'I never believed all this eccentric artist stuff until I met you. But I'll stay away from the exhibition if that's what you want.'

'Thanks, John. I'm sure it would be boring for you, anyway. Lots of Mummy's ex-friends will be there – she's trying to get back in with them. They're those rich women who raise money for charity.'

'Ladies who lunch?'

'Yes. And their horrible daughters.'

'Ah.' He grinned.

'They're all ugly.'

'I'm sure they are.'

'They're those people who get their pictures in the social diary of *U Know Who*.'

'Oh, yes; the ones you were giggling over with the girls in the office. What's-her-name, Mrs Poobottom?'

I snorted with laughter.

'Or is it Mrs Anchorarse?'

'Poo Anchorbottom – and her daughter, Fanny. They're organising it. Oh, and the Fitzwalton sisters are coming.'

He chuckled. 'Well, then I'm definitely staying away. I don't want to look too old in front of *them*.' He looked at me out of the corner of his eye. 'You're weird, Chloe. You make friends with pensioners and then tell me I look like a fossil – in my jeans!'

'But John, *black* jeans?' I cringed.

'They're back in fashion, you know. They're all the rage in Paris; you just haven't been shopping lately. We'll have to rectify that.'

I smiled. He *was* gorgeous, all in black. I hoped those doormen would be tactful.

Bling-Bling's nightclub was patronised by every movie star filming in Dublin, every mega-selling rocker and anyone who'd made the front cover of *Hello*. They always headed straight for the 'VIP Room' (the management actually called it that) and spent the night avoiding the attentions of local wannabes. On Saturday nights, the only people over thirty in the place were rich, famous or well known to the door staff.

I felt protective towards John as we approached the glamorous blonde with the stern expression who was shooing away wrinklies who dared to approach the entrance. Two guys who looked like Mormon missionaries playing truant stood behind her, ready to help if any of the rejects kicked up a fuss. But most people just went away looking embarrassed; it was early in the evening and the drunks were still in the pubs. I cringed as she did her traffic-cop handsignal routine with John and me – beckoning me on while putting her palm up in a 'Stop' sign towards him. 'But I know one of your doormen', he was saying.

I tugged at his sleeve. 'John, please!'

'His name's Clint.'

The door-belle removed her cigarette and blew smoke in his face. 'Would his surname happen to be Eastwood?'

The bouncers sniggered but moved forward, shoulders raised.

'No. Clint Scallion. He works in various clubs.'

Her face broke into a beautiful smile – the kind I imagined she'd give to Clint Eastwood. 'Clint Scallion – Scallywag! Of course I know him. He's working the floor. Go on in.'

John grinned and propelled me up the stairs.

Clint loomed out of the reddish haze, a formidable figure in a black T-shirt and jeans. 'How's it goin, Jonno? Chloe, I haven't seen you in ages. Why didn't you come to de weddin?'

'I didn't want to upstage the bride.'

John cut in: 'How *is* Brenda?'

Clint indicated his tummy.

I laughed. 'She can't have put on much weight in just a few weeks.'

'Not weight, you eedgit! She's up de pole. De sprog's due in November. Course, I didn't know till she told me; Brenda's always been a big girl.'

No wonder she'd been reluctant to do a spot of table-dancing at her hen party, I thought. I decided to buy her the most beautiful baby clothes John could afford.

'Have a drink with us', John said.

Clint smiled but shook his head. 'No can do; I have to stay sober on duty in case dere's trubble.' He put a muscular, hairy hand on each of our necks. 'Two crime families in de place tonight; they're celebratin deir Big Daddies gettin ourra de slammer – on appeal. Some fuckin hotshot barrister got dem off on a technicality. Bleedin lawyers – sorry, Jonno.'

'It's OK; I'm not defending criminals these days.'

Clint winked. 'You're better off away from doze scumbags. Especially now that you've got a bird to look after.' He pinched my waist.

'Ouch, that hurt!'

'Poor little skinny ting. You need to go down de gym, lift some weights. You can't have Jonno lookin out for you all de time.'

'Oh, shit', John was saying.

I followed his gaze. 'Isn't that your ex-client, John? Skoby?'

Clint gave a low whistle. 'Dangerous little fecker. And dat big bloke's his brudder – Dublin's answer to Al Ca-bleedin-pone!' He manhandled us over to the bar. 'Just stay dere and don't turden round until I tell yewse. I'll give de whole bleedin lorra dem a pass for the VIP room. Jackie Chan's goin to be in dere later tonite – he'll know how to deal wit dem if dey give us any shite.'

'There's no point in going onto the dancefloor anyway', I said as John pulled out a stool for me. 'No one goes to this sort of club to dance.'

'That's OK. They didn't when I was a teenager, either.'

'Maybe we should leave', I said. 'Listen, there's a fight in the VIP room.'

Even the music couldn't drown out the loud Cockney voice saying: 'Cawm down. Just cawm down.'

'Are you tellin me to calm down? Hey, Skoby, have you got dat razor?'

'Aaaargh! My facking face!'

'You should be payin me for fixin it; it was brutal.'

'Just oo d'you fink you is? The facking Kray Brothers?'

'That doesn't sound like Jackie Chan, I said to the barman.

'I think it's one of Steve Oldman's minders – you know, the lead singer from Jurassic Rox. He's got a house in Belgowan – to avail of the artists' tax break, of course. I mean, he's hardly here for the climate.' The barman sniggered.

'Oh, yes, he's one of my neighbours, sort of.' How ironic, I was thinking; my Daddy had left Belgowan to avoid paying tax (and private creditors of course) and now he was living in a nicer climate than the lead singer of a mega-selling rock band that must have been around since Daddy was a schoolboy.

'You probably wouldn't be into that kind of music; it's more for your boyfriend's age-group.'

'Cheeky little pup!' John said as the guy swaggered off to get us our drinks.

We heard Skoby's voice from the VIP room. 'Yewse lot tink yewse can cum over here for de crack – yewse don't even know what crack is. Dis is my bleedin cuntery and dat's my burd you insulted.'

'Just cawm down, mate.'

'I wouldn't've offered yewse doze E-nergy tablets only I tawt yewse looked a bit sickly. Jurassic Rox? It's Jurassic Pox you've got – hey, Stevo, you look like a wanker and your hair's like a rat's arse.'

'I'm having security call the police.'

We heard a roar of laughter. Then a wicked-witch voice. 'My son's a respeckerble pharmaceutical dealer, he is!'

John murmured in my ear: 'Skoby's Yummy Mummy, fresh out of the women's prison – or "De Burd Cage" as her son calls it.'

I laughed. 'She sounds like one of the Ladies Who Punch.'

'Ma, get me soliciror. I seen him over at de bar. I'm goin to sue dat scumbag for slander – he's loaded!'

'Let's go, Chloe.'

'Ah, John, why can't we watch the fight?'

But he was calling the barman over to pay him. 'Tell Clint to call me on the mobile when's he's finished', he said.

'He'll be *seriously* finished if the back-up biffs don't get here quickly', the barman said. He was taking off his apron. 'Hey, the drinks are on the house, OK?' He flitted out and down the stairs.

John dragged me out by the arm.

'Why do you want to talk to Clint later?'

'It's a surprise. I just hope he's still alive.'

We went to a piano bar, where I felt silly in my cropped top and low-slung jeans. John blended right in; even his jeans looked grown-up. A heavy-lidded woman was mumbling some never-ending jazz number, ignored by a crowd of men in suits and women in cocktail dresses, who were just drinking and staring into space. 'Chloe, stop sighing. People will think I'm playing footsie under the table.'

'Why do we have to wait until four?'

'Because that's when the clubs close.'

'Oh, yeah. We have to meet Clint. But why?'

He laughed and ordered a plate of scampi. 'This'll give you energy. It's going to be a long night.'

When the piano bar closed, he led me back to the car, casually flicked a soggy parking ticket off the windscreen ('These things crop up like mushrooms in Dublin; it must be the rain!') and let me in. 'You're going to need your seatbelt', he said. 'I don't want you hitting your head off the windscreen.' I didn't see what he meant until he took something dark from the glovebox and slipped it over my eyes. 'Shh' he said as I opened my mouth to ask him what this was about.

All through the jerky, never-ending journey, I worried that John might be one of those men I'd seen on *True Crimes*: strait-laced professionals who got rid of stress by tying their girlfriends up and...I shuddered. Maybe that was why Veronique had left him.

'John, I don't like this.'

'Shh.' I felt him take my hand in his, then kiss it.

The engine stopped and I lurched against the seatbelt, then heard his door slam. I felt a gust of cool air and then his arms, bundling me out onto hard ground.

'Come on, Chloe, hurry up. You're just mincing along.'

'I feel as if I'm being kidnapped.' I wanted to cry, but I just let him push me along, one hand on my arm, the other on my back.

I flinched as a car came close – very close. 'It's on the other side of the road.' 'I thought it was going to run over my foot.' 'Come on, up these steps and we're there.'

The smell was familiar. It overwhelmed me with a memory of something...but what?

The blindfold suddenly came off and I blinked in the bright light. We were in a marble foyer that seemed familiar. It was like in a dream. Someone even pinched me. 'Ah, you'll have to feed her up', a voice said from behind – Clint. He was grinning and patting John on the shoulder. 'I'll leave youse luvburds alone. Just remember, Jonno, you owe me a pint.'

Then I realised we were in the National Gallery. John was hugging me from behind and shaking with laughter that must have been trapped in him all night. 'I wanted you to enjoy it without having to worry about being accosted by the Fitzwalton sisters', he was snorting. 'Though – though I can't see the point now since you've invited – oh, Chloe! I can't believe you actually invited them to that exhibition.' He staggered across the floor, laughing. 'Just to brown-nose Pussy Anchorbum and her daughter, Arse.'

I didn't correct him; I was too busy laughing. It felt good after all that fear.

'Clint knows the security men here', he explained as we walked into the grand salon.

He followed me, holding my hand lightly as I flitted from one painting to another, my eyes devouring them; it had been so long since I'd seen my old friends. The place livelier than ever, now that the ghosts could gaze boldly back from their masks of dried oil on canvas.

I stopped under *The Wedding of Strongbow and Aoife*. I suddenly wanted to be part of it. It must have been the drink talking when I said: 'John, imagine making love under this painting.'

'Chloe!' We laughed so much we could barely stand up, but he steered me away from the orgiastic picture. 'The security guys probably have cameras on us right now – you don't want Clint and his mates watching a video of us in the back room of the *Shaven Head*, do you? Come on, let's have a good gawk at the Caravaggio and than we're out of here; I don't want to get the guys into trouble.'

We went up the stairs but, as I reached the landing leading into my favourite room, and smelt those old, old paint-people, I felt as if I had committed some terrible sacrilege. 'John, I want to go – now.'

'Yes, I'd say we've got about five minutes before the guys get nervous and ask us to leave –'

'No, not in five minutes. Now.' I glanced around the Italian Masters room, not daring to meet the eyes of the oldest ghosts of all. 'John, I feel they're all looking at me.'

'Of course they are', he said gently. 'That's the genius of great art, isn't it?'

I ran down the stairs and he followed me into the foyer. 'All right, den?' Clint said, and I noticed he was sweating as much as I was. 'Oh, Jonno, you're goin to pay for dis in pints – for me and de lads. We'll never wurk again if dis gets out.' I noticed the uniformed guard behind him was facing the wall. John squeezed Clint on the shoulders. 'We saw nothing.'

'Yeah, bit disappointin, isn't it? I tawt dere'd be summa dem pitchers of wimmin wit joy-normous tits.'

'Poor Brenda', I said to John as we got into the car. 'Clint's hands are like shovels!'

We pulled into a car park off the coast road just south of the city, and opened the hood to breathe in the last of the summer. The sky was full of stars and the sea made gentle slumber noises under its dappled navy blanket. 'That was the most beautiful thing anyone ever did for me. I'm sorry I acted weird.'

'You weren't acting; you are weird', he laughed and killed the engine. He opened our seatbelts and pressed the thing that made the seats recline. I lay on my side, facing him. 'I think you're corrupting me, Chloe. After a night of culture, all you want is this.' He kissed me. 'Want what?' 'This...'

He pulled me on top of him. His eyes darkened. I sighed as he pushed up my top, then unfastened my bra, flinging them onto the back seat as I removed his T-shirt. I gasped as my skin touched his, then moaned as he stroked my back, his fingers massaging the groove of my spine. We tore each other's jeans off. 'John, I want you now.' We climaxed at the same time and I let out a cry that seemed to have come from elsewhere.

Then he said her name.

He seemed to realise what he'd done almost as soon as he'd said it. 'Oh, Chloe, I didn't mean it...it was just a reflex action.' Like the last time, I thought.

'Make love to me again', I said, beginning to cry. 'We need to exorcise her ghost once and for all. Say my name this time. John, make love to me: Chloe.'

He had collapsed on top of me and was panting, his sandpaper jaw pressing into my flesh. At last, he leaned up on his elbows and faced me, his eyes haunted by more than one ghost. 'No. Not while you're crying. It would be a violation of you.' Now his voice was smooth, calm; his eyes still dark but torpid, like peat-water. I wanted so much to stir up what lay beneath...

'You're going back to her, aren't you?'

He rolled onto the driving seat, pulling on his jeans, belting them. I waited for him to speak. He was gazing out to sea as he spoke. 'Chloe, you're so young, you'll find lots of men to tell you they love you, to tell you how beautiful you are...how sexy. But Veronique is thirty-seven. She's not so sure of herself any more.'

I realised I had lost him because of my perceived advantage over my rival; it was the oldest trick in the world, and the cunning Veronique had played me the way a wily old fencing master defeats a vigorous young opponent – by feinting and double-bluffing.

She would never age, this wise, powerful old cat-of-nine-lives. She would just grow more alluring with the years; a Ligeia, living off the vibrancy of younger women – the conquests of her handsome, seductive husband. They'd feast on me for a while; he'd pass on the things he'd learned from our little summer affair, and she'd probably teach him something she'd learned from a lover in France. Hadn't she told me she had no problem in finding a man there? She probably had flings with older men to make her feel younger, just as John had used me to replenish his youth and, at the same time, let him feel in control of a woman.

He drove me home in silence. As I got out, he took my hand, kissed the fingers – and I slapped him.

I ran up to my attic, stood in front of the easel and inhaled the scent of oil and water paints; the ghost of my stolen painting. And as I breathed, deeply and slowly to avoid passing out, I imagined it was the perfume of Veronique. All that time I had been adding to the painting, nurturing it like a baby in the womb, she had been on the perimeter of my world, mostly out of sight, appearing only in glimpses like some kind of spirit called up by the clairvoyance of loneliness. She had come into my life at a moment when I had lost everyone and everything I loved, when my essence had been ripped cruelly away as if by an invisible hand. She had appeared as if by magic, transforming my style of painting from the classic to the grotesquely abstract. She had become my invisible muse, controlling me with her magic wand: her beautiful, charming husband. And soon even my real world seemed to be reflected only in a hall of warped mirrors, shimmering in the heat of an unusually hot summer.

And now the summer was over, and she had taken back her magic man, and the only trace of my strange experience was the lingering smell of paint in the air of the attic I would soon have to leave.

A blank canvas

When I woke, I realised I had fallen asleep on my knees, my cheek resting on the empty easel, arms embracing it. Poor thing, I thought; it looked so abandoned.

Mummy was in the kitchen, chopping vegetables and singing out of tune. She was wearing her pink tracksuit again; she looked like a huge magenta rabbit. I leaned against the doorframe, unsteady on my feet.

'Ah, there you are Chloe. You must have come in late; I didn't hear you. Poo was just on the phone; she needs help lugging in some big display boards and mounting them in the exhibition room. I told her you'd be fit enough.'

'No.'

She smiled, as if I had been joking.

'I'm not going to waste any more of my life on people I don't like.'

Now she frowned. 'What's brought this on, Chloe? You were happy yesterday evening.'

'I'm happier now', I said, wishing I meant it. 'I've decided to reclaim my life.'

She shrugged and continued chopping the vegetables. I grabbed a banana and went back upstairs to eat in my attic; I wanted to enjoy my studio without the painting for the first time all summer.

I spent the rest of the week avoiding people: I went to the gym during off-peak hours, walked around Dublin (but kept away from the National Gallery) and left my mobile off, except to call Daryus, who eventually agreed to meet me for a coffee one afternoon.

'I can't stay long; I have to be in town for a gig, he said. 'Wow –' 'Not the band; I've got a job as a security guard.' Oh, well, I thought; my little brother could do worse than turn out like Clint.

'You look more grown-up', I told him as I kissed him goodbye.

'Thanks', he grinned and swaggered off, his arms looking like oars, rowing away from me, the last person to leave me marooned on my little island.

After so much fullness, I felt empty.

I didn't go to the exhibition, of course. Instead, I hid in the upstairs bathroom until Mummy had grown impatient and driven off to help Poo hand out the wine and canapés.

Alone in the house, I lounged in the bath, reading a novel until the water got cold. I threw on a bathrobe and went downstairs to enjoy a lazy lunch of smoked salmon on rye bread, with chocolate for afters...and the last of Mummy's sparkling wine (well, she was turning into an alcoholic and I had to remove temptation). I skimmed through the local paper but couldn't bear to look at the job ads just yet.

Out of boredom, I switched on my mobile to see if anyone had called me. There were seven voice messages and twelve texts. I listened to the voice messages first; they were all from John.

'Chloe, I'm leaving the country. I just thought I should tell you. OK, bye.' That had been the most recent; that morning.

'You can't just go on ignoring me, Chloe. What if we meet again?' There was a smile in his voice that time, but it had been the previous night.

I continued to listen, reminding myself that each one had been left earlier than the last.

'I – I'll never forget you, Chloe. Goodbye.'

'Chloe, I'm sorry I said you over-reacted. It was my fault. Please call me.'

'Chloe, I think you over-reacted.'

'She's my wife. How can you expect me to just forget about her?'

And then the first one, which he had left at noon the day after that terrible night. His voice sounded hoarse, groggy. 'Chloe, I haven't slept since I dropped you off. I'm not taking the job. I'm going back to France with Veronique. It's better that way, but I – Chloe, I want you to know I'll always love you. Last night, when we made love, well – oh Chloe you've destroyed me!'

I felt the colour blaze across my cheeks, my whole body. I sat down on the floor and closed my eyes, trying to conjure up the ecstasy I'd felt before he'd said her name. But now the memories just mocked me; I heard his voice repeating 'Veronique' as if in a chant. I cancelled all the voice messages and read the texts.

They were much the same, except for the most recent, which said: 'Got a surprise 4 U. Please call.' He had sent it less than half an hour previously.

I hesitated, then decided I couldn't make the situation worse if I called. Anyway, I was curious.

He answered on the first ring. 'Hi.'

'It's me.'

'I know, silly; your number came up.'

'Oh.' I found myself smiling and then blushing furiously as I tried to suppress the smile; I was sure he'd know, even on the phone. 'What's the surprise?'

He chuckled. 'Can I come and see you?'

'Erm, I don't know. When?'

'Now. I'm only down the road.'

'I'm not dressed.'

'I've seen you undressed, remember?' He sighed, a smile in his voice. 'OK, you get dressed first. I'll come over in half an hour.'

Dressing for an ex is not the same as for a date. Not wanting to look as if I was trying to seduce him, yet badly needing to look my best, I frantically rummaged in my wardrobe. In the end, I threw on a pair of old jeans that sat well on my hips, and a slinky T-shirt I had bought in Italy. I carefully applied brown mascara that didn't look obvious. I thought about wearing perfume, then decided he'd think it was just for him (well, it would be, but I didn't want him to know that).

Then, feeling annoyed with myself for still wanting him, I stood in the doorway.

I felt my heart sink as Mummy's car pulled in. Just my luck; the big goodbye and she'd be there and I'd have to explain it was over, and she'd never let me forget; she had a habit of gushing about every guy I'd ever brought home, even the ones she'd disapproved of at the time. I watched her get out of the car, beaming and swelling up as if she had something important to say – I was sure she'd be full of news about Poo Anchorbottom. Well, I wasn't going to listen to it.

I looked at my watch. John wasn't coming at all; he'd had cold feet, I supposed.

Then the blood rushed to my cheeks as he drove up on the path. Mummy was standing in the drive, watching him.

They came to the door together. I ignored Mummy, who was waffling on about Poo Anchorbottom: '...such a stylish skirt...those shoes...her daughter Fanny, you know...' John was nodding but looking at me.

'Hi, Chloe.'

'John.' I was furious with myself for blushing, and I couldn't meet his eyes at first, because the memories were still so fresh. The last time I'd looked into those eyes they'd been gazing at me like an abandoned puppy's – and, moments before, they had been flinching from my nails...and not long before that they had been locked onto mine as we made love, just before he'd said her name.

I couldn't keep my eyes on the ground forever – certainly not with Mummy trilling: 'Chloe, are you going to let John and me in?' So I stepped aside to let her pass, then looked up and into John's eyes and realised he was desperately sad. I wanted to cover him in kisses and say I was sorry, that I didn't care how many times he said his wife's name, that he could still have a new life with me.... But now, even more than that awful night, I knew he was going back to her – like a bird returning to its gilded cage.

He didn't seem like the ogre he had become in my imagination over the past week. He was my John again – only a tragic version. And he was breaking my heart.

Mummy walked in and left us at the door. I suddenly noticed he was carrying something that made me choke back the tear that had been threatening to break free.

'She's the surprise I was telling you about', John said, with a gentle smile, as he handed the puppy to me. She was an Irish setter, exactly like my Scarlet O'Hara, the way she had been the first time Daddy had brought her home.

I hugged the warm little bundle, and she obligingly snuggled up to me, licking my face. 'This little creature totally depends on you', he said. 'You like that, don't you?'

I tried to say 'Yes' but it came out as a gulp.

'I brought her to the exhibition because I didn't want to leave her all alone in the car', he said, leaning down and kissing her head. 'She did a nice big plop on the floor – I'm sure some arty farty newspaper critic will think it's an avant garde installation and write it up as a work of genius. Mrs Anchorbottom just stared at it in horror.'

'She was probably jealous – there's only room in the exhibition for one Poo!' We laughed.

Mummy called from the kitchen. 'John, come in and have something to drink. Chloe, don't be so rude – keeping him at the door!'

'Can we bring the puppy in too, Bee?' Since when had John been calling my Mummy by her first name?

'You don't need to ask, John. Chloe, John and I had a wonderful time at the exhibition. It's a pity you weren't there.'

John was smiling at me. 'I know I promised to stay away from it, but I wanted to see what happened to your painting –'

'John, tell Chloe about her painting.'

'The Fitzwalton sisters bought it – for five hundred euros.'

I gaped.

'I'm sure it would have fetched more it had been auctioned. Mrs Anchorbottom just let them name their price.'

'I don't care how little they paid', I said. 'I didn't think anyone would want it –'

'I would have bought it for, oh, a thousand anyway.' He grinned. 'You'll have to do me another one, in return for the puppy.'

'She's worth more than a painting.' On cue, she licked my nose.

'I got her some bowls for food and water – I'll get them out of the car.'

As I waited, I asked Mummy about the fate of my painting. 'Did the sisters say what they were going to do with it?' I supposed they'd hide it in their attic.

'Yes. They said they'd frame it themselves and make room for it on the wall over their drawing room mantelpiece. They were really delighted with it, Chloe – and they seem awfully expert on art. They gave it a title. Here: Eleanor wrote it down for me to give you.' She handed me their card, on which Eleanor had scrawled: 'Still life with human figures'. In brackets, she'd added: 'Metaphysical satire with classic undertones and elements of cubism.'

Well, it was better than having no style, I supposed – but it sounded like Daryus's attempt to classify his music.

Now I tried to imagine my painting with a papier mache or tinfoil frame, taking pride of place in the Fitzwalton sisters' drawing room, among the other weird 'works of art', the inflatable sofa, the recycled car seat, those cats.... And the sisters themselves, living embodiments of De Chirico's *Disturbing Muses*.

'Chloe, dear, what are you laughing at? I'm sure the Fitzwalton sisters know what they're talking about. And I imagine they've got a beautiful house. They were a bit odd, though, like all aristocratic people.' (So they'd given themselves titles too? No wonder she was impressed.) She sighed. 'Actually, I'm relieved I spoke to them. I was worried that you were going crazy when I saw that weird painting – I was even going to ask Doctor Finklestein to take you on a no-cure-no-fee basis.' She beamed. 'But now I realise that it's an acceptable, artistic craziness.''

I cocked an eyebrow at John as he entered.

'Those Fitzwalton sisters', he laughed. 'You've got a strange fanclub.'

'What are you going to call her?' John asked as we sat on the beach with the puppy on my lap, both stroking her. 'Something Irish? Like the Fitzwalton sisters and their cats –'

'No!' I hugged her. 'Esmerelda.'

He laughed. 'Very canine name. And I suppose it is suitable for an Irish setter – emerald green and all that.'

'I'm calling her after the gipsy in *The Hunchback of Notre Dame*.'

'Naturally.' He had a mock-serious expression.

'Because she's going to be a nomad.'

'Oh, now I see how the name fits – kind of like "Rover", only more glamorous. Quite right, too; she's going to be a very elegant dog when she grows up.'

I smiled. 'We're going to travel the world together, if I can get her a doggy passport.'

John had gone silent. I looked at him. He had his face in his hands.

'What's the matter?'

'Don't do it, Chloe', he said quietly. He looked up at me with tearful eyes. 'Don't disappear. Stay here where I can find you.'

I cuddled Esmerelda to my neck. 'Why should I? You'll be in France – with Veronique.' He looked away. 'John, I'm tired of feeling trapped, isolated, passively waiting for Prince Charming to rescue me.' I smiled. 'I'm going to do a TEFL course: Teach English as a Foreign Language. It only takes a few months, and then I'll have a certificate that's recognised all over the world. I can even do the course free because I'm unemployed.'

'What will your Mummy say if you sign on the dole?'

I shrugged. 'I don't care. I can't seem to find a job – even a dead-end one. You wouldn't believe the number of interviews for fast food jobs I've failed. And I only got that job in the office because Mummy's solicitor put in a word with your uncle – and then he fired me.' I sighed. 'John, my life is going nowhere. I'm not sitting here while you make up your mind.'

He put his arm around me and I lay back against him. We made a nice little family: John, me and little Esmerelda. We sat there silently, John stroking my shoulder as I stroked the puppy.

At last he kissed my temple and spoke, quietly and seriously. 'Chloe, I didn't mean you should put your life on hold for me. You deserve better than a married man – or a divorcee who's still in love with his wife.'

I flinched and his eyes softened.

'I'm in love with you too, Chloe. And that's why I don't want to ruin your life. I'm a second-hand man, a hand-me-down.'

'Like the dress Veronique gave me?'

He smiled. 'A perfect fit but, well, not really your own. Chloe, you've got your whole life in front of you.' His voice trailed off. I wondered how many men would say that to me until I got too old for them to say it any more. My life seemed to be shifting like the sand beneath us, all traces of myself washed out like the footprints at the water's edge.

'And another thing: I think you're too clever to spend your life travelling as an underpaid teacher, sharing apartments with drop-outs and backpackers – with second-hand rucksacks from the Army surplus shops.'

'What a snob you are, John!'

'OK, I'm a snob. But I'm trying to save you from making a disaster of your life. You wouldn't be happy, Chloe.'

I sighed. 'I didn't know language teachers were so poor. I'm a high-maintenance girl, you know.'

He laughed and ran his fingers through my freshly-highlighted hair. 'I can see that. And as you mature into a high-maintenance middle-aged woman, you'll need plenty of money for hairdressers, make-up, clothes.... I should know; I'm married to a woman like that.' I looked up at him; he was grinning now. 'I'm lucky Veronique has her own money – lots of it.'

'I'm confused, John. Are you still saying I should be your kept woman?'

He shook his head and smiled. 'Well, if that's what you want –'

'Not if you're still married to her.'

'Hey, don't cry.'

'Sorry.'

'Don't be sorry.'

'It's just that – John, I thought you and she had decided to get divorced.'

'We had. Believe me.' He was looking at me steadily now and I wanted to believe him. 'Chloe, I haven't done this before. I know you think I'm the kind of man who has affairs and then goes back to his wife, but I'm not. I was always faithful – except, as she said, with my eyes.' He sighed. 'I can't avoid noticing attractive women, but in future when I'm with Veronique I'll keep my eyes on her. Well, I'll try.'

'You must really love her.'

'I do.'

'I never liked the idea of divorce anyway.'

He smiled. 'So unromantic, isn't it? I remember our argument about it in St Stephen's Green – you were so passionately against it. It seems so long ago.' He sighed.

'So how do you propose I get myself a high-maintenance lifestyle?'

'Well....' He paused. 'Chloe, I think you should finish your education.'

'But what will I study? I'm not going back to art college now; I'd need something that would guarantee me a career. And I hardly think the Fitzwalton sisters' buying my painting marks me out as a successful artist.'

He laughed. 'I meant go to university. Get a degree.' He hesitated. 'I think you should study law.'

'No! John, I've had enough of law. Your uncle put me off – and Janet, and Barry ...and Mummy's solicitor.'

'What about me? I like to think of myself as a rather moral person.'

I raised an eyebrow.

He shrugged. 'Apart from having an illicit affair – and collecting lots of parking tickets.'

'And bribing Clint to get those security guys to let us into the National Gallery at night...'

He laughed and kissed my cheek. 'And introducing you to one of Dublin's most vicious criminals – oh, that's another reason I've got to get out of "de cuntery": Skoby is trying to, eh, persuade me to take a personal injury case against Bling Bling's. According to

Skoby, Clint was less than gentle with him when he was chucking him out of the club. And he wants to sue Jurassic Rox and their minders for slander. Oh, by the way, he was very impressed by my scar.'

'I'm sorry.' I kissed his cheek. 'It'll heal.'

'I hope it doesn't.'

'Do you have to mix with criminals in your job in France?'

'No. Veronique's father's firm is strictly tax, probate and divorce.'

'Boring!'

He shrugged. 'Anyway I don't speak enough French to work as a lawyer. I just act as go-between for Veronique's *papà* and some English-speaking clients.'

'So you're even sacrificing your career for her.'

He nodded, his eyes looking vulnerable – like my puppy's.

I cried as we parted. He sat in the car with me, holding me close, kissing my lips, my neck, my eyelids, my hair. 'Chloe, I meant it when I said I loved you. I never lied to you. I'll always love you.'

Esmerelda wriggled up from my lap to stand on her tiny hind legs, her front paws scrabbling at our clothes as she frantically licked the tears from our faces. John laughed at last. 'Better not cry in front of the puppy.' He kissed her head, tenderly, as if she were a baby. 'We're like doting parents.'

'Just don't call me a "yummy mummy".'

'Oh, another thing: don't let envious women upset you.'

'I wish I could avoid unpleasant people.'

He stroked my cheek. 'You can't, Chloe. No one can. You can only walk away from them in your imagination.' He smiled. 'When anyone tries to hurt you, paint their picture.'

'And stick pins in it?' I laughed. 'I'm terrified of the supernatural, voodoo, that sort of thing.'

'Who needs voodoo when you've got the best weapon? – a paintbrush. Paint them as they are; paint the truth. Show it to them if they really piss you off; that'll hurt them.'

'And if they're clever it'll also heal them.'

He smiled. 'Will you do another truthful portrait of me?'

'Maybe.'

'Without lots of other people in it?'

I laughed. 'Do you want me in it?'

'Of course.' He blinked. 'Can I ask you another favour?'

I nodded, slowly.

'One last kiss.'

'On one condition.' I looked at him. 'That it won't be the last.'

He didn't answer; he didn't need to. We kissed until Esmerelda got bored and tried to join in.

John and I kept in touch and, seven months after he went back to the chateau in France, he told me Veronique had given birth to a baby boy. I did the math and realised that the baby was conceived during the summer I'd spent with John. He's still not certain the boy is his but doesn't want to offend Veronique by asking. They sent me a photo of little Jean and he just looks like a baby, so I don't know.

I tried to be gracious about it. I even sent them a present: a painting of the three of them, Veronique holding Jean as she walks away into the background.

As an afterthought, I painted Esmerelda in John's arms, the way she looked when she was a little puppy because that was how he'd remember her.

Veronique sent a *'Merci'* card. John emailed me to say he would put the painting over the cot – and to ask why I hadn't painted myself into the picture.

I told him I wasn't ready to do a self-portrait; it would be like giving birth to my own soul. I knew it sounded pretentious – but I was an artist, after all.

Easel life

It's been over a year, and Daddy hasn't come back – yet. Sometimes I see his picture in the gossip columns, or on the financial pages under such headlines as: 'Runaway tycoon living it up in rich man's paradise.' Sometimes he's pictured with Carmel and little Lexus, who is apparently going through the Terrible Threes. When I paint them, they're always in the distance – and I've come to like it that way.

Mummy and I didn't have to move to Clonbollard; we found a two-bedroomed flat down by the harbour in Belgowan, just five minutes' walk from our old house. I often wonder if it's the apartment John and I would have lived in. Mummy and I no longer miss the big house – though I usually pass that way when I'm taking Esmerelda for a walk. Sometimes a light is on in the attic; I wonder what the new owners have done with it.

Daryus is getting married to Mira next year. He and the band have reformed and they still plan to be the best punk-metal-whatever group ever, but Felim and Robert are studying to be engineers, just in case, and Daryus is very busy working as a security guard at all the rock concerts in Dublin (sometimes he works with Clint).

Barry took Skoby's personal injury claim against Bling Bling's and a slander action against the lead singer of Jurassic Rox, Steve Oldman, on a no-win-no-fee basis. Both cases were lost on technicalities: the management of Bling Bling's claimed Clint improved Skoby's teeth when he rearranged them; Oldman said he was just working on a lyric when he called Skoby an 'evil little prick' and Skoby's girlfriend a 'wannabe groupie'. 'My client is an artist', Oldman's barrister said, 'and art is fantasy masquerading as truth.' The jury agreed, though I think it's the other way around. Barry is now thinking of leaving the country.

I've started to visit the National Gallery again, in between lectures. I took John's advice and got a scholarship to study law. Aunty Helen says it's a waste of time, but I ignore her (and the begrudgers who say I'm a freeloader like my father).

Actually, I'm not really enjoying my studies at the moment because I find the law rigid and, well, unimaginative. But I've finally accepted that I need something solid in my life. I'm not a cat with nine lives, any more than Veronique was. Anyway even a cat needs a shelter.

If I ever make it as a lawyer, I'm never going to do divorces – though I might make an exception for John and Veronique.

I still paint. I've gone back to the classical style but the ideas are surreal. John is always in the foreground, Veronique walking away to the side with the baby.

Of course, I feel unworthy, when I think about the great masters whose styles I presume to emulate; I wonder if I'll ever be able to get down and stand beside those giants on whose shoulders I perch so precariously, as powerless as a child carried by her father.

The Fitzwalton sisters let me use their attic as my studio and supply me with materials – including rare, ancient paints they claim to have bought from a forger: egg tempura and little vials containing strange-smelling dyes.

They also buy some of my paintings. I spend the money on the hairdresser, clothes and, occasionally, drinks with Brenda and the others from my old job. When anyone says horrible things to me, I paint them exactly as they looked while they were speaking.

I still haven't got a boyfriend. Mummy says I'm better off single because I won't get my heart broken.

Enjoyed **Still Life**? You can now order:

Shampoo and Sympathy

A story about gossip, split ends and murder *by **Geraldine Comiskey***

No one goes to the hairdresser's just for a haircut. As everyone knows, a hairdresser is a combination of psychiatrist, confidante…and confessor.

Kay and Shay Sheeran's trendy salon, Ugly, has got the usual clientele of gossips and scandalmongers, with one exception. Because of its location in Dublin's poshest suburb, it attracts more than a fair share of "VIP"s.

The beautiful, the successful and the scandalous…all queue up to have their hair styled and spill the beans…. Long before the tabloids have got the news, Kay knows whose husband has run off with a visiting Hollywood actress and Shay has enough information to topple the Government.

The young couple stick conscientiously to the hairdressers' code of conduct: they never reveal clients' secrets. That usually means not telling a gossip columnist whether an actress is a natural blonde or not…or which famous rock star popped in for a change of image.

But when a bestselling author tells them that he has murdered his philandering wife, Kay and Shay are put in a dilemma. Should they break the confidential bond between hairdresser and client and tell the police? Should they tell an equally famous celebrity journalist who also happens to be one of their clients? Or should they keep quiet, pretend they never heard it and continue building their reputations as Dublin's most prestigious stylists?

As they are drawn deeper into the writer's real-life plot, Kay and Shay find themselves dealing with a grey area that they can't cover over.

Chasing Casanova

A novel about jealousy, attraction, falling in love…and running away **by Geraldine Comiskey**

Esmerelda Fox is the kind of girl other women love to hate – flighty, flirty and…foreign.

The women of Borgocasino, a little town in the Italian Alps, are not too pleased that she's moved there in search of men – their men.

But, at thirty-four, Esmerelda's been around the block once too many in her native Dublin, where she's dated more duds than studs…and she believes the Italians have "l'amore" down to a fine art.

It's an abstract art, however, and Esmerelda's tangled love-life includes a gorgeous TV soap star, a Sicilian sculptor with Roman hands and an urbane millionaire who sees love as a game.

Before she can say "buonasera", her life has turned into the title sequence of the Benny Hill show, as she is chased by a precession of Latin Lovers and their jealous wives. Everyone is hunting Fox.

And she still has to deal with the local "retro" feminist and a female boss who is more poisonous than Lucrezia Borgia.

In a country that created opera, fashion and the Mafia, just being a foreigner is weird, but being a foreign woman is positively dangerous….

Skin Deep by Geraldine Comiskey

Beauty is only skin deep...until everyone has it.

Doctor Raffaella Bianchi grew up knowing she was the most beautiful girl – in her family, her school and the little town of Borgocasino in the Italian Alps.
But she's never been tempted to sashay down the Milan *passarella* or even join the thousands of Italian girls who fight tooth and manicured fingernail for jobs as TV gameshow hostesses.
Instead, she became a surgeon in the local hospital. She is a kind lady and loves to help other people with her skills – whether with a sharp scalpel or a comforting smile.
But when the two plainest girls in the town try to commit suicide because their parents can't afford to give them cosmetic surgery gift vouchers, Raffaella realises that the only cure for some people is...beauty. She thinks back to her childhood, when she used to wish she and all the other girls in class were equally beautiful, so no one would feel envious.
So she trains as a cosmetic surgeon and offers her services free to anyone who wants to be more beautiful and can't afford it. Subsidised by her doting husband, Enrico, Raffaella opens a clinic and, soon, she is inundated with patients from all over the world.
But the "kindest cut" is a double-edged scalpel. No longer the preserve of those with good genes or plenty of money, beauty loses its exclusive appeal...and ugliness becomes a precious commodity. Suddenly, everyone wants to see unattractive people on screen, on the catwalk, sitting across the table from them on Valentine's Night.... What's the point in being the belle of the ball, when everyone is *bellissima*?

And what's Doctor Raffaella going to do about it? She has created the opposite to a monster, but she feels like Doctor Frankenstein.

Floozies by Geraldine Comiskey

It's not easy being the only dysfunctional member of a well-balanced family – especially when you're a forty-year-old social pariah with a 'princess complex' and a reputation for 'borrowing' other women's men.

Frida Carey is what every woman loves to hate and what every man is ashamed to know – a floozy. Now she's losing her looks – and, with them, the allure that used to make her irresistible to Mr Wrong.

And she's not the only one. Ignored in public by their married lovers, bullied out of jobs by envious female colleagues, shunned at weddings and Christenings, mocked by women's magazines, sabotaged by dumpy love rivals, floozies are under attack by respectable society.

But they're not going to take it lying down. No longer content to be gossip-fodder at the garden fence, Frida and her friends decide to set up a political party to fight for the rights of loose women everywhere.

Now the *femmes fatales* are fighting back.

Armed with killer fingernails, mascara and five-inch heels, the Floozy Party is ready to declare war on respectability.

But even a bad reputation has to conform to certain rules, and Frida finds it's not easy being a high-profile low-life.

Deadly *by Geraldine Comiskey*

A dead celeb has an image to keep alive.

The last critic to drive the knife into Karina Starr gave her the fame she craved…and the mother of her dreams

When Karina, the lead singer of a struggling Dublin girl band, is found viciously murdered, she becomes a cult icon. In death, she appears more talented, better-looking, a sweet girl loved by everyone – except her widowed mother, Gloria.

For Karina left a diary in which she accused Gloria of being 'the Mum from Hell.' Envious of her daughter's growing success, bitter about her own broken dreams, Gloria wanted Karina dead – or so the girl claimed. Now the diary is a best-seller and Gloria is the kind of mother any self-respecting rebel would be proud to have.

But Gloria remembers a different daughter to the one portrayed by the newspapers and social commentators: a cruel daughter who put on an angelic face for the public, a girl who inherited her father's savage temper – and who terrorised her mother.

Now Gloria is under suspicion, up against the police, the press, the neighbours, the other members of Karina's band (whose careers depend on keeping the legend alive) and the dead girl's growing army of fans. As she battles with her mixed feelings, she wonders if Karina will ever be truly dead.

Only when Gloria confronts her own childhood does she begin to unravel the enigma that was her relationship with her daughter. And gradually, the real Karina emerges, with the help of her ex-boyfriend, a girl she bullied and Cahal, a neighbour who is trying to put his own public past behind him.

As Gloria and Cahal fall in love, they discover that a problem shared is double trouble: a VIP won't RIP.

Made in the USA
Columbia, SC
01 June 2017